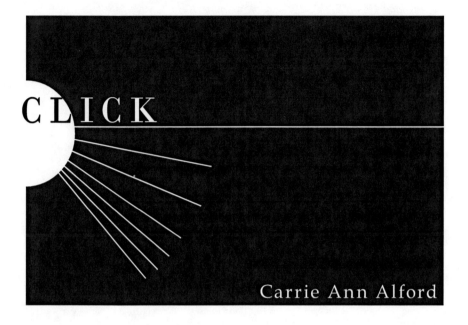

CLICK

Carrie Ann Alford

Bloomington, IN Milton Keynes, UK

authorHOUSE®

AuthorHouse™
1663 Liberty Drive, Suite 200
Bloomington, IN 47403
www.authorhouse.com
Phone: 1-800-839-8640

AuthorHouse™ UK Ltd.
500 Avebury Boulevard
Central Milton Keynes, MK9 2BE
www.authorhouse.co.uk
Phone: 08001974150

First published by AuthorHouse 8/2/2006

ISBN: 1-4259-4774-3 (sc)

Printed in the United States of America
Bloomington, Indiana

This book is printed on acid-free paper.

Dedicated to:

Dr. Rosalie deRosset

For teaching me that violence and grace go hand in hand

&

Mr. Cal Haines

For teaching me to be a journalist

And to both for encouraging me & nudging me along the path

to my dream of being a writer.

To Mom & Dad

For loving me no matter what.

"I will take back My new grain in its time
And My new wine in its season
I will snatch away My wool and linen
That serve to cover her ...
Assuredly,
I will speak coaxingly to her
And lead her through the wilderness
And speak to her tenderly.
There she shall respond ... "

— The Torah

I.

I was sitting at the bar. I swirled the thin stem of my martini glass between my fingers, finishing off my third martini in an hour. The murmur of a hundred conversations in a dozen languages swirled around my ears like the current of a river. I set down the glass, and waving off the bartender, half-hopped, half-fell off the barstool. I started to walk across the lobby to the door, trying to walk more or less in a straight line.

I stopped in front of the full–length mirror. I tugged at my white satin corset top and buttoned my black satin jacket. *Ugh, I've gained weight. My heels clack on the floor like horse hooves ... maybe oxen,* I thought. The highly polished sandstone–colored floor shone in the light of massive chandeliers and floor-to-ceiling mirrors with gold-gilded frames, a foot thick on each side. My blue eyes peered back at me critically from the mirror. I tucked a lock of my hair behind my ear. The rest of my long, black hair was up in a bun. I leaned in close to check for hateful gray hairs.

I should go in for a touch up when I get home. Gray shows so easily with black hair.

My attention turned from my reflection back to the lobby. I peered through the mirror at everyone mulling around. The lobby was thick with people in tuxedos and black gowns waiting for the American and Syrian motorcades to arrive so the partying could officially begin. It was an oasis of European culture in the midst of a burned-out Middle East. The newly christened and baptized–by–fire Secretary of State was in Damascus asserting a new administration's

1

already thread–bare promises to the region. Everyone else was there to forget their dusty lives for one night. Usually, I thrived in these situations. I could mingle, ask questions and laugh with the politicians and glitterati, all while snapping pictures and scribbling pages of notes.

Tonight, I was suffocating. I needed fresh air.

Toby, my personal fan club, trotted up behind me. I could always smell him a mile away. His breath reeked of falafel dripping with extra garlic and good German beer. His short stature was made up for by his athletic build, honey-colored features and out-going personality. He was always tan, quite a feat for a New Yorker. His dark blondish–brown hair and goatee were always perfectly groomed. His blue eyes danced with intrigue and mischief.

"Hey, I just heard the motorcade is stuck in traffic. I wonder if one of the limos ran over a camel or something," he laughed at his own joke.

"Thanks for the tip," I said. I backed away from the mirror and tried to walk around him.

"You look great," he said, sizing me up with one fell swoop of the eyes.

"Uh-huh," I rolled my eyes. I pushed another stray lock of hair back up under the knot. I was wearing a plain, tight but by no means daring black pantsuit with white satin corset peeking out from my blazer. A journalist has to be comfy, even in formal wear.

"I need air," I said, walking toward the door.

"Me too," he said and followed me.

"Great, you go to the left, I'll go to the right."

"Aw, come on Shelby, let me walk with you. It's dark and it's Muslim country, you're liable to be kidnapped," he said sweetly, batting his eyelashes at me. "Besides, I need to talk to you." He grabbed my arm and suddenly turned serious.

I turned to look squarely at him. "I'm going to walk through the gardens, down by the well–lit and gated pool. I think I can handle it." I took his hand off my forearm.

For a second I thought he looked nervous, jittery, but I brushed it off and attributed it to all the alcohol I had just consumed. He looked offended, but knew not to mess with me when I was in certain moods.

"Oh, okay then, but I really need to talk to you soon. I'll just stay here and look after your gear. Don't expect me to give you copies if you miss the action!" he said, trying to recover.

"Uh-huh, yeah, you do that," I mumbled and waved without looking as I walked out the door.

The crisp April air hit my face. It was an unusually cold evening, but I thought it was refreshing. I stretched my arms and took a deep breath. The smell of the cold fresh air mingled together with cigarette smoke. It was strangely sweet and inviting. I walked around the hotel to the extensive gardens that sloped gently down to a sparkling, sapphire–like pool. I was suddenly tired. I was tired of traveling and waiting hours for thirty seconds of work. It was getting harder and harder to write about corruption in City Hall and war in the Middle East, to constantly chase disaster all over the planet.

It's the same fucking story. People don't care about policy or what the President says. They only look at the Sports section ... Cartoons ... Obits ... photos in the Style section to see what everyone was wearing and who was dancing with whom. This is stupid. "What am I thinking?" I asked myself out loud. "I love my job. I must just be tired."

I threw my head back. The moon was full and sparkled against the black sky. I took a deep breath. The bartender had talked me into one too many drinks while waiting around. I needed to clear my head before everyone arrived and I had to be witty, charming and come up with the perfectly-phrased question for the Secretary to not answer.

I started walking again. I was on a beautiful, winding path through flowers and perfectly manicured shrubs. The pool down below sparkled in the moonlight. No one else was around. One of the streetlights lining the path flickered, sputtered and then went out.

I'd been in sketchier places in the world. The Damascus Sheraton was a five-star hotel and I didn't think anything of walking in a hundred feet of darkness. I toasted the full moon with an imaginary glass. Then, as I started to walk again, I kicked something. It rolled and rattled down the grated sidewalk into a crack. In the moonlight I saw a twinkle of silver. I crouched down as best I could in a corset and heels.

It was a roll of film. *Odd,* I thought to myself, *who would lose a roll of film back here? Oh well.* My curiosity got the better of me, and I picked it up. I started playing with it as I walked, tossing it up and juggling it back and forth in my hands. "Let's see if you are beautiful people or ugly people," I said holding up the film. "Maybe there are lurid, politically damaging pictures in there that will crack open an international scandal. Maybe I'll finally win one of those damn Pulitzers," I laughed. I have read way too many spy novels. I tucked the film into the inner pocket of my jacket.

It's funny how life works out. How you find things you aren't supposed to find when you are supposed to be somewhere else taking pictures of other people. In the moonlight I thought I saw the shadow of a person up ahead of me. I strained to see, trying to figure out if I was imagining things or if someone else was out for a walk. All I could see was the tree branches swaying softly in the breeze above the next lamppost.

"Oh, well, must have been the shadow of the tree," I said out loud to the imaginary person.

I walked back up to the hotel as the entourage was pulling up. Toby stretched out his arm, swinging my camera bag and notebook. "You have such a beautiful ass to save."

"Shut it." I grabbed the bag and bent down, furiously trying to get the bag unzipped and my camera in order.

After I snapped enough pictures, I put my camera back in the bag, slung it over my shoulder and followed everyone into the hotel. In the ballroom the diplomats and military brass pontificated on the future of Mideast relations, while I scribbled notes and managed to ask one question. I had no appetite for the festivities. After the speeches were over I decided to go up to my room and file my story. I took the roll of film out of my camera, popped in a new one and went to the desk.

"Hello, I am in room 512, do I have any messages?" I asked politely in my best German to the handsome, young, blond German guy working behind the desk.

"Mrs. Maxwell?" he smiled broadly, pushing his bangs off his face and straightening his posture.

"Yes," I nodded. Normally, I would have hung around and flirted for a few minutes, curious to find out why a good–looking German was working in Damascus. But, I was leaving at 5 a.m.

Being over 30 sucks, I thought. *When the girls find out how cute this guy is and all I could think of is work and bed they're going to die laughing.*

He rifled through the messages and handed me one.

Time: 10:30 p.m.
From: Brennan Maxwell

Message: *Hi Mommy, don't forget to bring back something from Syria. I miss you.*

I did the math in my head, 2:30 p.m. Central Time. I started to tear up, but quickly pushed the tears away. Sometimes it was very surreal thinking I even had a child.

Brennan is so much better off being parented by Michael. I probably would have completely screwed him up by now if I had tried to stay at home like a real mother.

"Definitely better off ... " I mumbled to myself.

"What?"

I looked up to see Toby standing in front of me again. "Nothing. Just talking to myself as always. I'm going up to file my story and go to sleep. I have to be at the airport at 5 a.m."

"Me too!"

"Toby, are you stalking me?"

"No!" he said, trying not to laugh. "You, uh, need someone to tuck you in tonight?"

"No," I smiled, "not tonight."

I walked over to the bank of elevators. Three men were getting into an elevator. One smiled and held the door open for me. "What floor?" he asked with an American accent.

"Five ... obviously same as you," I said looking at the numbers already lit up. I faced the doors and didn't pay much attention to them. I learned a long time ago to avoid anyone in a hotel elevator I don't need to know. We reached the fifth floor and I walked out.

"Night Shel, sleep tight," one said.

I spun around. They had already turned the corner. I walked down the hallway but they were gone. *Who would know me and let me stand in the elevator without saying something?* I was trying to remember their faces, *How did they know me?* It was almost midnight and I was too tired continue the train of thought or worry about some guy in an elevator.

I took off my shoes and padded down the other hall to my room. I tucked Brennan's note in my bag. I entered my room and took off my jacket. I took the mysterious roll of film out of my pocket and threw it in the bottom of my camera bag. I threw them both on the chair and put on my pajamas. I sent a couple e-mails, including one to my husband Michael to let him know I'd take a cab in the morning and he didn't need to pick me up at the airport. The other e-mail to file my story.

I started pulling bobby pins out of my hair. It came down slowly out of the tightly knotted bun, and I tried to brush it out. My long black hair was caked in hairspray and cigarette smoke. I scrubbed my face, trying to clean away the evening and the feeling of weariness sweeping over me in waves. I fell on the bed and tried to get some sleep.

II.

As soon as I lay down and started to drift off to sleep, some idiot started banging on my door. *Oh my God, I missed my flight!* I panicked. I looked at the clock. It was 1 a.m. I'd been asleep for about 10 minutes.

"This better be good." I stumbled to the door and opened it. Before I could see who it was, I felt my arm being jerked and I was thrown into a chair.

"Shel, you gotta get your gear and come now!" Toby said in a forced whisper.

"Toby, for the last time," I whined, "AP does not want pictures of the Secretary or anyone else drunk and stumbling off to bed."

He grabbed my shoulders and shook me hard. "Wake up! I wasn't kidding earlier when I said I needed to talk to you. When I was getting ready in my room earlier, I heard something in the room next to mine. People, talking, then a muffled noise and screams, but weird screams, cut short ... the door was open a little and I snuck in. Shel, two people ... dead. Huge mess. The police are here. They want pictures. We gotta get pictures of this. They look familiar, they're Americans. The dead people ... not the police."

I just stood there, staring at him, not able to comprehend what he was saying. He shook me again. He was breathing hard, shaking all over, and his hair was standing on end. Toby had never lost control of a situation in his life. His body language and tone of voice were unnerving me.

"Hey!" I finally said, more as a reflex than a response.

"Shhh," he whispered. He grabbed my camera bag and tossed it to me.

"Don't throw my camera," I tried to yell and whisper at the same time.

We tip-toed down the hall. I was still in my pajamas. The hotel security were there and a couple of police. They recognized Toby and saw our cameras and pulled us into a room.

"Aw great, now we're busted, and all I did was sleep," I slurred.

They tried talking to us in English since neither of us spoke Arabic. It was a little difficult straightening everything out. It was obvious they were unhappy about me–for many reasons–but Toby stood his ground. Apparently, they did not have a camera and were willing to cut us a deal once they saw our media credentials. Everything in the Arab world is negotiable when one party has something the other party needs. Toby took pictures for us to use, and I would hand my film over to the cops.

We were escorted into the room next door. The cops wouldn't let us out of their sight. They needed specific shots. I tried making a joke about not learning this in photography school. They didn't even smile. I was just grateful I was wearing a t-shirt and flannel pants and not some slinky nightgown. I was not, however, wearing a bra and started nervously tugging on my shirt and stayed hunched over. I did not want to end up in jail or standing before an Islamic court for modesty violations.

The room was pretty much in order. It didn't appear the killer had rifled through bags to steal anything or that there had been a struggle. The bed was unmade and a suitcase on the dresser was open with its contents spilling out ... but whose hotel room doesn't look like that? A formal gown hung on the bathroom door.

"Evidently, she didn't make it to the party ... " I said to no one in particular.

There wasn't much blood. There was a man wearing a tuxedo. He was flung over a female. I assume he had been downstairs and came up to check on the girl, or he hadn't made it down either. There was a creepiness in the way he was spread out on the bed, like a child stretched out pretending to be a superhero. I asked the police officer if that was how the man had been found. He nodded.

The woman was in a state of undress, sheer cotton top unbuttoned but it looked like it had still been on. She was wearing a matching underwear set, and her perfectly pedicured feet were hanging off the end of the bed. Her was hair disheveled as if in the early stages of sex, but the guy was fully dressed.

There was nothing especially gruesome except the accuracy and cleanliness of the shots. They had obviously been hit at close range. The woman looked like she never knew what hit her. I kneeled down to get a shot of the woman's face for identification. I gasped and dropped my camera.

It was Ameila Halverson. She was the daughter of the U.S. Ambassador to Germany. My cousin. Or more accurately, our mothers are cousins. I couldn't breathe. Amelia was like my twin, my second skin. I thought I was going to black out. The officers pulled me up and asked if I was okay. I nodded yes and tried to keep going. I hadn't seen Meelie, as we all called her, in six months, but we spoke two or three times a week by phone and email.

"You ... know her?" a police officer standing over me asked.

I looked up and nodded. I picked up my camera and slowly stood up. I felt my gag reflex kick in and thought I was going to be sick.

"She works for U.S." he said. "When her boss realize she not at party he send someone to check her ... the man, he part security ... Are you okay?" he asked without really looking over at me.

I was still doubled over, but managed to nod. I sucked in a breath through my teeth, hopped up on the dresser and started snapping away. The image was burned into my brain. I didn't recognize the man. He was lying across Meelie, like he dove over her, trying to save her.

This guy took a bullet to try and save Meelie. Who throws themselves in front of gunfire? Especially if it's too late? And why the hell is Meelie in Syria? No one tells me anything.

I hopped down and looked around the room for Toby. He came out of the bathroom. His face was white, drained of all color. The police saidwe needed to leave. I handed them the film as we left. Toby put his arm around me and practically swept me up. We rushed to my room. He shut the door with out making any noise.

"Change into regular clothes. We have to go, now."

His usual abandoned puppy–dog routine was gone. I was scared and in shock. I did what he said. He threw all my stuff in my bags. "Ready?" he asked.

I nodded my head. He grabbed my bags and we left. We stopped off at his room to get his stuff. "Here, put this on." He threw a Yankees cap over to me. I pulled my hair up and put the cap on, pushing it down as far as I could to hide behind it.

I was scared and wanted to hide, but I wasn't sure why. I'd had this kind of panic on the job before, but never because I knew the person killed. It was always some faceless, black blob out there ... some thing I was running toward when everyone else was running away. Now I was the one running away. I was mourning for Meelie and wondering if I had to be the one to tell her family and how much I had to tell.

We left the hotel at 3:30 a.m. We walked out the front doors and I looked down to the gardens. I remembered the roll of film I had found earlier. My brain was too hazy to tell the story. Toby was a foot in front of me, anyway. He pulled me along as if I was a rag doll bouncing along behind a child. My mind was racing, but

I couldn't form the thoughts into sentences. I felt like I was trying run while holding sand in my hands. It was seeping out. Everything was in pieces. Pieces were missing. There were things about what happened that didn't make any sense. We walked four blocks to the main square and found a cab. We climbed in.

"Airport," Toby barked.

"Sure thing," the cabbie said in a deep voice, trying to imitate an American accent.

Toby rolled his eyes and sat back in the seat.

I rolled down the window. It felt so good to have the cold air rush over my face. The hotel had felt stiflingly hot. I rubbed my sweaty palms against my dirty blue jeans. I zipped up my purple, alma mater Northwestern sweatshirt and tried to relax. A cab ride in Damascus could be as harrowing as a hotel with a killer in it.

"Why did you pull me out of the hotel so fast?" I whispered. "Why do I feel like I'm running through the bottom of the deep end of the pool?"

Toby looked deep into my eyes, slightly shaking his head no.

"Toby ... what the hell is going on? Why do I get the feeling you know exactly ... "

He put his finger on my lips; his left hand on my thigh and kissed me. My mind was swimming. I tried to push him off me and he backed off. He looked deep in my eyes and dried my cheeks with the frayed cuff of his red sweatshirt.

He put his finger up to his lips "don't say anything," he whispered. He looked up at the cabbie. "Sure is chilly out tonight. It won't offend you if we ... "

The cabbie laughed, "With Western tourists, no matter what happens in my cab, I always watch the road."

We looked at each other, then down at the seat. "What the hell did he mean by that?" I whispered. We both giggled and went "Ewwww."

He went back to nuzzling my neck and ear. He started whispering. He slipped a piece of paper in my hand. I cupped it in my hands and tried to read it in the dark. He pulled my head back up and started whispering in my ear. My eyes grew large and my jaw dropped. Toby kissed me to keep me from screaming.

"Don't worry. It'll be okay. No one knows." He wrapped his arms tightly around me, holding my head and back with his strong hands. He rocked me back and forth gently. I crumpled up the unread piece of paper tightly in my hand. I ran my right hand up his arm to the nape of his neck and started kissing him. It was a reflex. Safe and warm and it was the only thing that could relax me, short of alcohol.

. . .

We sought refuge in the first-class lounge at the airport. Toby gave the airline worker in the lounge our tickets and explained the situation. The guy found us two tickets on the first plane out. We found a soft couch and tried to relax. My muscles were tightened and starting to twitch. I felt hot and cold like I was coming down with the flu. I tried to concentrate on breathing deeply, but ended up sobbing. I squinted my eyes shut as hard as I could, trying to erase the events of the night from my mind. I buried my head in Toby's lap and curled up next to him on the couch. He peeled the baseball cap off and stroked my hair and rubbed my neck and behind my ears.

We left Damascus at 5 a.m. on a British Airways flight to London. We had to land and switch planes in Frankfurt because of some unnamed mechanical problems.

"Great, 'mechanical difficulties' is exactly what we need!" I howled. Toby clapped his hand over my mouth. My head was pounding. I was tired and my eyes were puffy from crying. I could hardly see straight.

"Shhh," he said. "They probably just ran out of gas. Happens to me all the time," he smiled. I didn't. "It will be fine. We'll go to the ticket counter and just hop onto another plane. Hey, look, the best German chocolate is in the Frankfurt airport. I'll buy you a couple bars."

He put his arm around my shoulders and dragged me toward the ticket counter. We were able to get on a flight to New York, but had to cross the airport to reach the other gate. We stocked up on chocolate at a stand half-way through the terminal.

We boarded the plane twenty minutes later and sank into the plush leather seats. I stared out the window, wondering how I fell into such a mess. Whatever *this mess* was. I didn't even know what the mess was! I felt I was stuck in one of the awful falling-but-never-hit-bottom nightmares.

Meelie is dead. I'm the one who took the pictures. Five hundred people in the hotel ... one hundred photographers ... and I'm the one they pick. I have to be the one to tell Uncle Jake she died while apparently having an affair, 'but don't worry, he loved her and tried to save her.' Uh, yeah ... there's no good spin on that one.

I felt haggard, dehydrated, drained like a wicked hangover. I squinted at the bright lights in the cabin. I put the cap back on and pulled dark sunglasses out of my bag. I asked Toby to put my bag up and stretched out my arms and legs as far as they would go in front of me. I couldn't shake an uneasy feeling that I was somehow involved in what happened more than taking pictures for the police. The mysterious roll of film kept coming to mind. I closed my eyes and rubbed my temples.

What is on that roll? Who was out there with me? And who the hell was that guy in the elevator who knew my name? Maybe he had just heard me and Toby talking. That has to be it.

"Shelby!" Toby yelled in my ear.

"What?" I yelled back.

"The flight attendant has been trying to ask you a question for five minutes," he laughed, our noses less than an inch apart.

"Oh," I said sheepishly. The entire first-class cabin was staring at me.

"Don't worry about it, Ma'am. What would you like to drink?" she asked politely in a clipped, king's English.

"A bottle of water and a glass of white wine."

She returned with a Heineken, small bottle of Chardonnay and two bottles of water. "Breakfast will be served in a minute. Would you like a hot or cold meal?"

I waved her off.

"Bring one of each," he said to her. He turned to me and said definitively, "you're eating."

"I'm not a child," I said sulkily, crossing my arms and looking out the window.

"Good to know. You're still eating something," he said sarcastically, going back to his newspaper.

I sipped my wine. I felt it running through my veins and seeping into my blood. I sank down into the seat and tried to empty my mind. "Mmm."

"Feeling better?" he asked. He looked over and patted my knee.

"A little. No sleep and photographing my dead cousin in a compromising situation may take more than one glass of wine. Pete better give me a big–ass bonus for this one."

"You're absolutely right," he said, handing me a chocolate bar.

I smiled. "God, I am easy to figure out."

"Not in the slightest. You're just predictable."

"Ah."

"Shel, maybe you should stay in New York for awhile."

I looked over at him, tearing off the sunglasses. "Why? And do what?"

"Wait for this to blow over. Figure things out. Strategize. Hang out with me and all your friends. There are going to be some great parties coming up," he said in a sympathetic, syrupy voice. He took my hand and tried to interlace our fingers.

"Are you on crack?" I asked, trying not to scream. "Parties? Wait for things to blow over? I need to go home. I need to make sure my son is okay. I need Michael ... "

Toby looked surprised. I surprised myself. I realized what I said and how much I had really meant it. "Yes," I said quietly, taking another sip of wine. "I need Michael ... I need my husband. I need to go home. I need to not end up like Meelie."

Toby dropped my hand. "Fine."

"Don't be an ass," I said icily. I closed my eyes and started rubbing my temples again. He tried to apologize. I ignored him and fell asleep.

III.

We arrived at JFK at 10:40 a.m. Toby gently shook me awake. "Hey."

I rolled over, not completely sure where I was. I rubbed my eyes and sat up. "Where're we?" I asked, slightly slurring.

"New York."

"Oh, okay," I said, half-dazed.

He walked me off the plane and over to the gate for my connecting flight to Chicago. "Stay here for a few days," he said, trying one more time.

"I can't. I need to go home. I need to see Michael and make sure Brennan's okay."

"But what if those guys are Gregory's thugs? What if that was a message and you're next? Do you really believe your crazy ex-husband is capable of leaving you alone?"

"They probably are, but it's my trap to walk into, not my six-year old son's. I have to go home."

Toby sighed and slipped my camera bag over my shoulder.

"What's that?" I asked. There was a sealed gray pouch lying on the top of my opened bag.

He kissed me on my cheek, "insurance. Tell Pete 'you're welcome,'" he smiled.

"The pictures," I whispered, unable to take my eyes off the package.

"Yeah. Hey, make sure AP doesn't rip off my tag line, okay?" he said in a strange tone.

19

I looked up at him, smiled weakly and nodded. "Of course, of course," I mumbled. I zipped up the camera bag and hugged him.

As I went up to the ticket counter to check in, he called out "keep the hat!"

I turned around, puzzled and I touched my head. I was still wearing his Yankees cap. He waved and walked away.

"Here you go Mrs. Maxwell, everything is in order."

I looked back at the woman behind the ticket counter. "Oh okay." I took my ticket and thanked her.

"They already boarded first-class. You can go ahead and board the plane. Have a nice trip," she said, smiling.

"Thanks, always nice to see someone in New York smiling," I said.

I boarded the plane and after stowing away my bag I went into the cramped lavatory. I grabbed what little bits of counter top there were and hung on like the plane was riding severe turbulence. Only we hadn't moved yet. I stared in the mirror and tried to recognize myself. Twenty-four hours earlier I'd been fighting off the beginning stages of a mid-life crisis. My biggest worry was being tired and my surprising, waning love of journalism. Now I couldn't breathe. I couldn't see straight. I turned on the water. The sad little stream was, at least, cold. I pushed up my sleeves and thrust my hands into the water, letting it run over and through my fingers, under my fingernails and down over my wrists. I cupped my hands together tightly and splashed the tiny pools of water on my face. Streams of water started running down my forearms. Two little waterfalls cascaded off my elbows and created puddles on the floor. I kept splashing. Over and over. I was soaked, but didn't feel any better ... any cleaner. I was trying to wash away blood that wasn't there.

. . .

I sniffled and cried softly all the way from O'Hare. I sat up and dried my face as the taxi turned off LaSalle Boulevard and onto a quiet side-street lined with huge oak trees beginning to bud. The air was drunk with spring. Flowers were trying to blossom, trees were budding and a sweet fragrance was in the air. The sky was electric blue. Wispy, cottony strands of clouds floated quietly by. It seemed the antithesis to my insides.

Isn't it supposed to be dark and rainy when someone dies ... is murdered?

Homeless men were feeding the birds in the park. A few people were walking their dogs or pushing baby strollers. Duke and Stan, two ancient black men, were playing their daily game of chess.

I wanted to scream out the window to them ... to everyone walking around like it was a beautiful spring day. I wanted to scream. *What's wrong with you people? Don't you know there's been a horrible death? Don't you see how miserable I am? How horrible everything is?* I bottled it up. No one noticed.

"You can stop here," I said. The cabbie pulled up to the curb. I fumbled around in my bag looking for my wallet. I finally handed him a fifty. "Keep the change."

"Thank you ma'am."

I opened the door and stepped out. He popped the trunk and hopped out. In one fluid motion he took my bags out and set them gently, side-by-side on the curb.

"Thanks," I said. I picked up the bags and headed to the gate. I punched in the code, heard the buzz and swung the door open. I took a deep breath, looked around at the immaculately clean and manicured little courtyard and started walking toward the back to my house.

"Well, hey there Ms. Shelby!"

I looked over to the gate across from mine. "Hi Mr. Chlopek," I smiled and dropped my bags in front of my door. My retired neighbor hated staying inside. He was the self-appointed neighborhood watch.

He had worked for the FBI for forty years and saw conspiracy at every turn. I could hear his wife from somewhere inside the house calling for him to shut the front door. He ignored her and bent down to pick up his newspaper.

"Kind of late in the day for you to be getting your paper ... " I said, realizing that it was mid-afternoon, although my body wasn't sure what time it was.

"Oh, yeah, well you know, doctor appointments this morning. Where ya back from this time?" he asked, waving his newspaper over his head, coffee sloshing around in a mug in his other hand.

"Oh, nowhere special."

"Ah," he said knowingly. "Same ol' same old, right?" he asked, tapping the tip of the paper on his nose and winked at me. His eyes twinkled with the memories of a time when he had been the one leaving his wife often, had been the world traveler.

"Yeah, something like that," I smiled.

"Mamma!"

I looked up and saw Brennan hanging over the balcony railing.

"Brennan, don't scream. And don't do that!" I called up to him. "Come down here. Hey, why aren't you at school?" I looked down at my watch again. It was later in the afternoon than I thought. *Of course, I have just flown backward through eight time zones on no sleep, so who the hell knows what time it is.*

"Okay! Already home from school today!" he called out again, louder than the first time.

I sighed, exasperated. Mr. Chlopek laughed and went back into his house. I unlocked the door, kicked it wide open and tossed my luggage into the foyer. I punched my code into the security pad by the front door. It never ceased to surprise me when I came home and my security code still worked.

"Mamma!" Brennan yelled again, bounding down the stairs. He hopped up and I caught him, all six years and sixty or so pounds.

"Good Lord you're getting heavy," I groaned.

"Yeah," he said.

I fell down, leaning against my luggage, door still open.

"Wha'd'ya bring me from Syria?" He pronounced "Syria" as "Ssyry-ahh."

"How did you know where I was?" I asked in mock shock.

"Daddy. I called."

"I know. I got your message. Where's your father?"

"Office," he said, hopping off my gut and bouncing up and down.

"What have you been eating?" I asked. *Where the hell is Katie*, is what I thought. I got up, brushed myself off and closed the door. "C'mon, help me push my bags back to the elevator."

We pushed the bags down the hall to the elevator and shoved them in. I picked him up and set him on top of the bags. "Take these up to my room and push them by the door, okay?"

"Okay!"

I laughed. He looked so cute. His eyes were a sparkling baby blue and his chestnut brown hair fell across his forehead like his father's. He pulled up his little blue jeans and pulled down his red sweater. I punched the button for the fourth floor, pulled the grating closed and waved good-bye. He waved back as the door shut.

I went up to the second floor. I walked into the kitchen and pulled a Slim-Fast shake out of the fridge and headed up to Michael's office on the third floor. I downed the shake in the one flight of stairs.

Michael and I had met at a dinner party at my parents' house two months after I had detangled myself from Gregory, my husband of one month. My father had "just happened" to invite him that evening and "we just happened to be" placed next to each other at the table. I was ready to never speak to my father again for setting me up with a stuffy lawyer who still looked eighteen. Michael asked me questions the whole evening. I don't even remember who else was at the party. I never had the chance to talk to whoever was on my left. His eyes sparkled and his smile was mesmerizing. He laughed at my jokes. He didn't laugh when the joke wasn't funny. He complimented my shoes. He called the next day and didn't ask me out for two weeks. I was in love before I hung up the phone. We were married the same weekend we met, one year later.

I saw him in his office, rummaging through papers and talking to himself. He was deep in thought. He was clenching his jaw and sucking in his cheeks, a bad habit he'd picked up while working for the Law Review at the University of Chicago. I leaned on the door-frame, more to keep me upright and on my feet than the side-effect of looking kind of sexy.

There was an inch of paper covering his desk and most of the floor. His dark brown hair was disheveled, his trademark bangs falling across his forehead and getting in his eyes. He mindlessly pushed them back. He was a brilliant lawyer; well-known for both his skill and less than lawyerly appearance at times. I smiled as I noticed his brown and green plaid shirt was half-untucked, there was a pencil pushed behind his ear and a large Mont Blanc pen clipped to his brown v-neck sweater. He'd never looked more gorgeous. It wasn't that he didn't care how he looked, usually, he just didn't notice. He could clean up real well and look imposing in a black three-piece, which was good, because at 35, he naturally had no gray hair yet and still had quite the baby face. His partners joked that he should go and get gray highlights so he'd look his age.

"Hey babe," I finally said.

He looked up and smiled. "Yanks, eh?"

"Huh?" I replied intelligently, once again forgetting the baseball cap. He pointed to my head with the pen in his hand.

"Oh right ... sorry, long story. We need to talk."

He walked over to the door. "Mmm. Okay," he said. He grabbed my waist and pulled me through the doorway, close to him. I caught the scent of his cologne. I took a deep breath and buried my head in his shoulder. He smelled like the North Woods: cedar, oak and earth, but sweet as well ... smoky campfires and the lake on warm summer days. It was the greatest smell I'd ever known.

"Could I breathe you forever?" I asked breathlessly, unable to open my eyes or lift my head. It was the same question I asked every time I returned home.

"That's the plan." He pulled me even closer, rubbing my back, "I could have picked you up, you know." He kissed the top of my head. My skin tingled from my scalp all the way down to the bottom of my toes.

I picked my head up off his shoulder and looked up at him. I was so tired my eyes ached and it was hard to focus on his face, it was so close to mine.

"I know, but it was the middle of the day. I didn't want to disturb you from work."

"I would much rather pick you up anywhere than ever do anything else."

I sighed.

He kissed me and every muscle in my body relaxed.

IV.

Brennan came bounding into the room. He put his little hands on our knees and squirmed and squeezed his way up in between us, unwilling to let his father have a monopoly of his prodigal mother any longer.

"Hi!" Michael and I said in unison. He peered up at us. We both looked down and started laughing.

I hadn't been home in almost three weeks. I had been finishing up a two-week investigative piece in Israel, the last trip of several over a year. I was hoping to get a fellowship and time off to write a book when I got the call from my bureau chief, Pete Harris.

The new Secretary of State was being thrown to the wolves. He was headed out for a trip to Syria for his first talk on Middle East policy. The world was waiting, holding its breath to see if the new administration would be as Mideast friendly as the rumors said they would. The new president didn't have much foreign policy experience. It was his 100 days marker and everyone was waiting for him to fall flat on his face.

The Washington bureau reporter who would normally accompany the Secretary on the trip was on maternity leave. Half the bureau was out with a nasty case of Asian flu going around Washington. Pete, in a rare psychic moment, just happened to call the D.C. bureau; he mentioned I was already in Jerusalem "and would be more than happy to go ... I was practically there anyway."

Right. So I went.

I felt like the country bumpkin trying to hang out with the cool kids ... even though I was a city slicker, and if I do say so myself ... at one point a cool kid. The Washington set all knew each other, had traveled over together on Air Force One and wanted me to believe they were the closest of friends. I was the outsider from the Midwest ... the sticks. I was invading their space. Since when is Chicago "the sticks"? If I ever get a job offer in Washington, I'm turning it down.

Michael picked Brennan up. "Hey. What have you been up to?"

"I took Mamma's stuff up to your room," he said proudly.

Michael raised his eyebrow and looked at me.

"We pushed the bags into the elevator and I sent him up and told him to push them out and leave them on the floor."

"Oh. Good job Bren."

He squirmed out of Michael's arms, jumping to the floor.

"Can I watch TV? When's Katie coming? Mom, come watch TV with me."

"Yes and soon," Michael said. Brennan ran over to the television in the office.

"Hey buddy, why don't you go downstairs and watch TV. That way you can watch out for Katie. Hey, where's Daisy?"

"I dunno," Brennan said, throwing his hands up in the air.

We tried not to laugh at him again.

"Why don't you go look for her and you two can watch TV," I suggested. "I need talk to dad for awhile. I'll be downstairs in a bit, okay?" I leaned down and kissed his forehead and nose. He wiped his forehead with his sleeve and scratched his nose.

"Okay!" he bounced back out the hall calling his dog, Daisy, a golden retriever three times his size.

"How the hell did we end up with something that cute and with that much energy?" I asked.

"Easy," Michael said, pulling me close again. "He got my cuteness and your energy."

"Ha ha ha. You are so funny."

"It's a gift," he said. He kissed me. "What time did you leave Damascus?"

"I left the hotel around 3:30 and got on the plane around 5 a.m."

"What? Why did you leave so early?" he asked, growing concerned.

"Uh, yeah ... we need to talk." My smile disappeared and my muscles started twitching again.

He looked at me. For the first time, he saw my swollen eyes and how drained I looked. My eyes could not focus on what was before me.

"What happened?"

"Can I take a shower first?" I asked, half whining.

"Yeah, of course. It'll be better to wait until Katie gets here to talk so she can keep Brennan busy."

"Is she graduating this spring?" I asked.

"Yeah, four weeks," he said, shaking his head.

"What are we going to do without her?"

"I have no idea. Beg her to stay?" He slid the pencil out from behind his ear and began running his fingers through his hair.

"Good plan. If she refuses, maybe you could throw yourself at her."

He smiled and shook his head. I always joked with him about the two of them having a torrid affair when I was gone. I half hoped it to be true so my conscience could be eased and Michael wouldn't be such a saint. It unnerved me how his perfection drew out all my impurities.

"Go take your shower." He pushed me out the door and smacked my butt.

"Yes sir."

I walked up the last flight of stairs. The fourth floor of the townhouse was the master bedroom suite. I smiled as I looked around to see nothing changed. The white, French Country king-size, four poster bed and armchairs were all in the exact same places as the day I first arranged them seven years ago.

There was a large vase of fresh red roses on my night-stand.

After we married eight years ago, I was overcome by a burst of domesticity. I didn't travel for over a year. I wanted to cleanse my house of my first nightmare of a marriage and start all over. I painted the walls white, bought mostly white furniture and redecorated the house, top to bottom in white and earth tones: blue, green, brown. We threw dinner parties at least once a month and stayed in most nights watching movies.

Brennan was born a year later. After two months I freaked out. I didn't want to take all six months of my maternity leave. I wanted to get out. My boss wouldn't let me come back. I panicked. Every day I was convinced I would drop Brennan or drown him or do some kind of irreparable harm. I was a party girl. I was the one who started working at 16 and never looked back. I relished my freedom, the ability to drop everything and leave town in an instant. I thought about leaving. I was a mess. I wanted to run away from home. Again, Michael's capabilities, natural knack for parenting and overall saintliness made me feel like a failure. I felt like I was slowly sinking in a pit of black tar. Everything I touched ... black ... a mess.

Michael quickly saw my depression, anxiety and eagerness to leave. He knew what I was thinking. He said he was not the kind of guy who thought he owned his wife. I was my own person. It was what he loved most. I was what he loved most. I was no longer the outgoing, lively person he had fallen in love with. He was in heaven having a son. As long as I came home at the end of each trip, he didn't care if I went back to work, back to traveling. The only thing I could do to break his heart is to leave forever.

"Loving someone till it aches and you can't love anyone else is the important thing, the rest of life is just details. How we arrange our marriage is just details," he told me. "Some people don't have to be together all the time or be in the same house every night to have a great marriage. Go. Live your life. I'll always be here when you come back."

He called my boss and talked him into giving me an assignment. I often wondered if he threatened Pete with lawyer-speak, but I never asked.

He left everything in the house exactly as I had placed it. He thrived on routine, on sameness. His disposition was perfect for a lawyer. He turned the guest–room into his home office. He was the special council to the mayor. He and the mayor were childhood friends. They talked all the time and about three days a week downtown was all he needed to stay in the loop. He did his private-client work from home.

He hired a college girl to help out as a nanny. He had wanted my input, but I didn't want to pick another woman to mother my son, no matter how little I was around. She was a sweet girl. After a year and a half she got married and left. Michael and I struggled through the spring. I stayed home most of the time.

Michael found Katie in the fall and was impressed with her maturity and connection with Brennan. She wanted to be a missionary, and was from the little Dryer Bible College near by, like the first nanny. She cleaned up with out being asked and continued after Michael told her she hadn't been hired to clean. She was a sweet girl who somehow already had the aura of a missionary about her. She was average height, weight and appearance. She had long light brown hair and green eyes. She didn't wear make-up or jewelry, but always looked pretty and put-together. She dressed like a stereotypical missionary in conservative, thrift-store clothes. I cleaned out my closet once a year and gave her several bags of clothes in a vain attempt to "help her." I am pretty sure she gives the clothes away.

Our families worried about Brennan growing up in an increasingly un-Jewish home. Michael and I pointed out that he went to temple more than all of them combined and Brennan would be fine.

I climbed into the shower. The hot water felt good. The steam swirled around and filled up the bathroom. I looked down and tried to imagine everything rolling off my body and down the drain. It didn't work. My shower lasted 20 minutes. My skin was raw from scrubbing. I still felt coated in an invisible film, unwashable with water.

I put on my bathrobe and walked into my closet. I tripped over my camera bag.

In an instant one word flashed in front of my eyes.

"Gregory," I gasped. "Why didn't I realize it sooner? He has to have something to do with this. Toby was right. Those guys in the elevator had to be his goonies." I groaned as I realized what it would entail if he really was part of this.

Gregory and I had met at some unremarkable charity ball. After six months of him chasing me I gave in. We had dated on and off for six months when I got my first big break as a reporter. I was working at the *Tribune* at the time and they sent me to Vegas to cover a convention with ties to Chicago. Gregory was at the convention. This should have been my first red flag. After the last day Gregory talked me into a black sequined gown and a night of drinking and gambling. By the time I hit the drunken carousing mark, Gregory had me in a wedding chapel ... he was deeply in love with my trust fund. Well, at least I was wearing black and not white. It took me four months to untangle myself from him and get the marriage annulled.

"The note. That fucker. Abusive ... maniacal ... sadistic ... " I started rambling off, pulling a pair of loose, black cotton pants on and tying the waist drawstrings into a bow.

Ten years and I am still paying. Why can't he just grow up and realize that stalking me will not get me to leave Michael and return to him? Ugh.

"Why can't he just drop dead?" I mumbled to myself as I pulled a dark green v-neck sweater over my head.

"Who should drop dead?"

I jumped with fright. Michael had come up to the room. He was leaning on the closet door–frame, hands shoved in his pockets.

"Sorry, didn't mean to scare you," he laughed.

"No, no I'm just on edge."

We looked at each other and simultaneously said, "Gregory."

"What'd the asshole do now?"

I took Michael by the hand and led him to the balcony. The French doors were open and a breeze fluttered the curtains and plants sitting on the balcony. The sun was already sinking and the top rays of sunshine shot over the Chlopeks' house and into our eyes if we looked straight ahead.

I slowly told him the whole story. My feet and hands were fidgeting and I was folding a little piece of my pants over and over in between my fingers. I couldn't look him in the eye.

He just sat there, trying to take it all in.

"What was in the note?" he finally asked.

I looked at him and took a deep breath, "too much." I got up and went back into the room. I rummaged through my camera bag and found the note. I came back out to the balcony and sat down.

I uncrumpled the note and tried in vain to press out the crinkles. "Basically it says it is from me and I killed Meelie out of a jealous rage. We were supposedly in some sort of twisted love-triangle. I had never seen the man who was with her before that night."

I finally handed it to him and sat there staring at him while he carefully read the note and chewed on his lip. I couldn't take my eyes off his face. It was like watching a train wreck.

"Michael?" I was scared that this was it. I had found the last straw that would finally break his back. He said he always wanted me to come home, but what about the crap I brought back with me? My ex-husband seemed to be a sticky residue we couldn't cleanse, no matter how hard we scrubbed.

He was angry that he'd lost me and my money. He wasn't smart enough to amass his own. It didn't help anything that he was also a lawyer for the city. He was vicious and vindictive to anyone proven smarter, more handsome or an all-around better human being than he. Which was pretty much everyone.

Michael looked over at me. Tears were in his eyes. I took a deep breath, waiting for him to say it, to kick me out.

He took my hand and pulled me over to him. I sat down on his lap. He put his arms around me. "I am so sorry you had to go through that. Are you okay?"

I nodded.

"I wish I could have been there with you."

He ran his fingers through my wet hair, pushing a lock behind my ear, curling strands slowly, deliberately around his finger. We sat in silence for several minutes. He took his handkerchief out of his pocket and dried my tears. He touched my nose and handed it me. "Blow."

"I wish you could've been there too. You're not angry with me?" I finally said. I took the handkerchief and blew my nose.

"Why would I be angry with you?" he asked, genuinely shocked. He took the handkerchief back and kissed my nose.

"Well, I ... I don't know, that I, maybe I somehow brought this on myself?" I stuttered.

"Hey Blue, don't ever say that again," he said. "No one could ever bring something like this on themselves. Now I really wish I would have picked you up at O'Hare."

I smiled at the sound of my nickname. Blumberg was my maiden name. Michael started calling me Blue when we were dating and friends and family picked up on the nickname. We sat there for a few more minutes in silence and tears. He was stroking my hand and started clenching his jaw again.

"We're going to get through this together. I think you're right. This has Gregory's slimy scent all over it. My secretary mentioned his brother was in the Middle East when I told her where you were ... which we all thought was odd ... "

"Oh my god," I whispered. I suddenly knew the voice from the elevator. "We need to get Brennan out of here for a few days. We need to show the note to my father and figure out what to do. I'm not worried about anyone in Syria. Toby had to have found the note before the cops. No one there would think I had anything to do with it. I may have to answer some questions, but I can do that."

"You call Pete, tell him you're back but you can't come in for a few days. It's the weekend, anyway. I'll call your father. Either your father or I will make sure we check fingerprints on this and make copies. We'll figure it all out."

"Okay. I filed one story last night before I left. I'll call my mother as well and have her take Brennan up to the lake."

"He'll be upset."

"We'll go up as soon as we can. Maybe Katie could go up with him," I said softly.

"I'll ask."

He stood me up and we walked back into the room. He pulled me close and kissed me so passionately it took my breath away. My knees buckled. "Welcome home," he grabbed me and laughed.

V.

"Hey Pete, it's Shelby." I threw myself on my bed.

"Where are you?" came the gruff, chain-smoker voice reply.

"Home. Nice to hear from you too," I said sarcastically. "Listen, I need to file some more articles on this murder in Damascus thing, I have pictures I'll courier over to you, but I need to do some more research and talk to a couple people. Can you give me a week to work on it?"

"What the hell are you doing?"

"It's a hunch, but ... "

"Hey, Shel, I know this chick was your cousin or something. I think that's too much a conflict of interest. Besides, Reuters and the *Times* are all over it. Don't worry. The story'll get out. Your job was to follow the Secretary and record his ramblings about the new administration's foreign policy. You did that."

"Thanks, but I was there. I think I may actually know who was at least partially involved in this ... " I tried to get him to say "yes" with out giving away too much, just in case I was completely off. The two rocks in my head sparked. I smiled and lowered my voice. "I have some first hand knowledge that the guys possibly involved in this are from here in Chicago. I spoke with them at the hotel and have some independent verification from a source here that they are the same guys." *Eh, so I stretched the fact a smidge. Well, it was generally true.* The spark went out and another thought jumped in my head. "Ooooh, by the way, before I forget, I am sending pictures of the crime scene over with the others, they are actually from Toby Jones,

37

I had to hand over my film to the authorities ... long story. Jones says to tell you not to stiff his by-line on those pics."

"What the hell are you doing with New York *Times* pictures? I'm going to yank your ass back down to intern level," Pete grumbled.

"Pete," I said tired and exasperated, "do you ever *listen* to me? Do you ever read the emails I send you?"

"Nope."

"Good to have that cleared up after fifteen years. Can you just trust me and cut me some slack, huh? Please ... just think, if I'm right ... think how juicy that would be ... how good it would make you look in front of all your little bureau chief friends. An exclusive on the murder of an Ambassador's daughter ... working for the Secretary of State ... murdered on an official business trip," I cooed into the phone.

Pete grumbled for a few more minutes but finally caved in and told me to do what I needed to do.

"You're a doll Pete."

"This better be good Blue. I mean solid fucking Pulizer gold. I get your head on a platter if you come up with bubkiss, got it?" he said as harshly as he could.

"Yeah, it will be. Bye."

I hung up and took a deep breath, rubbing my temples and saying any assortment of prayers I could grasp for from my murky memory. I even tried the Hail Mary, but I trailed off after "Hail Mary, full of grace ... " I sighed and punched in seven numbers.

"Blumberg."

"Hi Daddy."

"Shelby, where are you?"

"Home. Michael and I need to have dinner with you tonight. It's urgent."

"Oh God, he's finally leaving you."

"Uh, no, but thanks dad," I said sarcastically, tearing up again. "We just need to see you right away."

"I know, I know, he already called and set it up. Come over to my office, I have a meeting till six. I'll order dinner."

"Fine." I hung up.

. . .

I walked into the living room and found Brennan leaning on Daisy watching cartoons. He was absent-mindedly patting the dog, fixated on the TV.

"Where's Katie?" I asked.

He shrugged. "I dunno, she said she be right back," he said, not looking up at me.

"Oh, okay." I sat down behind him on the overstuffed brown leather sofa and grabbed some of the velvet pillows to prop up my feet. I made a mental note to teach Brennan responses other than "I dunno." One journalist and one lawyer and our six-year old was already slaughtering the English language. How embarrassing. Katie came in. "Hey Kate."

"Hi Mrs. Maxwell."

"How's the classes going?"

"Fine. I'm almost done," she said, smiling as broadly as only a graduating senior could.

"Do you have plans for the weekend?"

She thought for a minute, sitting down on the chair and a half next to the couch. "No, I don't think so," she said. She handed a cup of chocolate milk to Brennan and started scratching the dog's ears.

"We want to go up to Lake Geneva, but Michael and I have to get some stuff done tonight first. Could you go up with Brennan and my mother?" I asked. "If you need to come back tomorrow that's fine."

"Sure. I don't see why not." Katie had been up to our place several times and enjoyed the time away from campus.

"Great. You can take my car. If you'd like, you could run back to your dorm and pack and come back. Don't forget your bathing suit; it's warm enough to heat up the pool and use it."

A look of panic crossed her face.

"Something wrong?" I asked, slightly confused by her sudden panic. She loved our pool and was an excellent swimmer.

"Well, no, but ... " she stopped. I stared at her.

"Bathing suit worries?" I tried to tease her cheerfully.

"Katie coming to the beach! Katie coming to the beach!" Brennan put down his milk, jumped up and started running around and cheering enthusiastically. He ran around the room and then jumped up on the couch next to me.

"No, no it's just ... well ... I am nervous about using your car. I don't ever drive it. I guess I'm just used to taking Mr. Maxwell's car."

I laughed. "What kind of stories does Michael tell you about me?" That didn't seem to help. "Katie, don't worry. I'm not the evil step-mother type or anything. Someone needs to drive my car. Sometimes I wonder why I have it. We just need you to take my car. Don't worry, it'll be fine."

"Okay, if you don't mind," she said nervously. She tried to smile and relax.

"I don't mind. I should give it to you for graduation."

She looked slightly panicked again, but put her jacket on and left for her dorm.

When she returned we left for my father's office.

. . .

We walked in to the front office of Cohen, Sell, Blumberg & Poplinski, Real Estate and Estate Planning Attorneys. The receptionist called my father's secretary.

"They're in a meeting. It'll just be a few more minutes. Do you want something to drink?" she asked sweetly.

"Coffee?" I asked. Michael held up two fingers and she jumped up and scurried down the hall.

It was a standard law office. The walls and carpeting were dark gray. Expensive-looking replica Chippendale furniture was pushed up against the wall. It looked like no one had ever used those chairs. A square of leather couches and chairs sat to the left of the receptionist's fortress of a desk. The walls were covered in oversized paintings and prints of the English countryside.

Both conference rooms on either side of the lobby were in use. They both had impressive views of the North Loop and Lake Michigan. The walls in the rooms were lined from floor to ceiling with law books.

"Ever wonder why there is a fireplace in the lobby? Not to mention fifty–pound candlesticks with no candles?" I asked, easing into one of the leather couches.

"Oh that's easy," Michael said nonchalantly.

"Really?"

"Mmhmm. See, the candlesticks are to bludgeon non–paying clients with, and then they get thrown in the fireplace ... At least that's what we do at my office."

"You're a sicko."

"You asked," he said. He sat down next to me and smiled at his own story, stretching out his arms and legs.

Vera, the receptionist, came back with the coffee. At least, that's what she said it was. I peered into the black mug and saw a greenish–goldish liquid with powdered creamer floating in chunks around the edges of the mug. I looked up.

She smiled weakly. "Our coffee maker is broken and the condiment guy is new and keeps skipping our office. Sorry."

"No, no, it's perfectly good coffee," I smiled, stumbling over the last word. I set the untouched coffee down on a table.

"Into the fire!" Michael shouted, raising his arm and pointing his finger skyward.

"Excuse me?" Vera freaked out.

"Ignore him," I sighed, rolling my eyes. "Maybe we should wait by Gabbie's desk." I jumped up, pulled Michael up with me and led him down the hall. "Thanks Vera," I called back over my shoulder.

"You would think a billion–dollar firm wouldn't have problems with coffee," Michael commented loudly enough for everyone to hear.

"Could you behave yourself, counselor?" I whispered.

"Well, hello there, hello there!" Frank Jegerski rushed out of his office all teeth and handshakes. I tried to pull my hand out of the way. Too late. "What're you doin' here Ms. Shelby? Michael?" His face turned red and his large frame shook as he shook our hands.

"See what you did?" I hissed. I hid behind Michael.

"Hey Frank! How's the fast–lane world of corporate real estate?" Michael asked, slipping into lawyer mode and going toe to toe with Frank's blustery, over–the–top personality.

"Good, good ... "

"Great!" Michael laughed and cut him off. He grabbed Frank's shoulders and shook him lightly. "Good to hear it. We gotta go, meeting Mr. Blumberg, can't keep him waiting, you know!" he said, cocking his fingers into a gun shape and pointing down the hall. He spun around, grabbed me and pushed me down the hall.

"Good to see you!" he called after us.

"Good God, it's like running through a minefield," Michael said.

"Well, hello darlin'."

"Now there's a friendly face," I said. Gabbie walked up to us. She had been my father's secretary for twenty years. She was a petite and beautiful woman with silvery hair and bright blue eyes. Her face seemed timeless. She was as youthful as when I first met her. She was always pleasant, always had time to talk. I had always hoped that she and my father were having an affair and he would leave my mother for Gabbie and she would be my step-mom.

"Hi Gabbie! Is the meeting over?" Michael kissed her on the cheek and handed her a bottle of wine.

"Hi baby," she said to Michael. "Oh yes, yes, the meeting just let out. C'mon, I set up dinner in your father's office."

"Thanks," I said. We walked in to the office and sat down at the small table for four, set for three with real china and a white linen tablecloth. It was set in the back corner of the office, usually used for interviewing or meetings with clients. There were six different boxes of Chinese food and bottles of mineral water and wine on the table.

I had changed out of the casual sweater and linen pants after Katie left. I found my favorite suit, a comfortable pink wool suit and crisp, white shirt and pulled a mile of pearls out of my jewelry box. I couldn't go to my father's office in anything less than a fresh suit and pearls. Michael laughed at me. I made Michael put on a black suit.

"Blue."

We both looked over, my father walked in.

Michael stood up and shook his hand. "Sir."

"Sit down Michael," he said quickly, peering over his silver reading glasses. "I read in the paper about the double murder in the hotel you were at in Damascus. They haven't released many details,

43

but the *Times* says Amelia was one. I can't get a hold of Jake, what do you know?"

Although I actually did know, probably more than my Uncle Jake, Ameila's father, my father took the wire service getting news first a little too literally at times. He expected me to have the news first and answers to his questions about any news story he read. Most of the time, I wasn't the one who had written the story, half the time it wasn't even a wire story and I didn't know anything.

"I was there, the police asked me to take pictures. Meelie's gone. I didn't recognize the person she was with."

I took a deep breath, grabbed Michael's hand with both of mine and interlaced my fingers in his. We told my father the whole story.

He looked at me carefully, studying my face. "That all?" he asked skeptically. "Do you have this piece of evidence?"

"The note Toby found in the room? Yes, he gave it to me."

Michael pulled the note out of breast pocket. My hands were shaking and clammy. I really didn't want him to read it. My father was a realist. He'd lived through my college years, marriage to Gregory and traveling around the world for stories. He was frank and blunt and didn't care what I did. Most of the time, he'd already done it several times over, but there is a line for everyone, and even if I hadn't crossed it with Michael, it was quite possible my father would snap.

"Exhibit A," he said sternly. "Hand it over."

I took the note from Michael and handed it to my father. I twisted up my face as he unfolded the paper and read the note.

He sighed. "Aw shit, Shelby, is there no end to the stupid things you get yourself into?" He didn't look up. I didn't answer. He started reading, "Amelia and I ... same lover ... fighting over him and in a jealous rage ... killed them both ... off to commit suicide," he read half out loud, half to himself. "Well, whoever wrote this get points for creativity and obviously knowing the two of you." He looked up over his glasses again. "It's obviously not your handwriting."

My jaw dropped, but I couldn't say anything. I had expected worse, I knew the tongue-lashing would continue.

"Sir, in Shelby's defense ... " Michael started. My father held up his hand and closed his eyes.

He looked down again, setting the note face up on the table before him. He took off his reading glasses. Without looking at us, he said "I need to think. Eat. Both of you."

We picked at our food in silence. We drank the bottle of wine and wished for more.

"This is the only thing linking you to this, correct?" my father finally said.

"Yes. I believe so. Like I said, Toby found it in the room before the cops and snuck it into his pocket. I'm sure he would have noticed if there was anything else," I said quietly.

"You'd better dig a prayer book out of the dark corner of your closet. Going to temple tomorrow wouldn't hurt either."

We glared at each other.

"Don't start."

"Perfect time to start. And don't you talk back to me. You never got what's coming when you were a kid, your mother wouldn't let me, probably would've kept you straight. And in temple."

I rolled my eyes like a teenager.

"Thirty-one fucking years old and you still act like a child," he yelled. "God have mercy on your soul, even though he has no reason to."

"Ooo-kay," Michael said. "I think he's confirmed what I thought. George, Stella and Katie are taking Brennan up to Lake Geneva tonight. We'll go up tomorrow morning, wait a few days and come back."

"Good, this note says you're off to commit suicide, you need to be careful," he said, still staring at me. "You do know how to do that right? Being careful, I mean," he asked pointedly. He added, "I'm golfing all weekend. I won't have to hear your mother spin conspiracy nonsense."

"After temple," I said.

"What?" they both said.

"Well, you're going to play golf all weekend after going to temple, right? I mean you wouldn't order me to go when you're out playing golf?" I tried to look as sweet as possible.

"Michael ... "

"Yes sir?"

"Good luck." He got up and left the room.

We sat there in silence for about five minutes, staring at each other, the table, out the window.

"Well, that could've been worse," Michael finally said quietly.

"Yeah," I whispered. "We, uh, should get home and, uh we should pack and leave early in the morning. Maybe we can figure out how to get Gregory. Dad's right ... if I'm supposed to be off killing myself, it probably means there is someone out there waiting to help me with that." I started crying. I covered the white linen napkin with mascara and lipstick. I shook so hard I scared myself.

Michael stood up and came around behind my chair. He rubbed my shoulders and arms until I calmed down. He walked around in front of me, towering over me, looking down at me and smiled sympathetically. He sank to his knees and wrapped my hands in his. "C'mon. Let's blow this joint," he said and nodded toward the door.

"Why, Mr. Maxwell ... " I said pushing away tears from my eyes. He pulled us up together. He pulled a fresh handkerchief out his pocket and dried my eyes. He kissed my nose and led me out of the office.

"Good night Gabbie, go home," Michael said as he passed Gabbie's desk.

"Oh darlin', I am so sorry to hear about your cousin," she said sympathetically, hugging me gently.

"Thanks," I whispered weakly.

. . .

Brennan and Katie were already gone by the time we reached the house. Katie left a note on the front hall table.

Mr. and Mrs. Maxwell -

Mrs. Blumberg sent her car over to pick us up. Your car is still in the garage. We'll see you in the morning. Thanks for inviting me along for the weekend.

-Katie

I was suddenly overwhelmed with sadness. Michael practically carried me to the elevator. He took me up to our room and put me into bed.

VI.

It was still pitch-dark out when Michael woke me early the next morning. I looked up at him, blinking through a sleepy haze. I was warm and perfectly snug lying curled up under the covers. I had a chunk of comforter in each fist. There was a suitcase by the door.

"Hey Blue, wake up. I thought we should get an early start. There's coffee downstairs and a hot shower waiting for you." He was showered and dressed and ready to go.

"Grrrrughhh," I groaned and rolled over.

"Shel, come on, it's 6:30. Brennan will be up in an hour and expects to see us." He shook both of my shoulders and tried to pull me up. I opened my hands and let go of the comforter.

"Uhkey," I mumbled and rolled out of bed. Michael caught me and pointed me in the direction of the bathroom.

Twenty minutes later I was clean, if still a little damp, dressed in baggy gray sweats with "Northwestern" across the front of the hooded sweatshirt and a small N embroidered on the left hip of the pants. I grabbed Michael's crimson, University of Chicago Law baseball cap. I stumbled into the kitchen and filled my red and black car mug with black gold, slowly swirling in cream and almond syrup. I took a sip and felt the caffeine drip into my veins. I started to wake up and smiled in sweet satisfaction.

"You know," Michael said, walking into the kitchen, "it's not the caffeine working that fast, it's all the sugar you dump in there."

"Ha ha, it's sweet and blond, just like I like my men."

He shot me a dirty look. He hated that phrase.

49

"You drink coffee your way, I'll drink it mine." I said unapologetically and walked out of the kitchen and down the stairs.

Michael came down behind me. He had learned long ago not to take anything I said before 9 a.m. seriously. He opened the door to the garage for me, "I have breakfast stuff in the car. Your bag and sunglasses are on your seat."

"Mine or yours?"

"Yours, but I'll drive."

"Oookie," I smiled up at him, leaning like a seal against him. I kissed him once, my mood turning on a dime. "Lezgo."

"I love your version of the English language before you are fully awake," he laughed, his anger melting away.

"Uh-huh, lezgo Tonto." I walked into the garage and slid into the passenger seat of the dark–green, 1992 535i BMW, technically mine. I hadn't driven it more than 20 miles in the past year.

"Where's your car?" I asked. Our garage only fit one car.

"Out front on the street. Katie drives mine and she doesn't like to pull into such a tight space. She hit the garage once, I said it was fine, but she freaked out and started parking on the street. She refuses to take the car anywhere near the garage now. I try to get Kate to drive your car, but she refuses. Keeping your car in the garage keeps it nice and polished, anyway."

"Yeah, she mentioned she never drives my car. Why do we even have two cars, anyway?" I asked. He shrugged. I looked in the back seat to see a child booster seat.

"Well, it's good to know someone's driving her."

He looked over at me, and saw me looking at the backseat. "I just put that in."

"Oh."

"I do take it out about once a month for a Sunday drive with Brennan to make sure the gas and oil don't gum up."

I smiled, but felt completely left out of the family picture being painted in front of me. I sighed and started picking at my blueberry bagel.

Michael looked over and saw my face. "What?" he asked.

"Nothing. Just tired."

I turned on the radio and slipped in a CD. I pushed the button to open the sunroof and turned up the heat in the car. We were quiet for the two-hour drive up to the lake. I tried to push the picture out of my head of Michael and Brennan driving up and down Lake Shore Drive and around the city with the sunroof open on sunny spring days.

Stopping at the lake, going for ice cream, driving up to Lake Geneva? Maybe I'm not needed. Maybe it would be better if I just left and let them get on with their lives. All I do is run in and out and I always seem to bring trouble and chaos with me. It has to be frustrating for Michael and impossible for a six year-old to keep interrupting their lives. He's always happy to see me, but is it 'my love' or 'my friend'?

I fished around in my purse and found my cell phone buried at the bottom. I turned it on and punched in the numbers.

Michael looked over, I ignored him.

"Hey!"

"Hey, got a minute?" I asked.

" 'Course babe. What's up? I heard about Meelie. How horrible! And you had to be the one to find her!"

"How the hell do you know about that?"

"Cable, babe. I'm also not so far off the gossip buzz out here as you may think. My phone has been jammed for the last two days. I figured you'd surface and I wouldn't need to call you first."

"Thanks," I said gratefully. I sank down into the seat and wondered what the cable news was saying. "I'm almost to the lake, but I think we need to call an emergency session."

"Absolutely. We've already figured it all out. How soon can you be out here?"

"A week? I got some stuff to wrap up before I can get out there."

"No problem."

"I'll call the skirts and we'll be waiting for you. I'll call Bart too," we laughed.

"Thanks," I managed to finally say, while gasping for breath. "I'll call you Monday."

"Perfect. Bye."

"Bye."

"Skirts?" Michael asked.

"Yeah, Claire," I said, quieting down. "I feel like maybe I am just a whirling dervish who sweeps through town and wrecks your perfectly arranged world. Maybe I should just go out to Colorado and work this out with the girls."

"Shelby," he said quietly, pulled over to the side of the road and put the car in park. "If you need to rest and figure things out in Colorado instead of here, then you know I will stand behind you. But, don't you ever, ever tell me or anyone else you are in the way of my life. You are my life. You are Brennan's life. When are you going to get that through you thick head?" his voice raising and getting gruffer as he spoke.

I looked down at my hands resting in my lap. I looked over at him, he was staring straight ahead, gripping the steering wheel with both hands, his knuckles turned white. I hadn't seen him angry very often in the eight years I'd known him. I was a little frightened.

He sucked in a deep breath. "Shelby, please, whatever it is that you have been chasing all these years, please find it so you can come home," he said, his voice cracking as he said "home."

He looked over at me. His face was ashen. He gazed deeply into my eyes. His eyes were glistening, on the verge of tears. I felt as if he were looking straight into my soul–looking for something specific–and he wasn't sure he'd find it.

I blinked first. "Sorry," I said meekly.

"I know," he whispered.

He pulled my hand up to his lips and kissed the edge of my fingers. I curled my fingers around his, like an infant grasping at her parent's hand for the first time. He accepted my weak offering and pulled our hands down into his lap. He pulled back onto the road and ten minutes later we were pulling up in front of the house. Mr. Miller, the house manager, came out and helped us out of the car and took our bags into the house.

"Mamma!" I heard the familiar scream coming from deep inside the house.

"Brennan and Miss Katie are about to go swimming," Mr. Miller explained.

"Ah. How is my mother doing?"

"I am sure she is instantly better now that you are here to take care of Brennan," he smiled. "She started drinking mimosas at eight ... light on the orange juice. Brennan's probably glad you're here too.

"Ah shit, Shel, you are going to sit through the boarding school lecture this time. I've already heard it twice this month," Michael said, rolling his eyes.

"Hiya Mamma!" Brennan came running up to us.

"Brennan! No running," I said harshly.

He stopped dead in his tracks and looked like he was going to cry. "You sound just like Gamma."

I gasped. "Oh darling, I am so sorry!" I knelt down and motioned for him to come over. Brennan started giggling again.

"Why don't you go down to the pool and we will come out in a few minutes," Michael said and tousled his hair.

"Okay!" he said. He hiked up his little red swim trunks and scampered off.

We looked at each other and sighed. "Now you feel part of the fam again?"

I just stared at him. "How ... "

He kissed my cheek and took me by the hand to lead me up stairs. "Bags in the usual room?" He called down to Mr. Miller.

Mr. Miller looked up and smiled. "Yes sir."

"Tell my lovely mother-in-law we've got some business to take care of and we'll be down as soon as possible," Michael said.

"Yes sir."

. . .

"Hello," Katie said as we walked out on the patio. She shielded her eyes from the sun to look up at us.

"Hey Katie, how are things going?" I asked cheerfully, cheeks flushed.

"Fine. Are you feeling all right Mrs. Maxwell?"

"Perfectly marvelous, why?" I sang.

"You're all flushed," she said innocently.

At that moment Brennan shot up out of the water and dragged her underwater. Michael and I were sprayed by the backwash out of the pool.

"Brennan Michael Maxwell!" Michael boomed. A little dark head popped up. His face from the nose down was still under water, little fingers clinging to the edge of the pool. He was blowing bubbles in the water from breathing hard.

"What have I said about jumping on people in the pool?" he asked, standing a foot from the edge of the pool, hands on his hips. His six-foot, three-inch frame was imposing and darkened by the sun behind him.

"Don' do it," came the watery, muffled reply.

"Once more and you're out of the pool, mister," Michael said, relaxing and moving back from the pool.

"Yes sir."

Michael and I sat down in lounge chairs by the pool. There was a pitcher of mimosas, two champagne glasses and a large bowl of strawberries sitting on the table in between the chairs.

"May I?" Michael asked suavely, picking up the pitcher and a glass.

"Absolutely."

Michael poured the mimosas. We sipped and munched on the berries. We laughed as we watched Katie and Brennan splash around. We finished our snack and joined them.

. . .

I was drying off in my room, fighting off Michael's advances when someone knocked on the door "Come in," I said. "See, now aren't you glad we're not naked, draped across the bed?" I asked Michael. He just smiled like a Cheshire cat.

"Dinner will be ready in a half hour," Mrs. Miller said, peeking her head into the room. "Your mother is trying to serve your little Bible student a martini, you may want to get down there," she giggled.

"Oh God. Really! Could she be any more embarrassing?" I groaned.

Michael laughed himself off the bed. "Tell Katie to hang on, I'll be down in a minute."

He quickly tucked his shirt into his pants and finished buttoning his shirt and cuffs. He slipped his loafers on and slicked back his hair, which was extra wavy from being wet. He kissed my neck and pinched my ass. "I'll finish with you later. Want a martini?"

"You get down there!" I shoved him out the door. I rummaged through the dresser drawers to find a sweater and finished dressing.

The wall descending next to the staircase was covered in 100 years of family photos, all perfectly straight and in matching silver frames. The house had belonged to my great-grandparents. They had been major rivals with the Wrigleys. When my great-grandmother found out they were building a home up on the lake she demanded one too. "No prissy Gentile is going to upstage me!" is the quote attributed to her.

I had been sent up here every summer to avoid smog and my parents. I had even been in love with a Wrigley. He was tall and blond and the sweetest guy I'd known till Michael. He and Michael had actually been friends. They both went to the same school and played sports together. Chet and I sailed and waterskied together, wandered around town looking for trouble. We usually couldn't find any in the small summer resort town. We dated for two years and our first time was together Thanksgiving weekend our senior year of high school. We went skiing together with friends in Aspen. I knew I wasn't really in love with him, but I loved him in some way and he was my best friend. Besides, I was tired of not knowing what it was like.

Our families became alarmed at the long-term prospects when we started talking about going to the same college. His parents shipped him off to Europe for a year and then to the Naval Academy in Annapolis, Maryland. I stayed home and went to Northwestern University and kept working for the Associated Press. I had started hanging around sorting mail and making coffee at 16. By 18 I was actually learning how to be a journalist. I couldn't follow him to the East Coast. After I sent him my final letter, I cried for a week. I've never been able to decide whether or not that was too short or too long a time to cry over a guy.

I smiled sadly as I thought of Chet Wrigley for the first time in about ten years. I walked through the double, hardwood doors into the massive living room that ran the whole length of the house. It doubled as the ballroom back in the days when people threw those kinds of parties. The back wall was all glass, with two sets of French doors so people could walk out onto the back patio and look at the lake.

"Hello, Mother." I walked across the living room to her and kissed the air by her ear. I noticed Katie was sitting in the corner with Brennan watching TV. They both had Cokes.

"It's spring Shelby. Really, cashmere in April!" she said disgusted.

"Lovely to see you too, mother. Middle East was fine. Not dead yet, sorry." Michael handed me a chocolate martini and pulled me away from her.

"Stella, I just remembered something I need to talk Shelby about for a minute. Would you excuse us?"

"Humph." She screwed up her face and put her hands on her hips. "Fine. Don't spend any time with your decrepit old mother in her hour of need. Not to mention continually ignoring your only son. Why you should just send him to a boarding school where he can be around other children and learn how to be a proper young man ... and ... "

Michael tried to keep a straight face as he led me out of the room, through the set of French doors and onto the patio. My mother continued her soliloquy, increasing her volume so we could still hear her. We heard her finally break off and call to Mrs. Miller for another gin and tonic.

"How does your mother get her face to do that?"

"Hours of practice with the sorcerer in her secret dungeon," I said sulkily.

He shot me a look. I didn't apologize. "Shriveled, decrepit old bag in her hour of need my ass. The only thing she needs is to get laid for the first time in about 30 years."

"Shelby," he said sternly.

"Oh whatever, mister high-road. What did you want to talk about anyway? Or did you just want to separate us?"

"Both, but we need to be thinking, strategizing during dinner and talk afterward about what to do. I think you need to go back on Monday and start nosing around. But, we need to also keep you alive."

"Definitely. Alive is good."

"Dinner," Mrs. Miller's sweet tone floated out to us and we dutifully marched into the dining room.

The dining room was overly spacious on any occasion, but it was downright cavernous with only four people in it. The mahogany dining table easily catered to 20 guests. There was a matching sideboard as long as the wall it sat against, with a highly polished, beveled-glass mirror and glass top. There was a large arrangement of flowers and polished silver service for coffee and tea sitting on it. The chandelier was on at full light and the bright red, orange and yellow fresh flowers in the middle of the table were the only cheerful thing at the table other than Brennan, who was oblivious to the deep freeze around him and did most of the talking. The rest of us ate quickly in icy silence. Katie enjoyed being at the house, but my mother scared her to death. Rumor was, every time she had a run-in with my mother, she ran back to campus and learned all she could on the Jewish faith so she'd be ready for the next round of questioning. My mother pouted and made noises which I am sure were supposed to be muffled sobs, but it sounded more like a sparrow being choked. Unfortunately for her, I was all tapped out on pity for my mother.

After dinner, we escaped my mother and the house for an outing to find frozen custard, a Wisconsin specialty. We drove into town and found a place with picnic tables out front and a playground next to it. After inhaling his custard, Brennan dragged Katie over to the playground. Michael and I sat on a table, legs and feet dangling off the bench. As Michael finished off my peanut butter custard we strategized on how to get Gregory without leaving a trail. The final plan was to get him to crack and confess.

"It could be fun," I said, trying to be optimistic.

"Could blow up in our faces."

We sat quietly in the growing darkness watching Katie run after Brennan.

VII.

It was dark, yet foggy, murky ... I was grasping around the floor trying to figure out where I was. My hair was stringy, soaked in a gooey sweat and falling in my face. I kept pushing it back, but couldn't get it to stay. I found a table and pulled myself up against the gigantic table leg. I saw a little red light, blinking rhythmically. It was the machine! I started to fumble around, trying to open it and get the tape out. Suddenly, the tape shot up from the machine. Straight up in the air and came down on my head, then wrapped itself, serpentine-like around my shoulders. It worked methodically down, mummifying me. I could see no hands working the tape. I fell backward, unable to move.

"Shelby ..." came a disembodied voice from somewhere above. I strained to see who it was through the dark fog. Ameila!

"Oh thank God! Ameila!" I shrieked. "Help, oh help! Get this tape off me!"

She had the look of passive death on her face. I realized I could see through her.

She pulled a large pair of scissors out from behind her. I recoiled. The steel somehow glinted in the murkiness. The scissors were almost as tall as Meelie. I panicked and started vomiting.

She laughed. It boomed through my ears, making my eardrums quake.

"Meelie?" I said meekly.

She started cutting the tape. She was rough and sweeping. She forced me out of my cocoon. My arm came free and I tried to move,

61

but she cut off my fingertip. I screamed. She kept going. Cutting the tape and me. She sliced my cheek and took out a huge chunk of my hair.

"You were always more scabrous, more careless than I ... " was her ghostly reply, reading my mind.

My jaw dropped. I tried to scamper backwards. The floor became mushy and it was hard to move. I felt like I was being enveloped in gelatin. Ameila came close to my face, though I could feel no breath.

"There's nothing you can do. Reckless. Careless. You will bleed ... You will bleed more ... You will bleed more than I ... You will bleed more than I ... more than I ... more than ... "

"No!" I bolted upright in bed.

Michael woke up and yelled, "What?"

I looked over. I started patting myself down ... fingers, cheeks, hair ... all there. *Oh God what a nightmare!*

"Are you all right? You look like you've just seen a ghost."

My head snapped around and I stared at him. I was breathing hard, gasping for fresh air. "What did you say?" I whispered.

"I said, 'You look like you've seen a ghost,' " he whispered, trying to calm me down.

"I did." I pushed my hair back off my forehead and mopped the sweat from my face with my silk pajamas. I tried to control my breathing and recall the few details of the nightmare I could still make out.

Michael didn't ask any more questions. He simply lay me back down and gave me a long backrub. I kept my eyes open, watching the red numbers of the bedside clock click over. 4:13 a.m.

I slept restlessly for the next couple hours. I finally gave up. I slipped out from under Michael and out of bed. It was a little after 6 a.m. I stumbled around the room and into the bathroom. I found my sweats and running shoes and went out for a frosty, early-morning jog. I ended up at the Starbucks in town.

"Good morning, welcome to Starbucks," the college kid behind the counter said with a smile.

I pulled up my baseball cap and wiped off my face. "Hey," I replied breathlessly. "I'll ... uh,"

"Take your time," he said cheerfully.

I put my hands on my hips and doubled over. I breathed deeply, and started coughing. The warm air in the coffee shop made my lungs cough up and expel the frost I'd breathed in while running. The smell of coffee and pastries calmed me down. The coughing finally subsided and I caught my breath. I ordered a grande Almond Joy and blueberry scone with cream. I was about to consume twice the calories my little jog had worked off.

"Got the Sunday paper yet?"

"Morning drop-off of the Milwaukee Journal is 7 a.m."

"Thanks," I gasped. I looked at my watch. 6:50 a.m. "Kind of early to be open in April around here, isn't it?" I asked.

He looked up, continuing to make my coffee. "Naw, we get enough locals." He handed me my coffee and went back for the scone.

There were only three other people in the coffeehouse, spread out as if any less than six feet of space between them was taboo. I staked out an overstuffed purple velvet chair and a half, with a table next to it overflowing with old newspapers. I set down my food and headed over to the stack of papers a guy in a blaze orange jumpsuit had just tossed into the shop. I popped the plastic ring off the stack of papers and grabbed the paper on top. I handed the guy behind the counter a buck-fifty and headed back to my spot. I nestled into the chair, closed my eyes and slowly sipped the sugary-sweet coffee.

I started reading through the paper. "Not much national or foreign news in the Milwaukee Journal," I muttered to myself. I threw the paper on the table next to me. I looked up and noticed the guy in the corner.

It was like an old movie. He was sitting apart at a table in the corner by the window. He was wearing a fedora and holding up a paper full-breadth in front of him. He pulled the paper down, looked surprised to see me looking at him and quickly pulled the paper back up over his face. I snickered. I popped the last bite of scone in my mouth, slowly and carefully folded the napkin I was holding and set it and my coffee down. I walked over to the newspaper.

"So," I said seductively, "is Gregory keeping tabs on me for any reason other than to simply unnerve me?" I asked as I hooked my index finger on the top of the paper and slowly pulled it down.

The paper folded down into his lap. It was Gregory's brother Tony, the "sleep tight" guy from the hotel in Damascus. He was better looking than his brother and a smidge nicer. If I was going to make a horrible mistake, why couldn't it at least have been with him? He looked like Al Pacino in the first Godfather movie, when Pacino is still young and somewhat innocent, with that sad, abused-puppy dog look about him. Tony's large, chocolate-brown eyes made many hearts melt, but he was the youngest of three sons in an Italian family and had married at 21 to try and gain favor with his parents. His wife Juliana was a charming, beautiful girl, I felt sorry for her. She was ethnically Italian, but was an only child and well, her family was sweet and normal. She had no idea what she had gotten into when she married Tony. Friends in Manhattan said she was spending more time there and at their family home in Florence more and more. The rumor was she was convinced Tony wouldn't give her a divorce so she found reasons to make money for the family outside of Chicago so they would look the other way.

"Hey Shelby," he said sheepishly.

"Hey Tony," I said, smiling confidently. I hiked up my sweatpants and tightened them around my waist. "How's my favorite brother-in-law? Enjoy Damascus? I did." His eyes grew large and he started to say something. I pulled my arms behind my back and started stretching my chest over him. "I just love the Sheraton there ... don't you?" I became serious and took a step back. "Tony ... is Gregory trying to kill me?" I asked, putting my hands on my hips.

"Kill?" he stuttered. "Aw, come on Shelby ... no one is trying to kill you. Whadaya think huh?" he said in a thick Bridgeport-Southsider accent.

Unconvinced, but also not really wanting to know the truth either, I decided to just leave. I tried to muster up all the cockiness I could, to show Tony no fear. I knew the interaction would be reported back when Tony saw his brother. "Well, I was about to leave, anyway ... but you probably knew that. You never were much for watching the news or reading papers," I smiled and flicked his newspaper. I leaned over again, smiled broadly and said "I'd stop getting my snooping skills from old movies if I were you. Tell Gregory I'll be back in town tomorrow."

I winked at him and walked out of the Starbucks. I strolled down the main street in town, wondering how I had just come up with the balls to smile and wink at Tony Cortese. I resisted the urge to turn around, half-afraid Tony was going to come out of the Starbucks and shoot me. The street was now bustling with Sunday morning shoppers and couples heading to brunch. I pulled my phone out of my running pack and called Michael.

"Hey, where are you?"

"In town. I got up and went jogging this morning. I just left Starbucks."

"Filled with joy and cream I assume."

I smiled. "Yup. Wanna come pick me up?"

"What? No sweet blond guys around to give you a ride?" he asked sarcastically.

I was too shocked to answer. I just stopped and stood in the middle of the crosswalk until a large Chevy Suburban with tinted windows started honking at me. I mumbled an apology to both Michael and the Suburban and scooted out of the street and onto the sidewalk.

"Sorry 'bout that. Give me about 15 minutes. Where are you?"

"A block from Starbucks."

"Okay, stay put."

"Bye."

"I love you, Shel."

"Yeah, bye."

VIII.

I marched straight past the security guard and secretary. I threw open the highly polished mahogany door. It whipped back and I caught it in my palm, inches from my face.

"Hello, darling," Gregory said dryly. He looked up. His dull, expressionless eyes looked right through me. He looked back down and continued rummaging through the piles of paper on his desk. His only true talent in life was the ability to make a person feel inconsequential and unnecessary. "Took you long enough ... figured you'd be here last week with your little stage show."

Gregory ... always Gregory ... not Greg. According to his mother, Gregory was a powerful pope and Greg is a guy who bags groceries down at the local supermarket. Gregory was tall, but not imposing. He looked like Benicio Del Toro, but he was skinny, not muscular, tall and dark, but not handsome. He just looked beaten-up and trying hard not to show it. He had none of the finesse or sophistication needed to sail smoothly through a political career or public life. He was tolerated in social circles for his money and connections and family ... not because anyone really wanted him around. They didn't want their business to dry up, their extra helping of dessert, so to speak, to dry up or their loved ones whacked.

"What have you done?" I asked, trying to keep my voice even. I calmly, yet firmly shut the door behind me and walked toward his desk.

He sat down, picked up his cigar and propped his feet up. He was the only person I knew who could smile and look nauseous at the same time. "Poetry."

"What?" I stopped dead in my tracks. I took a step back in horror, unsure if I'd heard him right.

He waved his cigar around above his head with outstretched arms. "Oh, you know ... " he smiled.

"No ... I don't know. I'm not crazy," I hissed.

"It's like a personal greeting card, you know, it's like ... the eternal 'what do you get the person who has everything' question," he said wistfully. He paused, dipped his cigar in a shot glass filled with plum brandy, puffed thoughtfully on his cigar and continued. "Greeting cards are so impersonal these days. They never seem to say what you *really* want to express, you know?" His voice was calm, but strange, like he was trying to be emotional, but hadn't had any practice.

My head dropped into my hands. "Do you have *any* idea what you sound like?" I asked very slowly, afraid to look up.

He ignored the question.

"What, exactly, was the message you were trying to convey?" I was half-afraid of the answer. "Meelie was supposed to be me? The man ... Michael, or you? Both of us, all three of us? Did you kill her or not?" I threw my hands up in despair.

Gregory perked up. He smiled and started puffing on his cigar again. "Oh I don't know. You were always so much smarter than me," he condescended, wetting his lips. "The news hasn't mentioned the police finding any note. They seem to have no suspects. You, my dear, are standing here, instead of in a Syrian jail, so I assume you found the note."

"What note?" I asked innocently, face blank. I stepped closer to him.

He jerked his head back and contorted his face. "Uh, nothing, never mind,"

"Oh."

He changed tactics. He stood up, walked around his large desk and came over to me. He lowered his head and voice, slipping his arm around my shoulders. "I hear he prefers blondes."

"What? Who?" I ask, wiggling out from underneath his arm and backing away.

"Why, Michael, of course," he said innocently. "Oops, oh my, didn't he tell you about the Northwestern charity ball?" He pulled his fingers to his mouth, eyes widening. He stepped back.

I lunged at him. He scurried back behind his desk.

"Now you listen to me," I seethed and lowered my voice. I grabbed the other side of the desk and leaned over. "I don't know what you are up to, or what you are after, but I know you are always after something. And you are not smart enough to pull it off by yourself. Your goonies have been following me all over the globe. Damascus, Lake Geneva, Chicago, probably all over Jerusalem too, right? Tony was in Damascus and Lake Geneva." Pause. The light finally flickered on over my head. "Tony did this didn't he? He did it for you because you don't have the guts."

"Shelby, I know you think I am stupid, but if you think I am dumb enough to confess to you, you have another thing coming, big-shot journalist."

I backed away, unsure if I had heard him correctly. "Oh my god," I whispered. "You did it. You and Tony. You took a life for no reason other than sport ... to frame me. You are going to rot in an Arab jail."

He leaned in and smirked. "Is that so?"

"Mmmm."

"You're never going to pin that on me. My fingerprints were here, in Chicago with me."

"Your brother's were in Syria with him," I said cocking my head and mocking his voice. He turned red.

"You'll never pin it on him either. You have no evidence."

"Do I need evidence?" I asked, raising my eyebrows. "Are you saying without evidence no one will ever catch you?" I leaned in over his desk.

"Yeah, kind of what I'm saying. Lawyers like proof. Trust me, I'm a lawyer."

"Thanks for the reminder. Of course if you were a smart lawyer, you'd be working for a private firm or ... on the top floor ... " I grabbed his cigar off his desk and spun around on my heel.

He lunged at me at the allusion to his inferiority to Michael. "Bitch," he yelled at the top of his lungs like a little boy who's lost his toys. He was sullen and ungraceful and it was easy to avoid his lunging toward me. He chucked the shot glass at my head but missed by a foot. It bounced off the wall, cracking the glass on a picture on the wall and rolled across the floor. "You're the one who is going to get nailed. Rot in hell."

I opened the door, turned and smiled, "you first." I kicked the shot glass out the door and dug the smoldering cigar into the brass nameplate on the door. "Let the games begin."

I dropped the cigar, dug it into the carpet with my heel and walked out.

"Hey Grumpy," I addressed his red-faced secretary as I walked out. "I wouldn't go in there if I were you." Gregory slammed the door behind me. I kicked the shot glass again, sending it across the room.

His secretary shot me an evil look. "If you weren't ... "

I stopped and lunged at her, "go ahead, finish it."

"If you weren't a JAP with an obscenely rich father and husband to hide behind I'd kick your ass right out the window."

"But I am," I said wickedly. "If you've already called security, tell 'em I'm in my husband's office," I smiled at her, wanting badly to spit. "That's the Senior Council to the Mayor's Office."

I headed for the elevator. "Thanks for the card Greg!" I called to Gregory over my shoulder.

I reached for the elevator button but my arm jerked back, my shoulder almost pulled from the socket.

"You bitch."

I was spun around and smacked across the face.

"Hey Gracie, forget something?" I mumbled. My face stung, a searing pain coming from my cheek. I touched it with my hand and when I pulled my hand down it was streaked with bright red blood.

"You waltz in here, throwing your weight around, putting on a show to make everyone look at you," she seethed. "You throw him into a rage and then I have to put the office back together. You're a selfish, self-absorbed gloryhound who desperately tries to hang on to the man she threw away and doesn't love anymore. You trot your ass all over the world looking for lives to destroy."

She was a short, square Polish woman with a growing double chin and frizzy hair the color of dirt. Her face was bright red, arms flying and spit collecting at the corners of her mouth. If I hadn't been so scared by the threats and the name-calling, the squat and bouncing frame would have been comical. "Stop destroying mine or I swear to God I will hunt you down."

I gasped for breath and collected myself quickly. "Hey! Earth to Gracie," I screamed back, snapping my fingers in front of her face, making her corybantic. "Gregory is a lunatic with or without me. If your brain were half as big as your ass, you'd realize that! Get a real job for God's sake. What? He'll probably still let you come over and kiss his ass ... "

She slapped me again. She was wearing a ring with a large square gem, which had flipped around to her palm. It sliced my cheek a second time. It was covered in my blood. She didn't seem to notice.

The elevator doors opened and a security guard saw Gracie slap me the second time. "Mrs. Maxwell! Mrs. Maxwell! Are you all right?"

Gracie started sobbing.

I grabbed the guy's arm. "You didn't see anything." I pushed both of us into the elevator and punched the "door close" button with my fist.

"Are you sure you're all right? Your cheek is bleeding."

I put my hand up to my face again. I saw my reflection in the highly polished brass panels in the elevator. There was an inch–long gash on my right cheek. Blood was dripping down my face and streaming down my neck. Blood was quickly seeping through the collar of my white shirt. There was blood all over my hand and cuff. *Oh bloody hell.*

"It's nothing. I'm fine." I tried to smile, but couldn't. My cheek was swelling up. The doors opened up to the lobby and I started to walk out. "Could you go back up to my husband's office and see if he's there?"

"Of course. You don't want to go up yourself?" he asked. He was young and new and completely confused.

"No, no. I need to leave and meet someone, I'm running late," I lied.

I looked up at the guard and in a hushed voice I said, "I know you are confused. You have a code of conduct to follow, but please, when you go tell your supervisor you saw Gracie slap me, make sure if I have to come back in, that she's already been fired so I don't have to be in harm's way again," I said seriously, stepping in close to him. I put my clean, left hand on his chest and looked up at him earnestly. My wedding ring glinted in the reflection of his cheap "rent-a-cop" badge. I looked him directly in the eye. The tears I did not have to fake. "You know, I've seen this before. I've even heard from others in that office that she is not a stable person. But, you can't tell anyone that, second-hand information and all. I wouldn't dream of wrongly accusing someone."

He nodded seriously, puffing out his broad chest and trying to look very official. I tried to smile gratefully and pecked him on the cheek. A trail of blood was left on his white shirt. I turned and hurried out the front door.

It was 11:30 a.m. City and federal employees were beginning to empty out of their offices to enjoy their lunches in Daley Plaza. I thought twice about crossing the Plaza and turned around. I pulled my sunglasses out of my bag and tried to not look at anyone staring at me. I was still bleeding. There was a red light and four cabs lined up on Randolph Street. My cell phone started ringing.

"Where the hell are you?" Michael said.

"Daley Plaza. Greg says hi. We're all having brunch Sunday ... noonish ... Pump Room ... " I switched the phone to my good ear and hailed a cab.

"Shelby! You just left? The buzz is all over the building," he said, obviously agitated. "Are you bleeding?"

"I'm fine," I slurred. It was getting harder to talk with my cheek swelling up.

"Oh God, you are bleeding! Did he hit you?"

"Calm down. It was Gracie, but I don't think she'll be hitting anyone else anytime soon. Hang on. I got a cab." I told the cabbie the address and rolled down the window. I put the phone back up to my ear, "I'm here."

"Get out of here as fast as you can. Go home and rest, baby. I'll be home to take care of you as soon as possible."

"You're a dream. I'm on my way home now."

"I love you."

"Yeah, me too."

I hung up. The light was green, but the cabbie hadn't moved.

"Problem?" I asked.

"Ma'am, you're bleeding."

"Yes. I know. Don't worry about it, I don't need to go to the hospital or anything. Just take me home."

He looked very reluctant. I assured him I would pay him very well and not bleed on his upholstery. I gave him the address again, and gave him ten dollars as an advance payment for the ride. He pulled away slowly, oblivious to the honking horns behind him. He was probably the only cautious, speed limit abiding cabbie in the city and I wondered how it could be my misfortune to find him at this moment. I'd almost been killed, or given twenty-minute rides in half that plenty of times. Once I had a guy who ran stop signs and red lights while listening to a radio preacher talking about grace. I pushed myself up to try and see my cut in the rearview mirror and instead, I saw a black Firebird tailgating the cab.

"Goonies," I mumbled to myself.

"Excuse me?" he asked, looking more nervous than ever.

I looked up at the cab driver, "oh no, nothing ... wait ... do you want to have a little fun?" I asked, leaning over to the front seat. "Could you lose that car tailing us?"

"Excuse me?" he stuttered again.

I pulled out my wallet and threw a $20 on his lap. He smiled and hit the gas. I sank back into my seat and made another phone call.

"Hey, I'll be coming a day early."

"Well hello to you too," Claire said dryly.

"Problem? Because I was just bitch-slapped twice by Greg's whore and now I'm gushing blood!" I slurred. I touched my cheek again to check the bleeding. I pushed myself up and peered out the back window to see if the cabbie had lost the Firebird yet. He was still hanging on.

"Oh honey, you're kidding!"

"Ah, no."

"I'm with a client now, but I'll call you later."

"Bye," I said and snapped my phone shut. I tried to breathe deeply and relax. My cheek was still swelling making it hard to relax or breathe. I dropped my now–bloodied phone in my bag.

"Turn here!" I shouted to the cabbie. He hung a right on Wacker Street and headed north. The Chicago River was glistening in the sunshine and the Merchandise Mart rose above it on the far shore like an imposing castle. I rolled down my window and tried to get some fresh air. The cabbie hung a sharp right onto Wells Street to cross the river. I tried to grab onto the door handle to stop myself from sliding, but I couldn't grasp it quickly enough and slammed into the door on other end of the cab. I thought I caught a twinkle in the cabbie's eye as he looked back. I think I had awakened a sleeping giant. The Firebird was still following us. An idea popped into my head and I leaned over the seat.

"Turn left on Grand Avenue and then immediately turn right onto Orleans, then onto Ontario and if we're lucky the Firebird will either get stopped by the lights or end up on the Kennedy headed out of town," I said.

"Okay," he said.

We twisted and turned around the crowded Chicago city blocks of the Near North Side. This was my turf, where I had grown up. I knew every nook and cranny. I would loose the car eventually. The Firebird one–upped my best expectations. We turned at the last moment onto Ontario, an one-way street heading to the Kennedy Expressway. In an optical illusion or mental tweak, the driver of the Firebird quickly turned into the intersection he was in ... one block behind us. Ohio Street is also one-way. It heads out from the Kennedy, into the city. He was headed directly into traffic. I heard brakes squeal and the soft crash of two cars bending fenders in a low-speed collision. I instinctively looked back, but couldn't see anything. I closed my eyes and took a deep breath. The cab swung right and headed back east.

. . .

I stumbled into the house and into the bathroom on the first floor. My jaw dropped. My cheek looked like I'd been wrestling with a wild beast. I tried laughing at that thought, but couldn't. Gracie's ring took a chunk out of the right side of my face. There were two deep gashes, one large and one smaller one, which must have been the bottom edge of the gems scraping against my cheek. Compared to the larger gash, it looked like a minor scratch. My cheek was swollen and starting to turn deep purple. My head was throbbing. There were now several streams of blood down my face and neck, streaking down over and under the collar of my white shirt. The right side of my shirt was soaked and ruined. There was a spray of Brandy dotting my back and left sleeve.

I took the elevator up to my room. I stripped off my shirt and threw it down the stairs. I found my favorite plaid flannel pants and gray t-shirt and put them on. I found a couple painkillers left over from an old ski injury, took them and fell onto my bed.

I didn't hear Michael as he came up the stairs. He gasped when he saw me. It was so loud I woke up and tried to sit up. I immediately fell back down on the bed.

"I'll go get you some ice. Have you eaten anything?" he said horrified and probably a little sickened at the sight of the now-dried blood and bruising. The pillow was soaked and ruined. "You need to go to the hospital."

I tried to shake my head in protest, but he was already down the stairs. He came back up with an ice pack, wrapped me up in a blanket and took me over to Northwestern Hospital for stitches. The med student gave me 20 stitches and a month's worth of painkillers.

Michael drove me home and put me to bed. He set a tray with water and more ice down on my night-stand and arranged the pillows so I could sit up. "You need to let the swelling drain down out of your face," he said, pulling me up onto the pillows.

He handed me a couple of Tylenol, "I called over to Walgreen's, I can go get your prescription in a minute. I'll take Brennan with me." He gently put the ice eye-mask on me and fed me a Slim-Fast shake. He turned on some relaxing music and came over to rub down my shoulders and arms.

Brennan came up, peeking his head around the stairs.

"Hey buddy," Michael said softly. He patted Brennan's head and started to shoo him back downstairs. "Come on, let's go downstairs."

"Nnn," I tried to speak.

"You don't mind?"

I meekly shook my head no. Brennan gingerly climbed on the bed and very carefully crawled over to me. He kissed my kneecap and curled up next to me. We slept all afternoon.

When I woke up, around seven, Michael was back up checking on me. He was carrying another tray. He had evidently been changing the ice packs while I slept. He took the ice pack off.

"Swelling's down," he said smiling. "Feel better?"

"Yeah, you're a great nurse." I smiled back.

"Do you remember taking the Percocets?" he asked. I shook my head. "Want some dinner?"

"Yeah." I sat up further. Brennan came bounding in. "Well, I guess your nap was shorter."

"Mamma feel all better?" he asked. He was earnestly examining my scrapes and bruises with his big blue eyes.

"Yeah baby, I'm just fine." I kissed his forehead. "Are you okay looking at me like this?" I asked, afraid that he would be traumatized. Michael had never been able to handle the sight of blood or medical equipment. He hadn't done well at all when Brennan was born.

"Can we watch a movie?" he asked.

"Sure," Michael said. He and Brennan went downstairs to pick out a movie and bring up my dinner. They climbed up on the bed, Brennan nestled between us.

. . .

Half way through the movie Michael left to put Brennan to bed. When he came back up to the bedroom, he woke me up as he went into the bathroom. He came out with his silk pajama pants and no shirt. I smiled and tried to whistle. "Woohoo."

"Hey Shel."

"Hmm."

"I'd like you to do me a favor before you leave for Vail." He walked over to my side of the bed, leaned over and kissed my undamaged cheek.

"Nursing fees?"

He tried not to laugh. "I'm serious."

"Sorry."

He got up and walked around to his side of the bed. He looked serious again. "I want you to call Rabbi Feldstein." He climbed in to bed and tried to put his arms around me. I pushed him away.

"No."

"Aw, come on Blue," he sighed, frustrated, but expecting my answer. "Just talk to him."

"About what?" I asked, trying to shift myself away from him. I didn't want to pick a fight with him, especially while injured, but I felt the resistance building up inside, like an automatic switch and the words jumping harshly out of my mouth before I had any control of what I said or how I said it.

"How about everything that's been going on the last week?"

"I don't really think I want to talk to someone about this who I haven't seen or spoken to in eight years."

"Why is this always a fight with you?" he asked, I could tell he was losing his self-control.

"Because he'll just make me feel guilty about everything and try to get me to come to temple."

"He won't, I promise," his voice cracked.

I rolled over and looked at him. "You know he won't because you've already talked to him, haven't you?" I asked, feeling betrayed.

"Come on, please Shelby. It'd mean a lot to me. Please?" His frustration was giving way to desperate pleading. "I am worried about you. You have just been through something very traumatic ... you are still going through something traumatic. We think Gregory killed Amelia, he's trying to blame it on you and who knows what else ... the note did say ... " he drifted off, unable to finish the sentence.

"Said I was off to commit suicide," I whispered. I rolled over and stared out through the open balcony doors. The sheer, royal-blue curtains flapped softly like ocean waves. I was mesmerized by their cadence, rising and falling, the moonlight shimmering though the folds of translucent fabric. The light blue satin ribbon pulling the curtains back slapped and waved gently. I could feel the breeze on my face. It felt good as it floated over me and cooled my cheek. I had goosebumps and shivered.

He rolled over, nuzzled the space between my shoulder blades with his nose and slowly moved his head up, putting his chin on my shoulder. He slid his arm around my waist and warmed me with his body. I finally rolled over on my back so I could see his face. His chocolate eyes were wide and imploring, on the verge of tears.

"I'll think about it," I finally said.

"Thank you."

"I'd rather pay you nursing fees."

He tried to kiss me good-night, but I yelped in pain. He jerked back. A panicked look crossed his face. I started to laugh. He relaxed and laughed. Neither of us had ever been good at cuddling and snuggling in bed. We lay there happily intertwined in each other's arms, our legs a knot of knees and feet. I fell asleep with my head propped up on his chest, breathing along with his heartbeat and his breath on my ear.

IX.

"Rabbi Feldstein please."

"He's in a meeting, would you like his voicemail?" his secretary asked.

"Uh, sure," I said, grateful for voicemail and being able to just leave a message. In my opinion, voice mail is the greatest invention the world has ever seen. I left a simple message, "would you be willing to join me for lunch Thursday at Indian Hill? One o'clock?"

It was Tuesday morning. I slept in happy, dreamy sedation until Thursday morning.

. . .

Michael pulled up to the front door of the Indian Hill country club. I got out of the car without assistance. I looked around and asked the valet guys if the rabbi had shown already. They all shook their heads no. The sun was shining, not a cloud in the sky. It was an unusually warm and sunny day for the end of April in Chicago. The flowers were being planted by the grounds crew and birds were chirping happily in the trees. I turned my head to look around the parking lot again, pushed up my sunglasses and pressed my hands down my black capri pants, trying to straighten out the wrinkles. A soft breeze ruffled the sleeves and open collar of my black cotton Madras shirt and pulled strands of hair into my face. I mumbled something about my hair getting messed up.

"Where is he? If he doesn't show up soon, I'm leaving!" I stomped my foot like a child. "I got up out of my sickbed for this!" I declared.

"He'll be here," Michael said calmly. He flipped up his wrist and looked down, "we're early."

As if on cue, Rabbi Feldstein pulled up in a gold Buick with the windows down. "Where do I park?" he called out to us in a thick Chicago-Jewish accent.

Michael smiled and strode over to the driver's side door. "Here, the valet will take care of that! Blake, park it next to mine. Thanks." He and Feldstein shook hands as an already-tanned kid slid into the car and drove it away. The two men walked over to me.

"Good luck, Blue," Michael whispered in my ear. "I'll see you in two hours for drinks." I smiled and relaxed.

"Oh, so you're only playing the front nine?" I asked in a luscious, honeyed voice.

"Har har. You are so funny," he stole a kiss. "Have fun Rabbi, she's all yours." He parted for his golf game.

I smiled weakly, "My husband. Lunch?"

We were ushered into the main dining room. "Mrs. Maxwell, right on time," said another perfectly tanned kid, with perfect white teeth, close-cropped blond hair and wearing pressed khaki pants and a crisp white shirt with his initials monogrammed in dark blue on the pocket, which matched his silk tie. "Your table is right over here."

He led us to a table for four in a corner of the dining room with a full view of whom else was there. A fireplace with a hearth–full of large vases of roses and wildflowers was behind the table.

"Thank you, Garrett." I said to the host.

"Can I put in an order at the bar?" he asked.

"I'd like a Sauvignon Blanc ... Rabbi?"

"Ah, nothing right now, thank you ... Garrett," he said. Garrett smiled and left.

I looked at him. "You know, one of the reasons I let Michael talk me into this lunch with you is I always remember how kind you were to me, to all the kids. Brennan loves you."

"Well, thank you."

We sat in silence for a few minutes, perusing the menus.

"Hey Mrs. M., no munchkin today?" a perky blond bounded up to the table in a smart dark gray uniform.

"Hi Kirsten. No, the little one is in school."

"I don't suppose you want the chicken fingers?" she smiled.

"Ah, no," I said laughing. "Just the usual. I don't know why I bother to look at this thing," I said, snapping my menu shut and handing it to Kirsten.

"What's the usual?" Feldstein asked.

"Ooo, that's a large garden salad with extra tomatoes, croutons, black olives, the grilled salmon and a diet coke with lemon," she answered. "And for you, sir?"

"Kirsten," I said, patting her arm and strategically filling her ear with pre-approved gossip, "this is Rabbi Feldstein. He performed my Bat Mitzvah and wedding, both here at the club. We're just doing a little catching up."

"Oh how nice," she chirped. "Hey, I haven't seen you in a long time, been on one of your glamorous assignments?"

"Something like that," I said. I started shifting my silverware around the table, lining them up into a perfectly spaced row.

"Oooo, what happened to your face?" she asked.

I smiled and touched the bandage on my cheek. "Um, just doing my job," I said, trying to stay as close to the truth as possible.

"Oh. You know, I've been studying and practicing writing and taking pictures and I'm taking two language classes this semester and I want to be just like you!" she squealed.

I felt the color drain from my face. I smiled faintly, "ah, no you don't ... "

"Oh, I'm sorry," she said, ignoring my warning and turning to the rabbi, "You haven't told me your lunch order yet, Mr. Rabbi Sir."

"I'll have the grilled chicken, regular coke—no lemon," he smiled.

"Okay!" she scribbled quickly on her notepad, took the menus and left.

"Is there anyone over 17 working here?" he asked after she left.

I laughed. "A couple. Not many. There are several club kids whose parents want them to have a work experience, but the kids aren't smart enough to intern in a law office or something like that. Some are kids from suburbs around here who need to work. I love those kids. They're so real, so respectful. They knew my name and face by the second time they met me. I know people in this city who've been introduced to me twenty times and have a blank look on their faces every time we meet.'"

"I know what you're talking about."

We sat in silence for a few minutes. I nursed my wine while he chewed pensively on a crusty piece of bread. Feldstein was watching the golfers through the back wall, which was floor-to-ceiling windows, polished to a diamond-like shine.

"Fourteenth hole," I said.

"Yes, it's a nice course."

"That's what I hear. Have you played it?"

"Once or twice. You know, my regular foursome includes a priest and a minister."

I looked up at him and laughed. "I forgot how funny you are."

"What's so funny?" he shrugged. "Not bad golfers, nice guys ... we don't talk about religion much, you know ... "

Our lunch was served and we ate mostly in silence. I could see the speech forming in his head. I started picking at my salmon.

"So," he finally said.

"So," I replied.

"Michael says you've had a rough week. I am sorry to hear about Ameila, may she rest in peace."

"Yeah."

"Michael talked you into talking to me."

"Um, yeah."

"Why?" he asked. He carefully folded his hands together, pressed them together and up under his chin and looked directly at me, unblinking, but not harsh. Just waiting.

I set my fork down and picked up the glass of wine. As if a small wine glass was going to protect me. "Why what?"

"Why did you call me?"

"I love my husband. He asked and I agreed. Does that surprise you?"

"So, what do you want to talk about?" he said pointedly, looking me directly in the eye. No brownie points so far.

"I don't really know."

"Why don't you start with what happened."

Feldstein hadn't heard what had happened, only a cryptic phone call from my aunt saying Ameila was murdered. I was flustered at first, wondering how many more times I was going to have to tell this story. I began slowly, my voice shaking, the confident Shelby was crumbling. I felt my mind and energy slipping away as the story tumbled out.

"Michael always seems to know so much more, so much more about this stuff ... " I trailed off, wondering why I was still talking at all.

"What stuff? Religion stuff?" he asked.

"Yeah, God ... afterlife ... why we are here ... " I took a long sip and finished off my wine. I stared down at the glass and hoped desperately more wine would suddenly appear.

"Why are we here?" he asked, leaning over the table, face serious, his voice raised but yet hushed.

"Huh?" My head snapped up. Tears started to soak through the bandage; they were stinging my gashed cheek. I took my napkin and wiped away the tears. I hadn't realized I was crying. I quickly wiped my face with my napkin.

He smiled. "Shelby, I have no thunderbolt! No stone tablet ... " he trailed off, laughing, trying to get me to smile. I tried, he plowed on. "God didn't hand down a memo to me in my office before I drove over here. Only you can figure out why you are here, why you are the one who found your cousin and why you are here talking to me now. Hmmm?"

I slumped down in my chair staring at him. *So this isn't working.*

"Obviously, something is very wrong in your world, or you wouldn't have called and wouldn't be talking to me. No matter how much you love your husband. Right?"

I tried to look offended. I looked down at my hands in my lap. "No ... I have no idea what to do, what to ask anymore. Isn't that crazy? I get paid to ask questions and the only thing running through my head right now is 'why?' Not even why this happened, why Meelie ... just why."

"Shelby Blumberg Maxwell," he boomed in his thickest, Jewish accent, "I have known you your whole life. I actually took the bet that you'd do your Bat Mitzvah in English. But you didn't. I won a couple hundred bucks." He smiled. My jaw dropped. "You studied and you did it and it was fine. It was fine! Unfortunately, God's come a-knockin' again. So ... what are you going to do?"

"If God knocking means getting the crap beaten out of me, I'll pass," I said. My voice and face hardened.

"You think the beating is God or your life?" he asked pointedly. "Maybe ... if your life's been a great party, it's looking like the hangover's going to be a real doozie. Life is hard. It's supposed to be hard. It should be a restless thing ... an adventure that keeps pushing you forward. If you are living like you should, life will take you to places you'd rather not go. It's also Mitzvah. It's celebrating the gifts God gives us, no matter how long he gives them to us. We have to remember one thing though. We have to hold those gifts loosely, with open hands."

"Why? What gifts?" I asked against my better judgment. I couldn't help my curiosity.

"So it's easier for God to take them back when the time comes. Lemme tell you a story. You remember Jonah?"

"Jonah and the whale, Jonah?" I asked, eyebrow raised.

"Yeah ... Jonah and the big fish. The Hebrew translation is 'big fish' not 'whale.' Silly Greeks and their translations."

I sat there, staring at him and wondering what the hell he was talking about.

"Okay, so you're not here for a vocab lesson. Anyway, God tells Jonah to go to Nineveh. Mean, nasty capital of Assyria. Assyrians hated the Jews. Jonah knew it wasn't exactly a plum assignment, yeah? So he bolted. He tried to go two thousand miles in the opposite direction ... to Tarshish. Funny how things don't change, eh? Humans beg for proof of God and when they get it, they run in the other direction. Anyway, the point of the story is that God can find us anywhere, follow us anywhere and waits for us to do what he asks ... no matter how long it takes. Jonah ran because he was confronted with a picture of God and it didn't match up with the one he had. But, if there is one thing I've learned in my life it's that our picture of God and reality never match up–and that God is patient. When he wants something, he gets it."

"So ... what about the fish?" I asked sarcastically.

"The fish kept Jonah from drowning in the ocean. It kept him from running further away."

"So what? What about free will?" I asked, suddenly realizing it was probably not such a good idea to get into a theological discussion with a Rabbi and armed with absolutely no knowledge.

"Shel," he took a deep breath, "if God wants you to go to Nineveh, you're going. There is no safe way to Nineveh. There is no safe way to question God. The only thing you can do is figure out why you are in the belly of a big fish and how long you plan on staying there. So, now you have to figure out if it's a hangover, a coincidence or a serious message for you to listen to. Just be grateful that apparently God doesn't want you to drown. Let me know how it goes."

"Thanks, that is so helpful."

"What? I could be like my orthodox cousin in Brooklyn and tell you it's all your fault and the suffering is what you deserve for your life lived."

I stared at him, "my fault?" I teared up again.

"No. God does not dole out suffering and pleasure like Hanukkah gelt and lumps of coal. God is mysterious and full of wonder. He does not create people just to play with their emotions. You want to know what to do? You need help? Ask."

"Ask?"

"The posture of gratitude. You, my dear, are going to end up a pile of ash under a lot of dirt someday ... travel lightly. That's all I got." He slipped me a folded piece of paper across the table. "I need to get going. Thanks for lunch."

I sat there, staring at the fireplace, rubbing my temples, trying to take in what had just happened.

Did that just happen? Was that one conversation or, like ... six? Why did he tell me that story? What was he telling me? This was a bad idea. Big fish ... great, I'm supposed to take advice ... if I was even given any, which I wasn't, from a guy talking about a guy being eaten by a big fish! Feldstein is losing it.

It was like I was back in that dark and murky dream. Kirsten came up with the check and I absentmindedly signed it.

"Are you all right?" she asked.

I looked up. "You want to be just like me?" I asked softly. "No, no you don't. I've made such a huge mess of life. I'm a wife and mother who ... " I trailed off. She slid into the chair beside me.

"I'm a wife who is unfaithful and a mother who is never around. But my husband and son love me anyway ... which ... which just makes it all the worse because I don't deserve it. I don't deserve any of it."

I wasn't looking at her. I wasn't even really talking to her. I was finally unloading my feelings on the empty seat where Rabbi Feldstein had been sitting. "How can I believe in a God who was dumb enough to trust a job, husband and child to me? To me," I whispered, choking on the words. "I think I'm going crazy."

Kirsten sat there in silence, staring at the chair with me, soaking it all up. Finally, she said quietly, "Mrs. Maxwell ... your husband will be looking for you in the bar soon."

I looked over at her and then down at my watch. "Yes. Thank you." I reached out and grasped her hand and squeezed it. I stood up and walked out of the dining room. I walked along the stone path through the garden outside the back of the club. I looked down at my hand. I had grabbed the note from Feldstein without realizing it. I opened it up and read what he had written.

"Hosea, chapter 2, verses 14-19. That's in the Tanakh, Shel. The Torah is not a magic book or Ouija board. It questions us and waits for us to find the answer. "

I folded it back up and put it in my purse. I walked through the English gardens that formed the hedge of the 18th hole and looked for Michael.

Is God really after me? Why is he picking on a hopeless case like me? Why not a nice nun or Buddhist monk? What about all those freaky Christians ... don't they ask for this kind of abuse? This is not happening! Leave me alone! I stopped. My eyes were squeezed shut and I was clenching my fists. I opened my eyes slowly and looked around to see if anyone was staring at me. I took a couple deep breaths. I stretched out my arms, neck and back. My bones cracked. Gracie's beating was definitely having the desired effect. I cracked my neck once more and kept walking, feeling a little better.

I walked through the patio door into a room full of highly polished cherry-wood paneling.

"Hello Mrs. Maxwell," the young Hispanic man behind the bar smiled.

"Hello Jesus ... " I stumbled over his name. I tried not to roll my eyes at the irony of the name of the bartender on duty. I ordered a White Russian and went back outside to one of the patio tables. The large patio was beautiful gray slate with gray iron-wrought patio furniture. I sank into a chair. The patio was on the far side of the 18th hole, further to the left of the English garden. It was a buffer between the golfers and little old ladies walking through the garden and the kids splashing around in the Olympic-size pool and two wading pools. The pool caught my eye and I watched the small waves lap up against the dark blue tiles around the edges. The water shimmered in the late afternoon sun. I was in a trance and didn't realize I suddenly had company.

"Shelby."

I shielded my eyes and looked up. I could only see two dark silhouettes, partially blocked by the table umbrella. They stepped closer. It was two of Gregory's goonies. I felt a surge of fear and wondered how long they had been standing there.

"Hey boys. How much longer you going to be tailing me?"

"Gregory didn't really like your little speech," Vince Maggio said. Vince was a former football player, six-foot, five and over 250 pounds. One of those guys who doesn't really have a neck, or wrists. He was so big that he was just kind of melded together.

"Oh really?" I almost yelled.

"Head of security made Gregory fire Gracie. Said she should see a shrink. He's real mad Shel," he answered, remaining calm. No one really ever yelled at Vince.

"Well, you tell Gregory I didn't really like getting slapped by that big ox." I pulled my hand up to my face and pulled off the bandage, damp from crying, so they could see the two rows of stitches and deep purple, blue and red bruising. "That'd be 20 stitches boys."

"Gregory could retaliate just as easily as you marched into his office," Tony finally said. His face and eyes had a look of cold marble. I had never seen him look so hard, so much like Gregory. He must have received an earful from Gregory about our conversation. Vince just looked queasy when I pulled the bandage off.

"Tony," I said, standing up. It was kind of perverse, but my fear always melted away when either Tony or Gregory was standing right in front of me. Fear would bubble up into anger and I would gain a flagrant disregard for my own life. "You tell Gregory if he so much as touches one hair on my head or the head of anyone I know ... "

"Shel, I'm not being the meathead here," he said, cutting me off, but lightening up. "I'm here on my own, and I'm telling you Gregory is seriously pissed off. You might want to leave town for awhile. Vince and I are supposed to take care of you, if you catch my drift."

I studied his face. I backed off and sat back down. My fear returned as I looked into his eyes. "Yeah, thanks for the tip. Thanks," I whispered.

He nodded. They turned around and left. It suddenly hit me that I should have asked them how they even were allowed into the club, but they were gone.

"You all right, Ms. Shelby?"

I looked up again to see a friendly face. Jesus was setting my drink down on the table.

"I'm fine, honey, I'm just waiting for Michael to finish his golf game." I saluted him with the drink and took a long sip. He smiled and walked back inside.

"Hey J!" I called after him, not turning around.

"Yeah?"

"You shrink those tighty-whities on purpose, or is that how the management wants you to wear your uniform?"

He poked his head back out of the doorway and laughed. "Mrs. Klein and Mrs. Sell are coming in a few minutes for their afternoon canasta game, and honey, they tip vulgar amounts of money when I wear the tighter pants! They claim it puts them in a heavenly state of mind!"

"Viva capitalism," I said.

. . .

92

I felt lips brush against mine and I opened my eyes.

"Hey." Michael was leaning over me, arms on either side of me, his hands grasping the arms of my chair. The sun glowed around him, his dark brown hair looking golden, a halo hanging around him in the afternoon sun.

"It's about time mister. A girl can only be neglected for so long."

"Oh really?"

"Yeah."

"Buy you a drink to make it up?"

"Sure, but you'd better hurry. My husband is coming over here soon and he doesn't like good-looking men kissing me and buying me drinks."

"Naw," he smiled, "I asked him."

He kissed me again, pulled up off my chair and disappeared into the bar. He came back a minute later with an icy amber ale in a tall glass in one hand and a White Russian in the other.

He set the beer down. "Want another?" he said seductively, leaning over me to put the frosty White Russian on the table next to me and kissed me again.

"Could you two come just once without making out in front of everybody? Just once?"

"Hi Harrison," I said, pulling away from Michael.

"Hi Shelby," he crooned back. "I'm going to get a beer, I see my good friend has set the every man for himself model already."

"Sorry man."

"So'right. You want anything, Shelby?"

I shook my head and pointed to the full glass on the table. He was back in a minute, plopping down in the chair across from me, with his back to the sun and golf course.

"Where's Lily?" I asked, referring to his wife.

"Some girly bridal thingy, I think ... "

"Either that or she's with Hans," I said.

"Oh no, that's every other Tuesday, in the morning."

"Right."

"It's really getting so hard to keep up with everyone," Michael said in an old-matron–like voice. We all laughed.

"So how was the golf game?"

The guys expounded for twenty minutes on the grandeur of the game, the grass, tees, wind and air quality.

"So, not so great," I said dryly.

X. _____

On the way home Michael asked about lunch and I told about my run-in with Tony and Vince while waiting for him on the patio. "This is serious. If they are threatening me ... "

"Gregory is threatening you," Michael finished my sentence.

"Yeah. I think it's best to get to Vail as soon as possible. I need to see Pete tomorrow. I'd like to avoid Tony's accuracy."

"He could still find you there, you know," Michael said and started tearing up. He took my hand and held it the whole drive home. The wind came down through the open sunroof and rustled our hair. We listened to the humming of the world outside the car, whirring past us.

"Can you take some vacation time and you and Brennan can come out too?"

"I'll try."

"I want you to try," I said, rolling my head against the headrest to look at him. He looked over and squeezed my hand.

"I'll try."

"We could take a vacation like a normal family ... we could learn to be normal, right?" I asked.

"Sure we could." A huge smile spread across his face. "We're already more normal than anyone we're related to." He stopped at a red light and pulled my chin over to him. "C'mere Ms. Maxwell." He kissed me like it was the first time. Awkward, but full and adventurous.

"Oh ... my ... "

He smiled.

"Green," I said.

He looked up and saw the green light. We drove the rest of the way home in buzzing silence, looking out the front windshield at the road in front of us.

. . .

A note was taped to the front door. Michael read the note.

"I took Brennan to his swimming lesson, will take him to McDonald's after.

Katie."

"Are you hungry?" he asked after we were inside.

I shook my head no.

"Me neither," he said. He tossed the note over his shoulder. We looked at each other with that half-longing, awkward unspokenness of teenagers who have just fallen in love for the first time, but are still uncertain of the other's feelings. "Wanna finish that kiss?"

I nodded, suddenly unable to speak. He smiled like he was going in for the kill. The wrinkles on his forehead and nose crinkled up and his bangs fell forward into his eyes. I brushed them back. He grabbed me by my waist and pulled me to his chest. I felt snug and secure. I pressed up against him as close as possible, his arms tightening around my waist. It was as if we couldn't get close enough, as if osmosis might be the only way to get close enough. It was slightly terrifying.

His brown eyes shone. He started to nuzzle my neck. I closed my eyes and breathed him in deeply. He bushed my lips and softly brushed my injured cheek with his lips. "Does that hurt?" he asked. I shook my head no.

He moved over to my ear and played with my earring. I started to giggle and my knees literally buckled. He laughed and caught me from taking us both down.

"Maybe we shouldn't stand," he suggested in a deep, slow voice.

"Maybe we shouldn't," I whispered.

We pulled away from each other. Seeing the glimmer of mischief in each other's eyes, we raced each other up the four flights of stairs to the bedroom.

"Wait!" I screeched as we reached the top floor.

"What?" he asked, worried I was about to drop dead.

"Katie and Brennan," I said, sucking in my breath.

"They aren't here," he breathed a sigh of relief. He smiled and tried to pull me close again.

"No," I said, batting him away, "but they will be. Go leave a note for Katie saying something about us taking a nap or something and she should stay with Brennan."

He looked incredulous. I shooed him down the stairs, determined not to be overheard by a six-year old and a future missionary.

I kicked off my shoes and ran to his closet. I picked out his red satin pajama set. I went into the bathroom, baring my teeth to check if they needed to be brushed. I settled for a short swig of mouthwash. I brushed my hair a few times and went back into the bedroom.

Michael came back in. He walked me backward to my side of the bed. "Want a backrub?"

"What a stupid question," I said.

He ran his two index fingers down my neck and chest. He slowly unbuttoned the top I had just put on. He carefully slipped the top off and flung it over his shoulder. We both giggled like fourteen year-olds.

He sat me down on the bed. I lay down on my stomach, pushing a pillow under my chest so I could breathe. Michael sat down on the edge of the bed. He pulled open one of my night-stand drawers.

"Which one do you want?" he asked.

"Surprise me."

Michael fingered the brightly colored bottles of massage oil and pulled one out that smelled of peppermint and spices. He coated his hands with oil and started to slowly rub the full length of my back. Kneading me like bread dough with his fingertips, the knots in my shoulders and back melted away. He slowly and methodically massaged every last inch of my arms, fingers, ribcage and neck. He massaged my head with his fingertips and I almost fell asleep.

Orange and red rays of the sunset streamed over the balcony and through the doors, creating a fiery glow over the bed. It was as if we were swathed in a warm amber-colored stained glass bubble.

When he was getting tired and slowed down, I rolled over and grabbed his hands and began to massage them in mine. I looked up at him and smiled. We locked each other's gaze. All the pain was gone. My mind was empty of everything but him. The sun had slipped below the horizon and the room was dark. I sat up and pressed myself against his blackened silhouette. I showed my gratitude for the backrub for the next two hours.

We fell asleep pressed together on his side of the bed. The cool cotton sheets felt like satin against my skin. I purred in complete contentment. I had never felt so safe or secure as I did at that moment, half-unconscious, lying surrounded in Michael's strong arms, buffeted by his broad chest. I felt myself breathing in as he was breathing out. Breathing in and out each other's breath ... exchanging souls. Like the story of God breathing life into Adam and Eve. I was trying to breathe in as much of Michael's goodness as my lungs could hold. I hoped it would somehow seep through me.

. . .

I rolled over onto my back and stared at the shadows moving across the ceiling. Michael was still asleep and I was stroking his chest with my left hand. I looked over at the clock on my nightstand. It was 8:34 p.m. I remembered Brennan and Katie and my heart beat faster. My heart suddenly started racing. I looked up at the door. It was closed. My mind started going back over the entire evening. I slipped out from underneath his arms and found my pajamas, which had been flung behind the armchair.

I grabbed my robe, which was on the floor at the end of the bed. I ran my fingers through my hair and jogged down the stairs.

I peeked my head into Brennan's room. He and Katie were playing with legos. Daisy was sitting next to Brennan, thumping her tail back and forth on the floor. They looked up and saw me in the doorway. Daisy barked and ran over.

"Hi Mamma, feeling better?" Brennan asked. He ran over to me and I hugged him, holding him tightly in my arms.

"Yes. I woke up and wanted to see you. Did you have fun today with Katie?"

He nodded his head in an exaggerated motion. "Yup. We went swimming, went to McDonald's and have built a city with legos."

"Good." I put him down.

"How was your nap?" Katie asked.

"Good, I was just tired when we got back. I'm real sorry about this. Michael's still asleep, but if you want to go home, I understand. You probably have homework to do."

"Yeah, actually I do. I have several papers and projects to finish up before finals begin. I hope you are feeling better, Mrs. Maxwell."

"Thanks darlin'. You just say a prayer for me. You have the inside track right?" I laughed and shoved my hands into my robe pockets.

She laughed uncomfortably. "Not really, Mrs. Maxwell. If you prayed and told God what you want to say, he'd listen."

"I don't want to be the reason you don't get your work done," I said, ignoring her advice. "Go on now."

She smiled, got up and said good-bye to Brennan. Daisy and I walked her down to the front door and saw her off.

XI.

I awoke early Friday morning. It had only been one week since Toby and I were racing back from Syria. *I hope I never have another week like this in my life ... ever.* I got up and searched around for my bathrobe. I couldn't find it in the mess slowly oozing out over my room, so I gave up and went downstairs to make coffee in the my red satin pajamas and bare feet. I pulled up the pants twice and tightened the waist as I walked into the kitchen. I realized I had accidentally snatched Michael's pants instead of mine. We had matching red pajama sets with a gold M monogrammed on the shirt pocket and hip of the pants.

"Oops. Oh well. Maybe he won't notice," I said to myself.

While the coffee was brewing I went down to storeroom-turned-darkroom and started the developing process for the roll of film I had found. I was curious, but more than anything I was hoping against hope that God had actually shone down on me and given me the gift I needed to prove Gregory was behind this murder. It was just too big of a coincidence, too weird that I found a random roll of film behind the hotel right after the murder. Maybe someone got the pictures and wanted me to find it.

I went up to the office and started up my laptop computer. I found a legal pad and pen in Michael's desk. Although it was Michael's office, I had a small writing desk in the room, as well. It stood in stark contrast to the ocean of papers and books surrounding his desk like a tiny Pacific island. My desk was an antique, found one leisurely fall weekend up in Door County. Everything on my desk was neatly arranged. Journalistic reference books were piled up on the edge, a box of Puffs next to the books. Photos of Michael, Brennan and the Skirts were on the wall over the desk. My drawers were closed, the contents inside were organized. It was rare for me to go to my desk and not find paper or pen. *Michael must have run out of supplies and started raiding my desk instead of going to the store.* I took the tape recorder sitting on my desk and hooked it up to the stereo.

I went back down to the darkroom to check on the pictures. "C'mon, develop! Develop!" I shouted at the pieces of paper soaking in chemicals. I huffed out of the room and back up to the kitchen for coffee. I rummaged around the fridge for breakfast and went back up to the office.

I sank into the plush red chair at my desk and arranged everything before me. I drank my coffee and ate my warm, flaky croissant with brie, which flaked all over my computer and notes. I banged out four columns of copy in an hour. The room began to lighten up with the soft yellow and pink light of sunrise. I saved the article to three different disks and the hard drive. I printed out two hard copies and started making copies of the tape from the wire I had worn when I went to see Gregory.

While the tape was copying, I cleaned up my breakfast dishes.

"Hey, you're up early again," Michael said, coming into the office. He came up behind me, put his arms around my waist and kissed my neck. "Nice pajamas."

"Yeah, sorry."

"Don't worry about it. I just thought I was temporarily going insane when I couldn't fit into my pants. How long have you been up?" he asked.

"I don't remember. I guess I'm so stressed out I can't sleep anymore. What time is it now?" I took the third tape out of the tape recorder.

"Seven-thirty," he yawned. "Mmmm ... want some breakfast?"

"Actually, I already ate," I said sheepishly.

"Did you cook something?"

"God no," I laughed. "Not unless you consider warming a croissant in the microwave cooking. There's coffee," I offer.

"Thanks."

"I should go get ready. I need to see what shows up on the pictures from that roll of film and get over to the office as soon as possible."

"Thanks for saving me some coffee," he said and hugged me.

"No problem."

"I should go make sure Brennan is up for school," he said.

"Yeah ... I haven't heard any noise from his room. I let him stay up kind of late last night." I tried to hide my embarrassment at completely forgetting to check on my son this morning or thinking about getting him to school.

"Don't worry," he kissed my cheek, "I got him. You finish up here." He went down the hall to Brennan's room.

I felt a rising heat creeping up my neck and across my cheeks. Once again, I tried to push away the feelings of failure. I put my hands on my cheeks and forehead and sighed. I looked down at the desk and felt overwhelmed. I finally pulled myself together and put a copy of the disk, a hard copy of the article and tape in the safe and went upstairs to take a shower and get dressed.

As I came out of the bathroom and was getting dressed, I turned on the morning TV news, something I rarely did. I put on a pair of cream chinos and red sweater. I dug around the floor of my closet for a few minutes looking for my camera bag. I grabbed a pair of tall, brown leather boots and slipped them on. I heard the annoying morning anchor babbling about city hall so I perked up and went out and stood in front of the TV. She was talking about an "employee" who was suing her boss and the city for unlawful termination. I started to laugh. Gracie is suing Gregory because she was fired.

"Oh God, is that perfect or what!" I shouted out loud. I took camera bag and went downstairs.

I laughed all the way down to the darkroom. I sat on a stool and waited for the pictures to dry. The fuzzy images slowly came into focus. I pulled one off the line. I wailed like an animal being slowly tortured.

I opened the door to find a wild, terrified look on Michael's face. He apparently heard me all the way upstairs and flew down to the darkroom, pounding on the door as if he'd break it down before I could open it. He looked around quickly at the pictures but nothing was registering. I managed to pick up the picture I had dropped on the floor and with shaking hand, handed to him. He dropped it. We looked at each other, grabbing onto the tables for support, unable to stand on our own.

"Who do you think ... " I finally managed to ask after a few minutes.

He shook his head slowly. "I don't even want to know. But it does prove Greg is stupid. That is Tony, right?" he asked, unable to tear his eyes from one of the pictures. The picture was a profile shot of Tony pointing a gun at the bed. There were four more pictures about the same and two pictures of the two gunmen walking out of the room and down the hall, the guns dangling from their gloved hands.

I nodded. I began to collect myself and I pulled all the pictures off the line and slipped them into a manila envelope and into my briefcase.

"Where's the rest of the stuff?" he asked quietly.

"In here," I said patting my briefcase.

"I'll come with."

"No." I shook my head and pushed a lock of hair behind my ear. I grabbed the briefcase and slung it over my shoulder. I kissed him and said, "I love you, but this is my job. I am a journalist. I didn't do anything wrong and I don't want a lawyer in tow to make people think I had anything to do with this. I don't want you anywhere near anyone who could assume you're there to protect me. It looks like I know everyone involved. It'll be hard enough to hang onto this story as it is. Please, go to your office and I'll come over as soon as I'm done. I could be awhile."

He sighed, resigned but understood my logic. "All right."

· · ·

I arrived at the office about 8:30 and the office was already full and buzzing with activity. I slipped quietly to my desk, trying to avoid friendly conversation so I could finish my story. I changed it around, focusing on the pictures, trying to explain how AP had obtained the pictures without sounding stupid and documenting my every move for the last week.

After a half hour I threw my chair back and sighed. I tried not to sob. I rubbed my temples and under my eyes. *Am I being unethical? Should I give it up? Is this objective in any way?* I thought to myself as I quietly moaned and reread my story for the tenth time.

Every minute of the past week kept flooding back. Washing over me in tangible waves, I rolled the air in my mouth around. The memories were gaining a weight and life and essence of their own. If I could taste it, feel the events again maybe I could wrap my mind around what happened.

It was May 1st. May Day. Freedom for the common working man. "Too bad I'm not a Socialist. I could use a little freedom right about now," I said to myself. I pulled my copy off the printer and headed down to Pete's office.

XII.

"Is this for real?" Pete spit out, holding the pictures in his hands.

"I assume," I said. I sank into the battered, brown arm-chair by his desk.

"How the fuck did you get your hands on these?"

"I found the roll of film in the gardens behind the hotel when I took a walk around the block. I thought they were tourist pictures. I developed it at home ... this morning."

"You know who this is?" he asked, eyes as wide as saucers. Even in the grainy black-and-white pictures the gun shots were clear, deadly accurate and pre-meditated, with little blood or effort. Pete looked like he was going to be sick.

"Uh ... yeah ... that's my ex-brother-in-law Tony Cortese. The one on the bed with Meelie is Secret Service! That's why he is diving to save her," I said, smacking my head with my hand. I had forgotten the police officer who said a secret service guy was the other to die. I was saying it more to myself.

"Meelie?"

"Ameila Halverson, my cousin."

"Shelby, this is old news by now. Why didn't you get me these pictures a week ago? The *Times* reported he was detail five days ago. You've obviously been too busy to keep up with the news. Turn on CNN every once and awhile."

"Hey!" I said, upset at his bluntness. "I found the goddamn killer! Is the *Times* or Reuters printing pictures of the suspected killer? These things take time. I've had my life threatened, been slapped around and told to leave town for awhile. Not to mention this is the first week I've gone AWOL in fifteen years! Give me a freaking break!"

"But who the hell took these?" he asked, changing the subject.

"The guy she was really having an affair with."

Pete stared at me, completely confused.

"Of course!" I laughed at myself for being so dense. "We just have to figure out who that person is and how he took the pictures without being discovered. Right now, whoever he is ... we have the pictures and that's all that matters."

"Right. When you said you had more on the story, you weren't kidding were you?" he asked. He was flipping threw the copy of my article. The tape and computer disk sat next to the stack of pictures. "So, uh, what do we do next? Unless you're Linda Tripp, we can't use the tape. You didn't tell him you were wearing a wire."

"No problem. I wrote it based on the photos and other information I have. The tape is just background that verifies and substantiates the photos. I made a copy of the story on disk and the tape for the police. Could we get a copy of these pictures made here?"

Pete nodded.

"I'll take it all over to the cops. I made several copies of the tape and the article is also on my hard drive and I'll replace it with this new copy. The note, original tape and disk are in a safe." I left his office. Through the glass window I could see him just sitting there, staring at his desk.

I ran down to the darkroom to make more copies of the pictures.

. . .

"Hey, what's this?" asked J.P., the darkroom tech.

I looked over at him. He was staring at the roll. "What's what?"

"This ... " he handed me the roll "did you write this on the roll when you picked it up?"

I stared at the film casing. I was dumbfounded. *How had I missed it before? It had been dark, I just threw it in my pocket and hadn't really paid much attention to it again, in light of everything else that had happened.*

In small, perfectly printed letters and numbers in black ink was "TJ - NYT - 087."

My jaw dropped. I looked up at J.P. I shook my head and blinked, unable to believe our luck. "Don't let AP rip off my tag line ... "

"What?"

Slowly, a smile spread across my face. I bounced up and down for the first time in a week. I hugged J.P. and swung him around the darkroom "Oh! Oh! Of all the amazingly good luck!" I threw my head back, my arms over my head and laughed out loud. "What? What! Rufus! Don't you know what that is?" He shook his head, not catching on. He looked a little frightened. "What if *I* handed *you* a roll casing with 'SM AP 087' on it?" I stopped and grabbed his forearms and looked directly at him.

It slowly sunk in and he joined in my gaiety. His million–watt smile spread across his face. His dark eyes twinkled and he pounded the table with his fists.

"It belongs to a pro ... NYT ... the *Times* ... " he said.

I nodded. "Not only that, but I can tell you who. The only one from the New York *Times*, who was in Damascus and has the initials 'TJ', not to mention is connected enough to have a dalliance with an Ambassador's daughter without anyone noticing."

I hugged J.P. and told him I'd be right back. I ran to the elevator and took it back up to the newsroom. I burst into Pete's office.

"Toby Jones," I said breathlessly.

"For God's sake Maxwell, knock on the door before you barge in," Pete barked.

"Sorry." I knocked three times on his desk. I was still bouncing up and down on the balls of my feet. "Everyone marks off their rolls of film, especially when overseas to make sure the pictures stay straight. Right? Who doesn't learn quickly to devise a system so Jordan isn't misidentified in a caption as Saudi Arabia ... or whatever ... Look!" I dropped the casing in his hands and pointed out the markings. "TJ is Toby Jones. He was there. I saw him mark up his film the day before. That night in the hotel he said he needed to talk but I blew him off. I went for a walk and he wanted to come but I said no. I thought I saw someone in the shadows but thought I was just going crazy," I paused. I figured "crazy" sounded way better than "drunk on the job."

Pete stopped tapping his pen on the desk and leaned all the way back in his chair. He didn't look convinced yet. "Uh–huh." This was Pete's way of saying, "keep talking because right now you still got shit."

I continued. "He was there. Toby was in the room and somehow got the pictures and then dropped the roll of film for me to find it. When he told me to make sure AP didn't rip-off his by-line he was talking about these ... not the police shots. He'd already taken a set right as it happened! Go back and check the pictures he took that I already gave you. I'll bet a hundred bucks the casings have Toby's markings on them as well. He wanted me to have both sets so I'd know he took both."

I took a deep breath and put my hands on my hips.

Pete was still shaken from earlier, but picked up the phone and called for the other negatives and pictures to be found and brought to his office. I flopped down again in the old, beaten up chair by his desk. We tried to make small talk while we waited.

"Sounds good. Definitely could be ... I think you're right," he finally said. He picked up a pen and started tapping it mindlessly again.

Jason, one of the interns, knocked on the door and Pete waved him in. Jason handed Pete a large manila envelope and left. I held my breath while Pete pulled the negatives and pictures out. He studied the two sets of pictures and I looked for the markings.

I exhaled. "TJ - NYT - 088." I set it down and picked up another. "TJ - NYT - 089." I looked up, "it's the same handwriting. 087 is Toby's roll of film."

"Call him."

"I will."

"Today."

"Right."

"So, let me get this straight ... " he paused. He rubbed his forehead and exhaled loudly. "We start out with the Secretary's trip to Syria ... and we end up with an Ambassador's dead debutante daughter ... who also happens to work for the State Department ... and a smarmy gunman ... and you are related to both?"

I laughed nervously and pounded my fists together. "Technically, I'm not related to Tony anymore," I said weakly.

"Oh, well that makes it all so much better," he said sarcastically. "You still running off to Colorado?" he asked. He leaned back in his chair again and automatically looked over at the master calendar on the wall.

"Don't you think I've earned it?" I asked. I raised my eyebrow and rubbed my cheek.

"Whatever," he looked back at me and threw the pen on the desk. It bounced off and rolled across the floor. I picked it up, trying not to laugh, and gently set it on a foot–thick stack of papers on his desk.

"I'll have my cell on twenty-four-seven. I'll stay on this."

"No, no ... you've done more than enough. You're off this story. Just call Jones and let me know how it goes. If the police need to talk to you I'll give them your cell number, because you'll probably be parked at Bart's downing blackberry daiquiris."

"Thanks." I was upset, but knew better than to argue.

"Uh-huh. Now, get out ... you just doubled my work day."

I smiled, jumped up and left.

"Hey Shelby," he called after me.

I grabbed the doorframe and stuck my head back through. "Yeah?"

"You get that slappy girl fired?" he smiled. The newsroom had taken to calling Gracie "Slappy."

"What do you think?" I smiled back.

"Have fun with the granola-brains."

XIII.

I called Toby's apartment, office and cell, but left messages on all three when he didn't pick up.

CNN got a hold of the AP wire story I wrote and called. Some freshman producer with zero manners assumed I would drop everything and gush when he said I was wanted for an interview. I laughed. He was offended and started to snipe at me. I rolled my eyes. I have no patience with self-important cable television producers. I politely but firmly told him I was leaving town and if I had time when I returned, I'd have my lawyer husband call him and work out the details then. Then I hung up. Brennan was sitting on the bed. I winked at him. Daisy barked in approval of my decision. Brennan gave an exaggerated nod and folded his arms.

I spent the rest of Friday afternoon packing. It would have gone faster, but Brennan insisted on helping. Katie had asked for the day off to finish up schoolwork before finals.

"For all the traveling I do, you would think I'd be better at packing," I said to Brennan. He nodded in agreement. "Ugh. Sit here." I said, pulling him up onto my suitcase while I zipped it shut. I didn't need the help, but he loved sitting on suitcases while others closed them. I think he saw it in a movie once and was convinced this is what everyone does. He was always very insistent.

. . .

"Come on, Shelby, you're going to miss your flight!" Michael called up the stairs.

"I'm coming, I'm coming," I muttered as I stumbled down the stairs. "Tyrant." I mumbled under my breath as I entered the front hall.

It was five a.m. My plane left O'Hare in a hour and a half. It was still dark and frosty outside and it was permeating in to the house. The ceramic tile floor in the foyer was ice cold. Michael and Brennan were taking me to the airport. I always tried to fly on the first flight of the day to avoid delays and problems, but at that very raw and early moment when I actually had to be up and functioning, I often questioned my strategy and sanity.

The doorbell chimed and I thought I was dreaming. I spun around and stared at the door. Michael and Brennan were in the garage. I carefully looked through the peephole in the door. A dark figure was standing in front of my door. I was not imagining things.

I opened the door and gasped. A girl, a mirror image of me, except ten or more years my junior was standing on my doorstep. She was dressed in black from head to toe in a stylish, black leather jacket, pants and knit turtleneck. Her hair was black and straight and rested gently on her shoulders. Her piercing blue eyes stared at me, she said nothing.

"Can I help you?" I finally asked.

"Mrs. Maxwell?"

"Yes. I'm sorry, do I ... " I trailed off.

She reached into her jacket and pulled out a small white envelope. Without saying another word she handed it to me and left. I stood there in the open doorway, cold air rushing over me. After a minute I shut the door and opened the envelope. There was no writing on the outside of the envelope anywhere. It wasn't sealed. There was a small, square piece of white paper inside. The note was typed and centered on the page. It wasn't signed. I knew exactly whom it was from.

> *"Roses are red*
> *Sometimes black*
> *Violets are blue*
> *Sometimes purple*
> *You'll be all four*
> *When I'm finished with you."*

I dropped the note. I looked up and saw Michael walking down the hall. I stepped on the piece of paper.

"Was someone at the door?" Michael asked.

"What? No, I thought it was the doorbell too, but it wasn't," I said quickly. "I think it may be something beeping upstairs."

"Hmm. I'll go run through the house quickly. You go get in the car."

He ran upstairs and I scooped up the note and shoved it in my pocket.

. . .

"Take good care of Daddy," I said to Brennan.

"Of course," he chirped. I kissed him.

"We'll try to be out by next Saturday," Michael said.

We hugged for several minutes. Michael held me tight and clenched his jaw. "Everything will be fine," he whispered in my ear and kissed my cheek.

"You telling me, or you?" I smiled.

Before he could answer, Brennan decided we were done and stood on the chair and wiggled in between us.

"I need to hug Mamma good-bye," he said definitively.

"Ohhh, come here," I said. I picked him up and twirled him around a few times and dipped him over so he could put his hands on the floor. He squealed with delight.

"I want to go with," he said as I flipped him back upright and set him down.

A knot formed in my gut and my heart sank. Michael and I had been hoping he wouldn't say that.

"You have school," I said.

"That's okay. I think I've learned enough this year."

We stared at him and tried not to laugh.

"Well, who's going to travel with Dad, if you come now? And you have no suitcase."

"Daddy's big, he'll be okay."

"All right mister, that's enough," Michael said. "You will still miss some school when we go out to Colorado next week."

"Okay."

I kissed his cheek and patted his head a few times.

"I'll miss you. I love you, Bren."

"You better get on the plane," Michael whispered.

Michael and I kissed quickly one more time. Michael picked up my carry-on bag with his free arm and put it on my shoulder. I had a déjà vu moment and gave him a strange look.

"What?"

"Nothing. I'll see you next Saturday."

. . .

I tried sleeping on the plane. I used to pay for my own upgrade to first-class. Now, I have so many frequent-flyer miles I can upgrade for free pretty much every time I fly. As bad as I was at packing after over a decade of constant travel, I was even worse at flying awake. My flight routine consisted of ordering a glass of Chardonnay and a bottle of water as soon as I sat down. I drank the wine and put the bottle in my bag for later. I slipped on my headphones and listened to a relaxing CD and tried to be asleep before the plane began to taxi down the runway.

I popped my favorite CD in and settled back into the seat. I couldn't fall asleep. I watched the flight attendant go through the safety features for the first time in years. I finished off my wine and stared out the window. The clouds looked like mountains as they floated by below the plane. The sun shone brightly, reflecting off the clouds. I dug my sunglasses out of my bag and put them on. I pulled out a mirror and lipstick. I touched up the purple circles under my eyes with concealor and found a deep red lipstick to draw attention away from my tired eyes and the still healing, inch-long gash on my cheek. *I look like a prizefighter.* I sighed and threw the make-up back in my bag.

The flight attendant brought breakfast and set it before me. I mindlessly picked at the scrambled eggs and fruit in front of me as I stared out the window and thought about the Skirts.

"The Skirts" as we called ourselves, had been friends since as long as we could remember. We grew up within four blocks of each other and attended the private Lincoln Academy, or as all the students called it, "the Future Republicans of America Training Academy." The Skirts all managed to escape on graduation day unscathed and un-Republican.

I was the career-minded one. I had joined the school newspaper in junior high and loved it. I had to be in the center of the action, always the first to know the news. I loved the popularity that came with it and being privy to school news before anyone else. It was a rush. It was a sense of power and control. The others talked me into sports. I was too dangerous with a stick to play field hockey and I hated running at that time, so I ended up being goalie on the soccer team and a cheerleader. I didn't mind being a cheerleader. It kept me out of the house and in the loop for news stories.

Evelyn Cohen was the opposite of me. She was tiny and cute. Her petite 5'3" frame was lithe but muscular from seven years of cheerleading and a lifetime of step aerobics. She had dark brown eyes and perfect, thick, wavy brunette hair that was never out of place. My hair, a shade darker so it looked black, not brown, was frizzy and I spent hours blow–drying it straight. Her make–up always matched her outfits and her bags always matched her shoes. She was homecoming queen, prom queen, co-captain of the soccer team for three years and captain of the varsity cheerleading squad for two years. Every time the four of us got in trouble with our parents we could trace the leak to Evelyn. Her one weakness in life was a complete inability to lie or keep a secret. Her job in life was to be beautiful and impeccably dressed in the latest fashions from New York and Europe. Every spring break her mother and aunts took her to Milan, Paris or New York for the fashion shows. She always brought gifts back for the rest of us. One year we all went.

Vivian Pasquesi's weltanschauung snapped into focus on that spring break trip. Her life's work was set. Not her career path, not the job she decided she wanted, but her worldview was formed. She made it her life's goal to make enough money to be friends with all those people and have the jet-set lifestyle. The secret desire of her heart was to marry a European prince. When you grow up among the rich and beautiful of the Gold Coast, it is easy to be overshadowed for no reason. While it was Evelyn's birthright to be a "beautiful person," for Vivian, it did not come as easily as breathing. Viv was average height, hourglass figure, long, straight light–brown hair, hazel eyes and olive-colored skin which made it easy for her to always have a tan. She was like a bronze Roman goddess ... tall and athletic, captain of the field hockey team for three years and co–captain of the soccer team her senior year with Evelyn. She was class president all four years and usually the mastermind behind any major plotting.

Claire Adams was our token Gentile. While the school was split pretty much fifty-fifty, Claire was the only one in our inner circle. She taught us Christmas carols and gave us stuffed Easter bunnies, much to our lenient parents' ambivalence and grandmothers' horror. Her father was the minister at the large Presbyterian church where people went to be seen more than to see God. She was the stereotypical All-American girl with blond, curly hair and aquamarine-blue eyes. She had a quarter Illini in her and turned a dark reddish brown every summer. Guys literally tripped over each other and drooled in front of her when we hung out at Oak Street Beach in the summer. Vivian and I thought it was hilarious. Claire was humiliated. Evelyn would pout because guys weren't being stupid over her. Every summer she'd threaten to dye her hair blond.

For college, we partied our way through Northwestern together. We decided it was much smarter to be close to dad's wallet and on home turf for the prime college experience. The four of us had a suite for six ... I can't remember which father it was who pulled the strings for that one.

Evelyn organized the sorority charities and raised more money than any girl in AΣ history. She dated a Daley, a Wrigley (Chet's first cousin, Stuart), a Crocker, a McCormick, a Field, a Smithe and even a Leinekugel heir one summer at the lake before settling on a pre-law student with an East Coast pedigree as long and distinguished as anyone we'd ever met. Her mother started planning the wedding two years before they were engaged. Seven months after we graduated, they were married on the eighth night of Hanukkah at the Drake Hotel.

Vivian spent every summer interning. She worked for financial companies in Chicago, New York and London and did consulting and financial work for a large landowner/cattle rancher in Argentina her senior year. We went down to visit her, saw the penguins and gorged ourselves on Argentine beef. She decided she liked financial markets the best and went to NYU for grad school after our three-month tour of Europe ... a collective graduation present from our parents. After grad school she chose bond trading. She wanted to be close to Wall Street. She's never been married, and doesn't plan on it.

Claire's mother died our sophomore year of college. She had been suffering from a rare form of cancer for six years and finally decided she'd had enough. Claire spent the next two and a half years taking medical classes and volunteering at the university hospital. After graduation she moved to Vail. She joined her father who was already there pastoring a small mountain church and running a retreat center. She opened a spa resort for wealthy people who were stressed by their lives of idleness and cancer patients who needed alternative therapies. Her college sweetheart, a gorgeous, blond-haired, blue-eyed med student, followed her out to Colorado. At 26, after two years of marriage, he was killed in a freak ski accident. Claire hasn't skied or been in love since.

I spent college organizing AΣ parties and working for the Associated Press. By the time I was twenty, I had been hanging around for four years and had sufficiently driven everyone crazy with begging to learn their jobs. I learned to edit, write, report, copy-edit and take photos. I majored in journalism and minored in foreign affairs and languages. I learned French, Spanish and German. After graduation I left AP for two years to work for the *Tribune*. I had to get out. Explore. The world was waiting and I was going to record its stories.

Unfortunately, I covered flower shows, school–board meetings and all the other hideously boring stories given to rookies. After two years of paying my dues and writing stories for others to claim, I was given my first major break. A convention in Vegas. I was 23 years old. I was sent with two other reporters to Vegas to cover a convention supposedly a front for illegal businesses with Chicago ties. I think they gave it to me because I knew Gregory and his friends. No one at the paper knew we were dating. After my disastrous marriage and divorce, within the same year, affectionately referred to by everyone as "the drunken mistake" I left the Trib and returned to the comfort and familiarity of the AP's Chicago bureau.

XIV.

"We are about 10 minutes from Denver International Airport ... " the scratchy, husky voice of the pilot came over the intercom. "The temperature is a balmy 72 degrees, time is 8:20 a.m. Mountain Daylight Time."

After the plane landed, I made my through the airport and down to the baggage area. And waited. "Baggage guys have way too much power," I say to no one in particular, not meaning to say it out loud at all.

A college kid standing next to me with a skateboard and 20 extra yards of fabric hanging off him nodded in agreement. "Dude, so true. So fucking true. Heh, heh."

I looked down and suddenly became entranced with my watch and wrist, trying to figure out what time it was. *Mountain time is one hour behind ...*

"It's 8:30, right?" I asked the elderly woman on the other side of me.

"Yes it is," she replied politely. She took a step toward the baggage carousel, even though it hadn't started up yet.

Apparently, she heard my short conversation with skateboard guy and thinks I'm one of those crazy people who talks to everyone near them in public. Fabulous. I smiled sweetly, thanked her politely and adjusted my watch. Vivian's flight would arrive in a half hour from New York. The carousel whirred to life and bags began to pour forth. I finally saw my bags and grabbed them off the baggage carousel. I pulled everything together, and headed for the rental car counter.

"Hello. May I help you?" the rental car girl asked.

"Yes, thank you. I have a reservation."

"Name?" she asked, raising an eyebrow and sounding a touch snide.

"Right. Shelby Maxwell." *I know who I am ... you sure as hell should if you were any good at your job ...* I thought to myself. I tried to keep a straight face.

She clicked the computer keys with mile–long nails. She frowned, looking seriously at the computer screen as if cracking an international spy code. "Ah yes ... " she finally said, still typing. "Chevy Blazer."

Michael always tried to rent me the biggest, safest car he could when he called in the reservation. I smiled at her. "I don't suppose you have something a little more ... sporty?"

She frowned again, but found me cherry red Mustang convertible. I thanked her and mumbled an inane explanation about my husband. She looked down at my hand and stared at my wedding ring: two perfect emeralds and a diamond, square-cut and two carats each. She threw me an openly hostile look. I signed all the paperwork, took the key and humbly slunk away from the counter.

I reached in my bag and found my phone. I turned it on and thirty seconds later it beeped loud enough for people in the Salt Lake City airport to hear it. Voice mail from Vivian. She was wandering around the baggage area. She had forgotten which car rental place she was supposed to meet me at. I laughed out loud at a picture of a New Yorker dressed all in black and dragging around designer luggage in the Denver airport. I punched in her number.

"Hey babe, where are you?" I asked.

"Hey! I'm at some red company ... where the hell are you?"

"The pretty green one."

"You're funny," she yelled in frustration.

"Yeah, that's what I've heard. I've got the car all taken care of, just get down here so we can leave, huh?"

"Yeah, yeah ... I'll be right there."

. . .

I put the top down as we headed out of Denver toward Vail.

"I was hoping you would get a convertible," Vivian said. She opened her Coach bag and pulled out two silk scarves and two pairs of dark Jackie O sunglasses. "Here." She handed me a beautiful pink scarf. I pulled over to the side of the road and put the scarf over my hair and loosely tied it behind my neck. I took off my sunglasses and slipped on the ones Viv gave me. She handed me two mother-of-pearl covered clips to keep the scarf on. She put on an emerald green scarf and tortoise shell clips. We looked like we were in a 1950's movie. I slowly pulled off the shoulder and back onto the highway.

"Want one?" Vivian asked. She was holding a pack of cigarettes in front of me. "Get one now before Evelyn throws a fit."

"Naw, I've done real well since I was pregnant with Brennan."

"Hell, if this past week isn't a time to smoke, I don't know when a good time is," she said, lighting up.

I smiled. "Yeah, I know. It's tempting, but I'll regret it."

"Suit yourself," she puffed away. After a minute she looked back over to me, "you've become a real Mother Fucking Theresa, you know that?"

The warm spring air filled the car and we turned up the radio and sang along. The sun shone through the clouds. The gauzy clouds looked like cotton being slowly pulled apart into wispy shreds as they scraped over the top of the Rockies. We drove west, straight toward the peaks, still snowy. As we began to climb higher in altitude I could feel the tension falling behind me.

My white eyelet cotton shirt and scarf fluttered in the breeze. Vivian took off her black, satin button-down shirt. She had a tight, emerald green camisole underneath that matched her scarf. She rubbed on some sunscreen and lay back to soak up the sun.

I put a Chris Isaak CD into the CD player and turned it up. Vivian and I sang along and dreamed of Chris. She lit up another cigarette and smiled contently. An hour later we pulled into Honey's, a diner in West Lionshead. I could see Claire and Evelyn at a booth by the window. They waved. We waved back and went in.

Over gallons of Irish Crème coffee, mounds of pancakes, French toast, fresh fruit and powdered sugar we giggled and all talked simultaneously to catch up on the last few months. I explained the scar on my cheek. The girls instantly took to the new nickname for Gracie. Evelyn was five months pregnant with her third, and found out it's finally a girl. Claire was engaged to a ski resort owner ten years older than her. Vivian updated us on Toby.

"He's been acting so bizarre ... " Vivian started.

"Post-traumatic stress," I cut in.

"Yeah, no shit ... " she cut back in. "I've only seen him once in the past week ... he's not answering calls from anyone or going out at all. I went down and checked on him and he opened up only after I banged on the door for ten minutes and threatened to blow down the door."

She leaned in over the table and lowered her voice. We all leaned in to hear her. We all knew Toby from Northwestern. He was two years older, but a Sig ... our brother fraternity ΣΑΣ. Evelyn thought he was repulsive. Claire tried to "fix" him. Vivian and I stopped speaking for six months, after we found out we had both been sleeping with him at approximately the same time. He had broken up with both of us and after a drunken night of questioning my self-worth a sympathetic frat brother confessed. After recovering from our mutual mortification of not being able to see it, and having a guy play us like that, we made up and have used Toby as a cabana boy ever since.

"His apartment was disgusting," she continued. Toby and Viv lived in the same building on Central Park West, two floors apart. "He was in boxers and a dirty t-shirt. I immediately walked over to the phone and called my maid service. I threw him in the shower ... helped him get dressed. He's pretty messed up over Meelie and what he saw in Damascus. He was practically catatonic. I couldn't get him to talk much and he absolutely refused to talk about her. He flinched like a rifle was going off when I even mentioned her name ... or Shelby's."

"Yeah ... am I crazy or was he messing around with her?" I asked.

"I heard he was the real reason she was spending so much time in New York last year," Evelyn said. "She couldn't have cared less about all those UN subcommittee meetings! I heard she didn't attend half the meetings she claimed to be at."

We all stared at her. I start choking on my mouthful of bacon. Evelyn never gossiped. She believed it was beneath her, a deadly sin and the number one way to make enemies. If Evelyn said she heard something, it meant it came straight from Meelie.

"What else did you hear?" I asked slowly.

"Well ... I don't know if ... "

"Aw shit, Evelyn ... this isn't the club!" Vivian yelled. "Meelie's not going to care!" All the senior citizens who were sitting around us sipping coffee looked over and glared. She smiled at them, and lowered her voice again. "Evelyn, if Meelie told you something, you need to tell us. She's dead and Toby's a fucking mess."

"She said she loved him," she said, half whining like she still didn't want to tell us. "But then he started to back out ... like he always does ... she found out at a party that he was flirting around with other women right there under her nose. So she left. She said she wasn't going to put up with it. She went back to the Embassy in Bonn.

Then, right after Inauguration day, because she was reportedly so miserable no one wanted to be around her, she ended up with a job at State in Washington. Her father arranged it to get her out of the embassy. She didn't want to go, so she didn't tell many people. I found out when I called her up in Germany, because Ted was going to be there, but I was told she wasn't there. I'm not really sure what her job was. When she found out she was going with the Secretary to Syria, she called Toby's office to see if he'd be there as well. I told her to stay away from him but she wouldn't listen ... "

"Evelyn, Toby didn't kill her," I said. "But he may have saved her from becoming a cold case file."

Now they were all staring at me.

"I don't have all the pieces, but I know he was in the room that night ... probably the bathroom, it's the only thing I can think of ..."

"How do you know that?" Claire asked.

"I found a roll of film and developed it and it was pictures of the murder as it happened and the film casing had Toby's markings on it. I was at the hotel and saw him at what must have been right after. He was acting a little strange, but mostly himself. At the time I just thought he was being himself. Now I think he was trying to get my attention to tell me ... but I blew him off. Anyway ... I know who did it."

"Who?" they said in unison trying to keep their voices down.

"Tony Cortese was the trigger man and Gregory planned it."

"That sick fuck ... " Vivian whispered. She banged her palms down on the table. A waitress gave us a dirty look as she walked by. We all apologized and hoped we wouldn't be kicked out. "How did they even know that Meelie would be there?"

"I don't know that ... they may not have known. She may not have been the original target. I have my conversation with Gregory on tape and pictures of Tony pulling the trigger," I continued.

We sat in silence, sipping coffee. The air began to fill up the whole place like water. We felt its presence and weight pushing against us. I realized I was holding my breath. I exhaled slowly.

I saw Toby before me. The picture painted by Vivian. The various Tobys I saw in Damascus, becoming more and more separate and defined—the hotel, the cab, the airport. My mind was unable to put together all the different scenes. A stifled cry began to bubble up from my innermost parts.

I began to see and slowly recite out loud the gruesome painting of Meelie's death. Not the check-list of 'this happened, then this, oh yes, and this' as I had for Michael, my father and Pete, but the way you recall a memory after twenty years of gold dust and haze have set it. The point at which you begin to remember things in prose and poetry.

"When you see a murder—a dead body for the first time—it is as if time stops ... slides backwards, sideways ... stretches to a point of deformity ... perversion. You are trapped, like seeing the world through a piece of dark stained glass. Red, maybe blue, anyway, you can see, but it's dark ... murky ... not real. It steals away your soul. There was a high-pitched ringing in my ears, a choking somewhere in me ... like being strangled, but from the inside. You know ... like when you are pregnant and feel the baby push on your ribcage from the inside for the first time? The moment I saw Meelie's face ... all color drained from the world and there was that pushing from the inside out feeling ... " I trailed off to a whisper, my voice cracked.

We all sat in silence. I sucked in air and continued. "I feel like there are these cracks and crevices — that every time I tell the story, the further away I get from it — more and more of the detail, the color, the consistency of the story is lost into these cracks and crevices. Like the first time I went to Israel. Remember? I was so jet-lagged when I returned and every time I showed my pictures and told the stories, the stories changed. Evolved. I looked at pictures and got some of the details wrong ... thought it was a different picture, event ... It wasn't that I was lying or exaggerating ... it just changed, the longer it went on. Well, now I look at the photos and try to remember. I try to remember the truth. I try to wade through all the versions and misstatements to remember the truth ... " Pause. My voice was high and strained. It sounded unfamiliar to me as I talked.

Like a child playing with a helium balloon, I sucked in a second breath and continued. "I am losing my mind. I'm having nightmares. Visions of God watching all of this up above ... stirring his finger in the pool of eternity and it is slapping me around ... "

Evelyn and Claire let out clipped, high-pitched gasps. I was exhausted.

For you write down bitter things
against me
And make me inherit the sins of my youth.
You fasten my feet in shackles;
You keep close watch on all my paths ...

Why do I put myself in jeopardy
and take my life in my hands?
Though He slay me,
yet will I hope in Him ...
Indeed,
this will turn out for my deliverance.

~Book of Job

XV.

After brunch, we drove up to Claire's house. It was on the high road above Vail, nestled in the mountains overlooking Vail and Lionshead. The house was typical for Colorado, a log cabin kit, not the smaller A-frame model, but low and long, with a three-quarters second story. The back of the house was all glass. The full-length windows captured the full view of the valley. The front of the house looked out at the mountains jutting straight up. To the right, or north side of the house was a hiking trail and then beyond that ski trails ... run by Claire's new fiancé. Since it was early May, the mountains still had a filmy layer of snow, albeit icy slush. Only brave, stupid or professional skiers were still zipping down the mountain for one last run before summer.

The wellness center, next to the house, accommodated 10 guests as well as various offices and healing rooms. It was also mostly glass, taking advantage of the views on all sides. Claire had a garden in the back, as well as a "natural–setting" pool and hot tub.

Both house and center were decorated with nature. Exposed wood walls were covered with antique skis and gold mining equipment. Placards with Bible verses and quotes to induce deep thinking lined the kitchen, halls and bedroom walls. The furniture was unvarnished pine, covered with natural fabrics. Fresh flowers in beautiful, colored vases were placed in every room of the center and house. In the summer, the flowers came from Claire's own garden.

We took our usual rooms. The room Vivian chose was upstairs. It was decorated in green and cream plaid and had rich, dark furniture, including a queen-sized sleigh bed. Evelyn's room was across the hall. The sweet pink room was filled with white pine furniture trimmed with painted pink flowers. A four-poster bed with a gauzy canopy, tied at the corners with white ribbon from Tiffany's sat in the middle of the room. Both rooms had French doors out to a second-floor balcony.

Claire's bedroom was the master bedroom. It was large, with a large bathroom, a closet the size of a small room and the only television in the house. It also had a large fireplace. It was decorated in rich, dark reds and greens, plaid fabrics and dark cherry wood furniture. Family photos and pictures of the four of us, our families and other friends lined the walls of Claire's room. There were many, many photos all over the house and wellness center. Claire told clients they needed to find friends to get them through life. She used us as examples.

Her father's small room, on the first floor, looked like a monk's cell in a monastery. Simple, brown and cream, a few tintypes and photos hung neatly on the walls. A wooden cross, given to him by a homeless man in Chicago, was hung in the place of honor above his single bed.

My room was off the front foyer across from Mr. Adams' room and study. I loved it because it had a stone fireplace. The curtains, sheets, comforter and blankets were indigo blue. A handmade blue and cream quilt was always folded neatly at the end of the bed. Old teddy bears and a pair of ice skates decorated the fireplace hearth. There were pictures lining the mantle of my family and Claire's through the years. I threw my luggage down by the fireplace in my room and fell onto the bed. I think I fell asleep before my head hit the pillow.

. . .

"Feel better?" Claire asked as I walked into the main room. She was curled up on an overstuffed, blue–jean covered couch reading a book.

"Yes. Thank you." I wandered into the kitchen to find a diet soda.

The back half of the first floor was one open room with furniture creating partial divisions between the living room, dining room and kitchen. A high, long bar with stools separated the gourmet kitchen from the living room. A counter wrapped around to separate the kitchen from the dining room. Huge chandeliers made of some kind of antler hung over the dining room table, which seated fifteen comfortably, and one over the middle of the living room area. The dining room table was a nine-foot long oak door, turned into a table, with benches on either side for chairs. The table was in front of the wall of windows at the back of the house. Diners feasted on scenery and sunsets while eating Claire's simple, but fabulous cooking. The side wall of the dining room spread into the kitchen and became built-in shelves and cabinets from floor to ceiling. The kitchen pantry was large enough for three families, all of the clients at the wellness center and whoever else dropped by during ski season. The other main wall, on the other side of the open area, was the living room wall. It was a massive stone wall. It curved around into a fireplace. It created the wall separating the living room from my room and the fireplace in my room backed up to the living room fireplace. When there wasn't a fire going, you could see from one room into the other.

I sank into the matching blue–jean covered couch across from Claire and tossed a red, corduroy pillow to the other end of the couch. "Where's Viv?" I asked, tapping on the top of my soda and cracking it open.

"She crashed like you. Evelyn had a craving so she headed off to the store," Claire said, looking down at her watch. "She should be back soon."

"What time is it?"

"Four."

"Dang."

"Don't worry. You looked pretty wiped back at Honey's. If you hadn't immediately fallen asleep, I would have suggested a nap."

"You're the greatest."

"That's the rumor."

I sat for a minute, sipping the soda and mentally arguing with myself over whether or not to mention my conversation with Rabbi Feldstein with Claire.

"Something wrong?" she asked, knowing there was, but being gracious as always. She always let the other person admit it or not. She never pried. She bookmarked her place in her book and set it down on the coffee table.

"Well ... maybe not 'wrong,' but I didn't tell you guys everything," I paused and put the soda on the coffee table in front of me. I noticed the crystal coasters. They had been a cherished wedding gift to Claire's mother. Each had *"Adams"* engraved in the middle. I had always loved them. They reminded me of Mrs. Adams. "I met with Rabbi Feldstein for lunch last week."

"Oh?" She sat up a little. Claire came with us to Temple services on Friday nights so we all could go out after. The rest of our families all belonged to the same Temple. It was a large, very Reformed congregation concerned with keeping up basic Jewishness ... just not all the details. Of course, being the good friends we were, we rarely returned the favor by going to church with Claire on Sunday mornings. But we did go to many over-hyped, over-sugared youth events with her. We all secretly resented her because she seemed to enjoy and fully participate in both Temple and Protestant worship and events. She made us look bad ... in two different religions.

"Yeah. I'm not sure exactly what he told me, but I wasn't ready to talk yet. Michael asked me to meet with him ... so I did. I tried to start talking about something ... anything ... but I didn't know what I wanted to talk about. He asked me 'why are we here?'"

"He asked you that?" she giggled.

"Yeah, can you believe it?" I laughed and threw up my hands. "I kind of brought it up first I guess ... I was grasping at straws ... hell, if God is behind all this for whatever reason ... it may just be the most plausible reason I can think of. I guess I just want God to finally exist for me because I don't think I can live in a world where this kind of thing happens randomly or for no reason. You know? Even if I hate the answer and end up hating God, at least it's a reason. Something other than molecules banging into each other. He smiled and told me, 'Shelby, I have no thunderbolt! No stone tablet ... '"

"No stone tablet ... that sounds like Feldstein."

"Yeah, wait ... it gets better ... classic Feldstein. Then he said, 'God didn't hand me a memo.'"

"Nice. What did you say?"

"Nothing. He said only I can figure out why I am here, why I was the one who found Meelie. I just slumped down in my chair and stared at him. I was like, 'no shit, so this isn't working.' He said, 'obviously, something is very wrong in your world, or you wouldn't have called and wouldn't be talking to me. No matter how much you love your husband. Right?' I tried to look offended, but he ignored me."

"Wow. So what do you think?" she asked, pulling her legs off the couch and sitting up straight.

"My jaw dropped. He said, 'unfortunately, God's come knocking' and asked me what am I going to do ... only, I didn't know then and I don't really know now, either. It's like I have all these pieces ... at the hotel I knew there were all these pieces, but I didn't have any of them, that I knew of. Now I have some, maybe most ... but I still am so confused. I don't know what to do. I don't want to do anything. I just want to wake up and have it be 5 a.m. and I am in my hotel bed in Damascus and I get up and get ready and calmly go to the airport and go home because none of this ever happened," I sighed. "I told him, 'If God knocking means getting the crap beaten out of me, I'll pass.'"

I left out the part about Jonah and the big fish. I still wasn't sure what to do with that, and I didn't feel like a Sunday school lesson from Claire.

"God's not beating the crap out of you," she said. "I know what you mean though. I've definitely felt God was out to get me at times. When my mom died I thought God had taken her on purpose, just to hurt me and my dad ... like we failed a test and he decided we didn't really deserve her after all."

"That is exactly what I feel like. Like Meelie's gone because of me; that Michael and Brennan are going to leave ... or be taken away because I've failed. Feldstein said that if God's not trying to tell me something it might just be time to pay the piper. 'Life's been a great party and it's looking like the hangover's going to be really nasty' he said. He said I have to figure out if it's a hangover, a coincidence or a serious message from God. 'Let me know how it goes' he said. Let me know how it goes ... " I trailed off. "I wish someone else could finish this off and let me know how it goes!" I said and put my hands over my face.

Claire gave me a sympathetic look. She came over and sat next to me. She put her arm around me and we just sat there.

"There's one more thing," I said softly.

"What, darlin'?"

"He gave me a note ... something to read ... oh crud, what was it? What did I do with that note?" I asked myself.

"What did it say? Read what? A book?"

"H, I think. Begins with H ... Torah, right. His note ended with a snide remark about how it was in the Tanakh."

"Right ... Tanakh ... is that part of the Torah?"

"Hell if I know ... probably."

Claire got up and went over to a bookshelf. She pulled a Bible off the shelf and started riffling through it. "Aha! Yes, of course."

She walked back over to the couch and sat down. I stared at her and waited. My mind was a confused blank.

"The book of Hosea is probably what he told you to read."

"That rings a bell."

"It's a beautiful story ... kind of sparse on details. Hosea is a prophet in Israel, after it splits into the two kingdoms. God asked him to marry a wife, Gomer ... "

"Gomer?"

"Uh, yeah ... aren't you glad that name fell out of fashion," she laughed.

"No kidding."

"Anyway ... Gomer is unfaithful ... She married Hosea but kept up her partying lifestyle and affairs with, apparently, many men." I flinch. She pauses and continues in a soft tone. "But they have three children and their lives are a mirror, a living metaphor for the people of Israel and God's love for them. It's a love story that isn't simple and sweet and PG. Hosea and Gomer are real ... they suffer and probably drove each other crazy ... but somehow, something made them work it out. He goes to find her one last time and apparently she returns for good. She's redeemed ... reclaimed. The story is pretty sparse on details, like I said. We are never told what happened to make Hosea go get her or what made Gomer return. You are left to assume it was God working in their lives. It's supposed to show how the nation of Israel someday returning to the land and to God. We don't know how ... we are just supposed to believe it can and will and does happen."

We sat there for a few minutes. I tried not to take the story too personally, but I couldn't help but draw all kinds of crazy comparisons.

I know exactly what Gomer was doing.

I looked up at Claire. "I know why she left Hosea," I finally said. "It's hard being around a prophet ... a man of God when you are not ... when you are a failure and hopelessly flawed."

"Oh darlin'," Claire said. "That is not the point of the story. The point of the story is we are all hopelessly flawed ... but God comes and gets us anyway." She hugged me. "Okay, so I know you are probably not believing any of this ... you don't really have to." She pulled away and looked at me. "But if you want to ... to read more, to study ... my father's office is full of books. You may find something that helps. Feel free to use his office while you're here."

"Thanks. That helps, I guess," I tried to smile.

"Hey! Did you two start the sharing and bonding without us?" Viv said. She and Evelyn were standing in the kitchen. Vivian was leaning over the bar. Evelyn was pulling steaks and fresh veggies out of a brown grocery bag.

"How long you two been standing there?" I asked.

"Since you were hugging. What's Claire talking about?" Evelyn asked.

"Yeah, why would you want to read anything in her father's office?" Vivian asked. She made a face like she had a bad taste in her mouth.

"I'll tell you over dinner," I said.

. . .

The next morning we went to the best day spa in Vail for a full overhaul. After four hours of being massaged, exfoliated, buffed, manicured and pedicured, I was as relaxed as I'd ever been. The girls wanted to go shopping, but I wanted to go back and be by myself for awhile. They were reluctant to let me out of their sight. They were afraid one of Gregory's goonies was in Vail waiting for the perfect time to finish me off. I waved them off. In my new-found blaséness I shrugged them off.

"I'll look behind every tree and mailbox, I promise. If you see anyone lurking around just come back to the house," I said. "I promise I'll lock all the doors and keep the windows closed."

I walked down to the bus stop and waited. I noticed a guy standing across the street in front of a Western clothing store. He was just standing there staring straight ahead. I tried to casually look around for other people around me he could be staring at. There was no one else at the stop and no one walking behind me. I suddenly felt very exposed. I strained my eyes to see if I recognized the man. *This is crazy! I can't freak out every time I see someone staring off into space and assume they are out to get me.* The bus pulled up and I got on. I looked through the window as I sat down and saw the doorway of the shop was empty. I looked around but didn't see him anywhere. *See, he was just some poor guy waiting for his wife to finish shopping.*

I walked in the house, stood in the hallway. I tried to shake off the feeling that someone was watching me, following me around. I stared at Mr. Adams' office through the open doorway. It was tucked in the front corner of the house, across the front foyer from my room, as you walked in the front door. He was in Pasadena for a conference, Claire explained yesterday when we arrived.

I cautiously entered the room, almost tiptoeing as if I were breaking in, or violating sacred space. There was a grand picture window that looked out at the mountains rising straight up in front of the house. Since most of the action happened in the main room in the back of the house, the office was a serene nook. A sanctuary. The walls were lined with bookshelves. Some shelves were covered in knickknacks, which I assumed were gifts from his parishioners. It was easy to figure out which gifts came from parishioners in Chicago and which came from Vail. The books were colorful and lined the shelves in some kind of order, maybe by subject or author. I had no clue. They rose and fell like jagged edges from shelf to shelf. Tall, short, thick, slender. I didn't recognize any of the titles or authors. I couldn't even understand some of the titles. Some of the cases held thick volumes of mass works. They looked like Michael's law books to me.

A plain, unadorned desk sat in the middle of the room with the chair facing away from the window. The desk was about five feet long with a smooth, rectangular surface and nothing on it but a computer, a picture of Claire and a picture of his late wife, both framed in unvarnished wood frames.

I pulled one of the many Bibles off the shelf. "KING JAMES VERSION" was stamped in large gold letters across its spine and front cover. I had heard of this one. I was confused by the row of Bibles. I was unsure if they were all different and why they were all different sizes and thicknesses. I opened it, found the Table of Contents and flipped through till I found Hosea.

I started reading. "And I will betroth thee unto me for ever; yea, I will betroth thee unto me in righteousness, and in judgment, and in lovingkindness, and in mercies. I will even betroth thee unto me in faithfulness: and thou shalt know the LORD ... "

I stopped reading and stared at the book. I snapped it shut and went back to the shelf. I looked at the row of Bibles again. I put King James back on the shelf and pulled three more off the shelf. I sat down at the desk and opened them all to the same place and lined them up in front of me. I found one that was actually in modern English. It had "NEW AMERICAN STANDARD VERSION" in silver on the spine and "HOLY BIBLE" in silver across the front cover. I wished Claire or her father was there to explain, but I also wanted to be alone. I hesitated for a moment, staring at all the open Bibles before me. I started reading again. I tried to pick out the story of Hosea and Gomer and figure out the story among all the bizarre and inexplicable stuff. I needed to prove Michael and I were nothing like this dead prophet and his whore of a wife.

"Contend with your mother, contend, for she is not my wife, and I am not her husband; and let her put away her harlotry from her face ... I will strip her naked and expose her as on the day when she was born. I will also make her like a wilderness ... I will have no compassion on her children ... For she who conceived them has acted shamefully."

That's harsh. Claire thinks this is a great story? It damn well better get better.

I skipped down a little and kept reading. "For she said, 'I will go after my lovers, who give me my bread and my water, my wool and my flax, my oil and my drink.'"

I started reading to myself out loud, mumbling the words in disbelief.

" 'Therefore, behold, I will hedge up her way with thorns, and I will build a wall against her so that she cannot find her paths ... She will seek them, but will not find them.

... For she does not know that it was I who gave her the grain, the new wine and the oil, lavished on her silver and gold ... Therefore, I will take back My grain at harvest time and My new wine in its season ... no one will rescue her out of My hand ... I will punish her for the days of the Baals.' "

Baals? I'll ask Claire later.

" 'Therefore, behold, I will allure her, into the wilderness and speak kindly to her. I will give her vineyards from there, the valley of Achor as a door of hope. She will sing there as in the days of her youth ... It will come about in that day,' declares the LORD, 'In that day I will also make a covenant for them and will make them lie down in safety. I will betroth you to Me forever; Yes, I will betroth you to Me in righteousness and in justice, in loving-kindness and in compassion, I will betroth you to Me in faithfulness ... I will also have compassion on her who had not obtained compassion, and I will say to those who were not My people, 'You are My people!' and they will say, 'You are my God!'"

I pushed back from the desk, spun the chair around and stared at the mountains behind me. The mountains were my security blanket. They rose up so solidly ... a stalwart, a bodyguard puffing out its chest in protection of me. They were resolute and forever, unmoving and unmovable. The mountains were my shield, my security. I could not be hurt, injured here. They kept the world and all the "bad stuff" out. Away from me. I felt secure and hidden when in Vail. It was probably why I came here for vacation every chance I could get.

I started sobbing. Not the unsettled, strained, nervous sobs of the airport lounge or my father's office, but release. It was as if there was a presence in the room, pressing in on me, ever gentle, indulging my tears. I had felt it more and more as I read on. It was warm and electric and wrapped all around me. It held me as securely as the mountains did. I shook and doubled over. The tears splattered on my smooth, polished feet and dripped off onto the floor. I felt the pressure floating up and out of the room through the ceiling like steam coming off a pot of boiling water ... or smoke coming off a burnt sacrifice on an ancient alter. Swirling upward and outward toward heaven. A burnt sacrifice. That's exactly how I felt.

Meelie was the one who was killed, but I was the one feeling charred and sacrificed.

XVI.

"Good Lord, what's wrong?" Claire asked. She, Evelyn and Vivian had run into the study when they heard me crying.

I screamed from fright. I hadn't realized they were back. Claire saw the Bibles on the desk and came over to me. I had somehow ended up on the floor in a ball next to the windowsill. She wrapped her arms around me and picked me up. She stood me up and motioned for one of the others to bring over a box of Kleenex from a small table by the door. She hugged me tightly.

"I'm fine," I tried to say. I pulled back a little and Claire let go. "I'm fine. Really. It's more of a release than anything else. I've been crying a lot lately. Making up for lost time I guess ... " we all laughed a little. I was never a crier. "I was reading this stupid story Claire told me about yesterday. I was hoping to prove Rabbi Feldstein wrong ... Claire wrong–that this story is completely different than ... than ... " I trailed off.

"Oh honey ... you're not a whore!" Vivian said indignantly. "I don't know why Feldstein and Claire filled your head with that awful story. You're a good person. You're one of the greatest people I know," she said definitively, smacking Claire.

I looked up at her and grabbed a tissue. Mascara was probably streaming down my face like Army camouflage. "I'm not sure how to take that, Viv."

"C'mon, let's go to Bart's," she said, undeterred. She grabbed my hands and pulled me up.

"Viv," I sighed, staring at her. "I am like that story. It's not nonsense. I've been thinking all along there was more to what was happening than what I could see. Now I am sure of it."

She rolled her eyes. "Fine. Let's go to Bart's and you and Claire can have a Bible study later," she huffed. "Until yesterday you didn't even believe God existed! You're Jewish, what the hell are you doing with a pile of Bibles?" She flung her hands over her head in exasperation.

"Come on Vivian, that's not fair," Evelyn said quietly. "Let's just drop all this. We are here to spend time together and support Shelby ... not get in a fight. Let's not forget what she's been through. For all we know there could be someone out there waiting for the perfect time to ... " she trailed off, unable to finish the sentence.

"I'm fine, guys really," I repeated. I felt they were all having a conversation about me, over my head like they were the parents and I was the child. "Let's go to Bart's," I smiled and put one arm around Vivian and one around Evelyn.

• • •

Bart's. A local institution. Bart's was a bar and grill in the middle of Vail where the locals congregated. The outside tables had bright yellow umbrellas with labels of mineral waters and beers on them. There was live music several nights a week. In the summer musicians set up outside and the parties lasted well into the night. The stage inside was being set up as we arrived for dinner.

A teenage hostess with a too–tight black dress and platinum curls piled on top of her head greeted us as we walked through the door. A large group filled the bar area off to the side, but there weren't any other people waiting around for tables.

"Who's playing tonight?" I asked.

"Her name is Georgie Armstrong. She's kind of new, but very cool voice. She has a very Melissa Ethridge sound to her," she said, cocking her head to the side. I watched her head to see if the curls would come tumbling down. Not one curl moved.

"Cool," I answered, finally tearing my eyes away from her head. I smiled and hoped she hadn't noticed my gawking. *I don't need anyone else thinking I am a wacko.* We all nodded in approval, as if we knew her and were connoisseurs of hip, indie music ... or Melissa Ethridge for that matter.

We were shown to a table not far from the stage. We sat down and the hostess handed us large menus. We didn't open them. We didn't need to. The waiter came over and set four glasses of water down on the edge of the table.

"We're ready to order," Vivian said. He looked up at us, startled and a little confused.

"Oh, oh okay." He pulled a notebook out of the pocket of his apron and the pen from behind his ear.

We ordered the same thing we always ordered. Two orders of grilled chicken with fresh tomatoes, green, yellow and red peppers and onions. It came with black beans, cooked to mush with bacon and diced tomatoes and large helpings of Spanish rice. Two orders of steak, one well-done, one medium rare with sweet chutney/salsa and the same beans and rice. We split the four dishes between us so that each of us had half a piece of chicken and half a piece of steak. We have never been able to finish all the side dishes.

The waiter returned after a few minutes with a basket of fluffy, hot fresh-made bread, three blackberry daiquiris and an ice tea for Evelyn. The daqs quickly melted the tension from before. We were talking and giggling as if nothing had ever happened. That was how it worked. Our arguments were sometimes serious, often stupid, but never lasted very long. It helped that arguments never included all four of us, usually only two, so there was at least one person to referee and bring us all back together. It also helped if there was alcohol around.

"Hey Viv."

We looked up to see Bart behind Vivian's chair. He kissed her cheek and started to massage her shoulders. He was wearing blue jeans, a blue–jean shirt and black cowboy boots that were scuffed and cracked. His skin was brown and leathery, but his brown hair and closely cropped beard were free of gray. No one was really sure how old Bart was. Not even Vivian, who had been carrying on a seasonal affair with Bart for about ten years.

"Hello Bart," she smiled.

"Hi Bart," the rest of us cooed.

"Y'all back kinda soon after ski season ... "

"Yeah, just a girls weekend, so to speak," Evelyn piped up.

He laughed. "'Cept it's the middle of the week. I wish I had you girls' lives for just one week, I swear."

"You can have mine," I said. Claire slapped my arm.

"Yours is the most adventurous, Shel," he said, laughing harder.

"Adventure's only fun when you survive, Bart," I said sarcastically and sounding more drained than I had intended. Claire kicked me under the table. I threw her a dirty look.

"What about me?" Vivian said, trying to look hurt. "Oh doll ... Shel is adventurous, Claire is the beautiful healer, Evelyn is the adult ... " he winked, she tried to look offended, "and you lovey are the sexy one." He kissed her shoulder, squeezed her hand and waved good-bye to us. "Gotta go see my other tables."

"Are you still sleeping with him?" Evelyn whispered.

Vivian tried to be coy ... a skill she excelled at with everyone but us. She finally broke down and admitted that in a moment of weakness in February she had gone to his place.

"So that's where you were!" Claire and I said in unison.

"What?"

"Aw hell Viv, come on, give us some frickin' credit," Claire laughed. "We knew you hadn't come home. We never believed your story about coming in late and not waking us up."

"Yeah, I heard you come in at four in the morning. My door is right off the foyer, remember?" I said.

"But ... but, you sleep like the dead," she said, genuinely shocked.

"Well, babe ... I woke up that night," I laughed. Unable to contain myself, I confessed the truth. "Actually, Michael heard you because he is a very, very light sleeper. He freaked out because he thought everyone was in the house. He got up and opened the door and saw you. His getting up out of bed woke me up and when he came back to bed I asked what was wrong. He said he thought he had heard a burglar, but it was just you coming in. I told Claire in the morning in the kitchen, right before you walked in and saw us."

"Oh."

Evelyn changed the subject. "Ooo, the baby just kicked!" she squealed, rubbing her tummy. We all ooohed and ahhhed and started talking about baby stuff. I was pretty sure the baby hadn't kicked. It was just Evelyn's way of changing the subject off something unpleasant and onto herself. Not that she needed to be the center of attention, she usually was, but never minded when she wasn't. She just hated conflict. Evelyn *was* the adult, as Bart said. She was not usually the reason we got together, except for her wedding. She was the one always supporting the rest of us. Of course, we hadn't really fawned over her about the baby yet; she was probably feeling neglected. It was definitely her turn, no matter what was going on in my life.

The food arrived and we all became quiet while we ate.

Around 9 p.m., after the food was long-gone and we'd moved on to Top Shelf margaritas, Georgie Armstrong took the stage. She was cute and outgoing, but not annoyingly perky. She hopped onto a tall barstool and pulled up a beautiful acoustic guitar. She was laid-back and chatty with everyone sitting around her. She had an infectious laugh that put everyone at ease. She was very casual, wearing loose-fitting jeans and an oversized, boxy brown wool sweater with two dark green stripes around the middle. She was wearing wool socks that matched her sweater and Birkenstock sandals. She definitely fit in in Colorado, even though she had a southern accent.

She pushed her short dark brown hair back off her face, and said "al'righty y'all ... let's get started."

She started strumming the guitar. It made a rich, bluegrassy-bluesy–rock sound I'd rarely heard from anyone playing in a bar. She played for an hour. The last song before her break was called "Isaac." I heard the forceful music and lyrics and sat up straight. The words pierced straight through my heart. I felt like she'd written the song about the last two weeks of my life.

After she was done I went up to her and introduced myself.

"Hey, you're great," I said.

"Hey thanks!" she beamed. "I'm glad you liked it."

"Do you have a CD?" I asked.

"Two. Why?" she asked. "Want one?"

"Yeah!"

"Really?" she laughed. "Wow! That's great!" she seemed genuinely surprised to hear I wanted to buy her CD. She dug around in a bag. "You're in luck. I have both with me."

"Which one has that song you sang right before you went on your first break?"

"Uhhh ... " she threw her head up and thought for a minute, "what song was that? Oh yeah. I know," she said and smacked her forehead. She flipped the CDs over and looked over the song titles. "This one." She handed me one of the CDs.

"You know what, I'll take one of each."

"Really? You are so cool." She handed me the other CD and clapped her hands.

I couldn't help but smile and instantly like her. I wanted to be friends with her. She seemed so down-to-earth and comfortable with herself. *Let's face it, I want to be her.*

"No, no," I said, shaking my head. "You are the cool one. Can I buy you a drink or something? I'd love to talk to you about your songs," I said. I pulled two twenties out of my wallet to pay her for the disks.

"Sure. I don't think I have exact change for you," she said as she took the twenties.

"Well then, you'll have to keep it. C'mon. What's your poison?" I said, leading her over to the bar.

"Just a Coke."

"Really?" It was my turn to be shocked.

"Yeah."

"Hey Mason," I chirped to the bartender "two Cokes."

"No problem Shelby." He smiled and winked. He grabbed two glasses and filled them with soda. "Cherries?" he asked.

"Of course. Georgie? Maraschino cherry in your Coke?"

"Oooo, is it good?" I nodded. "Okay," she laughed. We took our Cokes and sat in the back corner of the bar area where it was a little quieter. "Okay, not to pry, since I don't know you, but was

153

that bartender flirting with you?" she asked as soon as we had sat down.

I laughed. "Mason? Oh, he's harmless. Damn cute, but way too young." Mason was 21 years old, covered in muscles and a deep tan from skiing, glistening, white teeth and sandy brown hair that was naturally streaked blond. He had a surfer vibe to him. Every one loved Mason. He was the good-looking kid who didn't know it and had no time to worry about it because he was always working. He was training for the Olympics.

"Okay, now my turn to be nosy," I said, "is Georgie really your name?"

She laughed. "It's short for Georgia. My parents are very unique people, is the short answer."

"Say no more. I understand."

Georgie and I talked for an hour about her music. I gave her the phone number at Claire's and invited her up sometime. She gave me her number and thanked me for the Coke and conversation. I felt ten pounds lighter for having been in her presence. I think I floated all the way back to the house.

XVII.

Isaac

Feels like I've fallen flat, my back's against the altar
And you are standing over me with eyes that break into my soul
Are you the priest who has come here to sacrifice me?
Will you use that knife to kill me, or somehow make me whole?

And who are you?
Is this really how you love me?
Can it be that you're my father?
Who are you?
Will you wound me like a killer, cut me open like a doctor?
Is this knife only to hurt, or is this pain to set me free?
What is it you're taking this time out of me?

I've lived too long with this bitterness of mine
I am shaken by the sorrow, I am weakened by the pain
And these idols I've erected in the temple of my heart
They are growing like a cancer, they get bigger every day
But tell me ... where were you?
When I was dead and buried, did my time down six feet deep
Where were you?
On the third day will you resurrect me up to live eternally?

If I die, again tonight, what awaits me in my grave?
He who holds on to his life, will loose it, he who dies will save
Save myself, I know I cannot save, I cannot save myself
If I yield, if I fight, if I live, if I die
I know I, I know I, I know I am a sacrifice

I was doin' fine, I never knew that I was broken
And I don't think my health is worth the pain of operation
I guess I ought to feel it's an honor to be chosen
But I think you might have warned me just how bloody is Salvation
Tell me ... where are you?
Do you know what it's like to feel the blood sweat through your skin?

Where are you?
Would it be that you are willing to come heal me once again?
If I die again tonight, what awaits me in my grave?
He who holds on to his life, will loose it, he who dies
You who died and rose to life, only, only you can save
Save myself I know I cannot, I cannot save myself
If I yield, if I fight, if I live, if I die
Or if I yield or if I fight, if I live or if I die
I know I, I know I, I know I am a sacrifice.

"Shelby, phone for you!" Claire called out from the kitchen. I was sitting in my room listening to Georgie's song over and over again.

I got up and poked my head out into the hall. "Is it Michael?"

"Toby."

"I'll take it in here," I called to her. I went back into the room and turned off the CD player. I sat down on the bed and grabbed the phone on the night–stand. I flopped back onto the bed, my feet dangling off the edge of the bed. "Hey."

"Hey, happy Monday," came the faint reply. It didn't sound like Toby at all.

"Toby? Where are you?"

"Lying on the floor of my bedroom, next to my bed, looking into my bathroom."

"In my apartment would have sufficed."

"Sorry. I'm lying here in my boxers and one sock."

I stared at the phone and tried not to laugh at Toby. "Um, I'm not really sure what to do with that information."

"See … I was trying to get dressed and I could only find one sock, so I thought maybe one was under my bed and then I needed to lie down for a minute. Then I saw the piece of paper with your name and Claire's number on it. So I thought I'd call you back. Sorry it took so long."

"No problem." I took a deep breath, put my free hand over my eyes and cut to the chase. "You took those pictures and then tossed the roll onto the sidewalk where I'd find it, right?"

He was silent for a minute. "Yeah. That was me. I wanted to hand them to you and tell you everything but you seemed to be in kind of a bad mood."

"No, just an exhausted drunk."

"Yeah, I could smell the gin." He laughed a little. "Shel, I don't know what to do here. Scared shitless doesn't even begin to describe it."

"Yeah, I don't know what to do either."

"I saw your story. The *Times* picked it up, so did the *Post*, *Globe*, *Trib*, LA *Times* … "

"Really?" I sat up.

"Yeah and Shel, I'm scared. Your fucking story is all over the country. Those pictures have my initials and *Times* credit. I'm worried those guys are going to find me."

"I'm so sorry Toby. If it makes you feel better, they're going after me, not you. I've already taken one beating and was threatened twice last week."

"No ... "

"Yes. Okay, maybe that doesn't make you feel better. I don't know," I stopped for a minute. I swung my legs back and forth against the edge of the bed and stared out the window. "But the police should have Tony by now, at least ... right?"

"Shelby, do you ever watch the news?" he laughed.

I was notorious for never watching news when I wasn't there covering it. I found cable news either overwhelming or ludicrous. "You know what it's like out here," I said.

"Yes I do, and I know full well Claire has a television and cable. Not to mention the Denver *Post*. Really Shel, some people just leave the TV on in the background ... "

"Leave me alone."

"Sorry."

I sighed and pushed a lock of hair behind my ear. I rocked back on the bed again and propped myself up on my elbow. "No, no it's fine. This is not really what we should be talking about anyway."

"You're right. I assume your messages were referring to the pictures."

"Yeah, they really freaked me out, you should have warned me!"

"I tried."

"Right." We lay there for a minute, two thousand miles apart. Neither of us talked, just lay there and listened to the silence. I couldn't picture Toby or his apartment. I just saw black, with this disembodied voice on the phone. I rolled over on my side and started picking at a loose thread in the quilt.

"I haven't left my apartment in over a week. Vivian is the only person I've seen," he finally said.

"She told me."

"Oh ... right. So are you still working on the story?"

"Pete's not real thrilled with the ethical conflicts since I am related to Amelia and was related to Tony. He yanked me on Friday, before I came out here. It's probably better ... anyway ... I've given Gregory and Tony too many reasons to hate me already. I just hope they're safely locked up before I get home."

"Yeah, I don't think you should go back to Chicago until you know they can't hurt you. The police arrested Tony, but I think he's out on bail."

"Probably. Horrible family. Michael and Brennan are coming out to Colorado this weekend. We'll probably stay another week and then see how it looks."

"I wouldn't go back at all if I were you," he said. He sounded like he was tearing up. His voice was scratchy and hoarse again.

"Well, we'll see," I said delicately.

"Shelby, I just want you to know ... " he broke off. I rolled over on my other side, my arm going numb from lack of blood and supporting my full weight. I waited. "I just wanted you to know I loved her."

I didn't know what to say. I started picking at the quilt again.

"She hadn't returned my phone calls for months. Then she wasn't in Bonn anymore and no one would tell me where she went. I was so happy when she tracked me down and said she was willing to work things out. I rushed up to her room that night. It was my first chance to see her ... she'd been with the Secretary all day. She was getting ready for the party. She looked so beautiful. She was half–undressed, getting ready for a bath. I came in and we started talking. She went into the bathroom and turned the water on. We started kissing and then we could hear voices, outside the door, an argument. Then banging on the door. We assumed it was her boss, so I hid in the bathroom with the water still running in the tub so I wouldn't be heard if I made any little noise. I pulled my camera into the bathroom so he wouldn't see it. Only it wasn't her boss ... "

"It was Tony," I said softly. I was trying hard not to cry. I took a deep breath and rolled onto my back again. I rubbed my forehead as the vivid pictures of the hotel room blazed in front of me again. It was so real I could have reached out and touched her room.

"It was Tony. I remember he was so calm. I could see him–the bathroom door was open a little–his face was hard, but calm. It was weird. He didn't notice me. He didn't seem to notice anything. She didn't recognize him. She was trying to talk to him. She had no idea who this guy was or why he burst into her room. But he just pushed her on the bed and didn't say anything. One of the secret service guys rushed in from the hall, he must have been the guy Tony was arguing with. Tony raised up his gun. The guy dove in front of her. I grabbed my camera and started snapping pictures. I was scared to death that I would be found ... that Tony would hear the clicking. But he didn't. I think the water and gunshots covered up my noise. Everyone from the rooms around Meelie's was already downstairs. No one was around to hear. Maybe people on other floors, but they wouldn't have known what the sounds were, people in the Middle East hear gun shots all the time, right?" I wanted to correct him that that was mainly Israel and Palestine, but I didn't want to break his narrative. "He fired at such close range and only twice ... it really wasn't that loud. I held my breath until he left and then threw up on the bathroom floor. I ran over to the bed, but they were both dead ... one shot through the heart of each."

"Oh God," I whispered.

"I didn't know what to do. I was so scared. I took the key, locked the door and ran down to find you. I kept clicking the camera as I ran down the hall, ripped the film out of my camera and put it in my pocket. I realized I had forgotten my bag in the room. I slipped back in to get it. That's when I found the note I gave you. Tony must have planted it in the room as he left. It was on the dresser."

"So that's how you found it before the police."

"It was just lying there on the dresser. I don't know why I noticed it, or how I noticed it hadn't been there before. I just picked it up and glanced at it. I couldn't believe what it said. I shoved it in my pocket and left. After you went outside, I went out the other door on the other side of the gardens and cut through. I dropped the film when you were looking up at the moon. The light burning out was a bonus."

"I thought I saw someone between the bushes, but I couldn't be sure."

"After you went up to your room I went into the ballroom and mingled with Meelie's family and friends. They all kept asking where she was. All I could say was, 'I don't know.' Finally, one of the secret service guys tried to find the guy who had been killed and noticed Meelie seemed to be missing as well. Two agents and her boss went up to the room and that's when they found her."

"And you were there when the police arrived and convinced them to let us take the crime scene pictures."

"Yeah."

"And you knew it was Meelie, but didn't tell me before we got in there ... "

"I am so sorry, Shel. I should have told you. I thought if you knew you wouldn't go in there. I couldn't go back in there alone."

"I'm not mad at you Toby ... well, at least you are currently so far down the list of people I'm angry with, you don't have to worry. I'm just worried about you."

"I'll be okay."

"You're just saying that." I rolled over and tried to get up, but hit my arm on the night-stand. I yelped.

"What?" he panicked.

"Nothing. I just slipped and hit the night-stand while trying to stand up. I guess I don't have enough bruises yet," I said sarcastically.

"Be careful with yourself."

"What kind of reckless fool does everyone take me for?" I asked, rubbing my red arm. "It seems like lately everyone has been telling me to be careful."

"Sorry."

"It's not you. Viv will be back on Saturday. Will you please give her a call and let her help? She's really worried about you."

"We'll see."

"Toby ... "

"All right, fine ... I'll call her."

"Thanks."

XVIII.

"Hello, may I speak to Georgie Armstrong, please?" I asked politely. *Why do I feel like a junior higher calling the popular girl in school? Because I want her to like me. I hate people not liking me.*

"This is."

"Hey, this is Shelby Maxwell, we met the other night at Bart's and ... "

"Oh, Shelby! Hey, how's it going?"

"Hey, my friends and I were just wondering if you'd like to join us for dinner? They'd like to get to know you too." I bounced up and down on the balls of my feet in the middle of the kitchen.

"Tonight?"

"Yeah, tonight. Can you make it?"

"Sure! Can I bring anything?"

"Oh no, you don't have to bring anything. Although, you could bring your guitar ... if you don't mind."

She laughed. "No problem."

"Great. How about six? Do you know where the Vail Wellness Center is?"

"Yep."

"It's the house right next to it. Claire runs the center."

"Cool. I'll be there."

"Great, see you then."

"Great, I can't wait."

. . .

We feasted on huge slabs of ribs dripping with Claire's completely unhealthy brown-sugar barbecue sauce. There was a stock pot full of baked beans, enough grilled corn for half the state and gallons of ice tea. Some of the guests at the wellness center joined us for dinner, along with Georgie. Claire thought it would be a good idea to have her give a concert for the guests. We moved over to the living room and sunk into the couches, a couple people sprawled out on the rug. Georgie noticed several of the guests weren't wearing shoes.

"Mind if I take my shoes off?" she asked Claire.

Claire laughed and shook her head no. "All we care about here is comfort!"

"All right, you are my kind of girl!" she answered and kicked off her shoes.

She charmed us for about almost two hours with stories from touring two-bit venues and bars around the country and with her songs.

Her wit and abundant energy were infectious. While people had always said I had an overabundance of energy, I knew it was never like that. I was always busy. I was always rushing and doing and going. Georgie had a natural energy bubbling up from somewhere inside her, sustaining her, not just propelling her forward. Every story ended with her sweet Georgia drawl giving way to a chuckle of surprise. Not that every story ended well ... or everything worked out ... but she seemed to find gratitude in every situation. I was envious. Which was probably the wrong response. I wanted to sit at her feet and listen to her stories and learn all her secrets of life. I fought the urge to run and get my notebook and start scribbling notes.

"Okay, okay ... I have one last song and then I should go," she finally said. "I actually wrote this today, so I apologize if it's rough. I wrote this after talking to Shelby the other night. I've been kicking the tune around for awhile, but couldn't find the right words to go with it. I had this line running though my head. I stayed up and wrote out these words. They just poured forth like I had nothing to do with it other than transcribing them onto paper. It was freaky weird, ya'know? So, here goes. I hope you don't mind. It's called *God Does Not Remember.*

She stood up, pushed her hair back and pulled up her sleeves. She started strumming, rocking back and forth, letting the cadence of the music carry her to the song. Her hand moved back and forth across the polished Gibson guitar in a staccato, yet fluid motion.

She started singing. Her voice was beautiful, light and airy, but simultaneously full and rich and deep. She picked up the tempo as she sang, and then it fell again. Her voice was like a soft pitch, a looping, lazy roller coaster. I was lost, transported into another world.

Such a burden, to carry such a load
She is half the woman, half a child
Still so young, to feel so damn old
She is just too old to want to cry
People say, this will never go away
It's there branded on your face
And you will always take the blame
Well that's a lie, child

She closed her eyes, threw her head back and belted out the chorus, rocking back and forth, keeping perfect time with the stomping of her foot.

God does not remember,
He's forgotten all your sin

God does not remember,
Never brings it up again
God does not remember,
The monsters in your closet do not scare him

She is familiar, with the cruelty of life
Screwing up, they'll remember it forever
She thinks she's nothing, but the image she projects
And it's hard to always hold it all together
When even the most innocent mistake
Leaves you flattened on your face
Ain't got no idea of grace––no idea child

God does not remember,
He's forgotten all your sin
God does not remember,
Never brings it up again
God does not remember,
The monsters in your closet,
All the skeletons and ghosts
In the graveyard of your soul
Keep you broken down and screaming out
While you dream of being whole
God does not see you like that
God does not remember
God ... does not see you like that

Tears rolled down my cheeks, but I paid no attention. I had
stopped trying to hold the tears back. I was no longer concerned
with sopping up the damp, salty streams that just kept coming.
Images were swirling around me, flashing before my eyes. It was

not an end-of-life, montage thing. I was at peace. Deep in my core, the pushing and screaming and angst had finally subsided. I was leaning forward on the couch, only the tips of my toes touching the floor. Every last fiber within me was straining, desperate to believe Georgie. Yearning to believe she was singing the truth.

As soon as Georgie finished Vivian excused herself to the back deck for a smoke. The rest of us said good-bye to Georgie. I walked her to her car.

"Thanks for coming," I said as we walked out the front door.

"I had fun. You have great friends," she replied.

"Thanks for the song," I smiled.

"Thank you for the song." She stopped in front of her beat up old Nissan. She threw her arms around me and hugged me. I was taken aback at first. I was not used to people I've just met hugging me.

"Thanks for everything, Georgie. You've helped me more than you'll ever know."

"What? What did I do?"

"You were here."

"Please girl, I didn't do anything special. You just keep up your search. Truth started pursuing you long before you realized it ... and it'll be there, waiting ... as long as it takes you. You can't rush revelation. Life's a journey and it takes exactly as long as it takes. But redemption ... finding the truth and knowing it ... well, you just feel it. It has a weight, a feel to it ... a sweetness. You'll sink into it and know you never want to leave again."

"I don't know ... I ... I just, well ... I'm just a screwed up Jew, who for some reason I cannot explain, wants what you've got. Does that make any sense? It doesn't to me. I've never wanted to be anyone else ... ever. Not that I want to be you or know what it is that you have that I don't ... I just know you are the coolest person I've ever met."

She laughed. I just stood there and stared. I was a little offended. I had just bared my soul and she was laughing.

"Oh, oh ... I'm sorry, I'm not laughing at you," she apologized and put her arm around me. "It's just that 'cool' is not a word I would ever use to describe myself. And I definitely would not call you 'screwed up.' But I do know what you're talking about. I felt that way once too. Heck, I still feel that way all the time! When I was in high school there was a woman I knew who I wanted to hang out with all the time because she was the coolest person I had ever met. The thing ... the thing you can't put your finger on is grace–something you didn't deserve but once it's been given, it can never be taken away from you. It's knowing you're forgiven every time you ask and being so grateful you can't help but love others as much as you've been loved. But I do have some bad news ... "

"What?" I asked, my eyes wide.

"Well, first of all, when grace first finds you it can throw off your whole life. You question your sanity and wonder why things weren't good enough the way they were. And then things can get down–right scary as hell. Unfortunately, once God's found you ... decided to let you know he wants you ... you only have two choices: accept it or run away and make the whole process a lot longer and messier."

"Jonah ... " I whispered.

"Yes! Exactly! Perfect example, just remember that at the end of the story, even though Jonah spent the whole time arguing and running from God, God still saved Jonah ... and a whole city full of people. At the end of the day, there's no better place to be than where God wants us," she smiled. She stopped and looked down at her watch. "It's getting late ... I should go."

"Yeah, fine ... good ... sure," I said. I waved good–bye as she drove away. A small voice inside, my deep gut feeling, was telling me what she said was true. I'd been seeking out the truth my whole career. Now I felt as if I was hearing it for the first time.

What she said made complete sense. She said the same thing as Feldstein. So why I am scared to death and ready to run in the opposite direction?

I walked around the side of the house and found Vivian still out smoking and leaning on the railing. She stared out into the pitch darkness. A cold breeze skimmed over the mountains. It was silent, except for the occasional rustling of leaves in the breeze. I walked up to the railing and put my foot up on the bottom board.

"Hey."

"Hey." Vivian didn't look over. She took a long drag on her cigarette and kept looking out ahead of her.

"Viv, are you okay? I mean ... I know you're not much for the religious conversation, but you seem more bothered than usual."

She looked over at me. Tears were rolling, unimpeded down her cheek. She pulled a pack of cigarettes out of her pocket. She silently offered me one. I knew it was a test.

"Aw hell, why not," I tried to laugh and took the pack from her.

"I thought you were reformed," she said in a dead monotone. She flipped a small pack of matches up between her fingers. I took them and handed her back the pack. I lit up, spit on the match and let it drop to the deck.

"The way down doesn't disappear once you've decided to reform."

"That's deep as shit, Shel."

"Viv, I'm not really in the mood for games. So spill it."

Her eyes flashed. She stomped out her cigarette and faced me for the first time. "You and me. It was always Claire and Evelyn, you and me. You are my best friend. I've known you my whole life. I know you better than anyone. But in the last 48 hours I've felt like

169

I don't know you at all. You never believed in any of that religious bullshit before ... just seems a little hypocritical to turn to it now."

She stopped. She lit up what was probably her fourth cigarette and turned back to the expansive blackness beyond the deck.

"Viv, I love you. You are my best friend. I can't imagine life without you. But this one time, you weren't there ... and instead of being jealous, you should be grateful. You should get down on your knees, kiss the ground and thank the goddamn stars above you weren't there ... that you don't have to live with this picture burned in your head for the rest of your life."

"I'm not jealous, you bitch. I'm scared."

"What?"

"What? What do think it has been doing to me to know that you are running from someone who wants to take your life so you can't tell on him. Maniacal ... sadistic ... And now, on top of everything you want to go and get all fucking religious. I don't know which is worse ... " she trailed off. We stood there, smoking into the breeze. "Either way ... I lose my best friend," she whispered.

"Now who's being the fucking hypocritical idiot?" I asked.

"Hey! I'm serious!" she screamed.

"Hey!" I screamed back. I grabbed her shoulders and looked straight at her. "I'm not going anywhere. Okay? Gregory is not going to kill me and I would never believe in God–or anything else–that made me give you up."

She pulled back and tried to smile through her tears. "I am so scared," she whispered.

"So am I ... so am I," I whispered back. I wiped away her tears with my thumb, "but nothing is ever going to come between us. Can you get that through you thick skull ... " I smiled. Then a second later it hit me.

"What's wrong?"

"I ... uh, I ... " I gasped for air and put my head in my hands, crying and laughing at the same time. "I just said something to you that Michael's said to me a hundred times."

"Michael's a good guy," she smiled at me.

"Hey! You two got everything worked out yet?" Claire called out from the door. We looked over at the door and saw her silhouette. "We got a movie all cocked and loaded."

"We're coming!" we both call back. We put our arms around each other and helped each other back into the house.

"We'd better come back out first thing and clean up these cigarette butts before Claire and Evelyn freak out," I said.

"Absolutely."

XIX.

"We're up here," Evelyn called from the top of the stairs.

Vivian and I walked upstairs and back to Claire's room. They were setting up snacks. On the bed were two pairs of neatly folded flannel pajamas. One set was ice blue and had a card with my name written neatly on it. The other was mint green for Vivian. Claire was wearing pale yellow with white trim. Evelyn was wearing pink.

"Do you have any idea how hard it is to find pajamas for a pregnant woman that aren't hideous?" Evelyn asked. We all laughed at the idea of her in a cottony tent outfit.

Viv and I changed and hopped into Claire's king-size bed. On the two night-stands were bottles of white wine, Kleenex and bags of Oreos and M&Ms. We had learned, younger than we should have, that white wine comes out of sheets and carpet easier than other alcoholic drinks. We learned this-and other things we probably shouldn't have-from Claire's housekeeper who was sympathetic to our youthful experimentations.

Claire had our favorite movie, *Love Affair*, ready to go. Not the 1950s version with Cary Grant, or the modern retelling with Warren Beatty, no, no ... we only watched the original. The 1939, black-and-white version with Charles Boyer and Irene Dunne. All four of us have been in love with Charles Boyer since we first saw the movie back in high school on late night TV.

We snuggled together in the bed and passed the sweets and Kleenex. Balled up Kleenex soon littered the bed. We each had our favorite lines to recite along with the characters. We always cried when the sweet, old grandmother takes to the girl and then she sings for the grandmother. Then, of course, the end of the movie ... immortalized by *Sleepless in Seattle*, when Rita Wilson's character is trying to explain it to the men. They don't get it and she's sobbing.

"Ever wonder why he never asks her questions? You know, at the end when he realizes she's paralyzed, I mean," Vivian asked while the video rewound.

"Yeah, really ... " Evelyn sniffled. "If that happened to me with a guy, I'd be all over him wanting to know why he didn't just tell me. How can she love him if she keeps it from him?"

"Pride," I said softly.

"Yeah, pride," Claire echoed.

"You think you are doing what is best for the other person, but you don't know what the other person needs, or what is best for them, because you aren't talking to them ... because you think you know, all it does is keep love apart." I said.

"That's so deep," Claire said, chewing on an Oreo. "But, maybe he's smart enough to know questions will just get in the way. He loves her and he doesn't care anymore, now that he's found her again. He's willing to let all the questions, the past ... slip into the past ... out of sight out of mind. Because finding her was the important thing, nothing else, ya'know?"

"Questions will kill you if you let them," Vivian said. She raised her wine glass to toast us. "May each of us be lucky enough to find someone who will never question ... will always let the past slip into the past and love us no matter what."

I started crying. I had an Oreo in each hand and a pile of Kleenex in my lap.

"Oh darlin', what's wrong?" Claire asked.

I was in between Claire and Vivian. Evelyn was on the other side of Claire.

Vivian took the cookies out of my hand and set them on the night–stand. They both put their arms around me.

"I ... I ... I have that ... what Viv said ... I have that an' I've been taking advantage of him for so long. I can't believe he puts up with me. I can't believe his hasn't left ... hasn't left in the last two weeks ... " I hiccuped and started hyperventilating.

"Oh darlin'," Claire said again. "You don't take advantage of Michael. You love him. I've seen you two together."

"Yeah Shel, I'm sorry I said that, I didn't mean you. Michael's great. You have the greatest husband on the face of the earth," Vivian said.

"No, no I do but I don't appreciate him like I should. I come and go as I please and just expect him to keep everything going ... keep everything the same for when I come back. Be there when I come back. I don't even let him pick me up at the airport. What happens when I come home and he's gone. He's just given up and gone. I'm a lousy mother and a horrible wife."

"No you aren't," Evelyn piped in. She had climbed over to the middle of the bed so she could face me. "You're just burned out from everything that's happened lately. You're just tired. We shouldn't have watched this movie tonight."

"Yes, exactly!' Claire said. "You just need more time."

"That's the problem ... I've always thought I had all the time in the world. Now time is running out. I'm at the end and I haven't paid attention at all."

"Stop that! Stop saying that!" Vivian screeched. "You just told me tonight that you aren't going anywhere and I expect you to keep your word ... you always have."

I sniffled and cried softly for awhile longer. Around 1:30 a.m. Evelyn and Vivian went to their rooms. Claire convinced me to spend the night in her room. I drifted off to sleep around 2 a.m. but slept restlessly. I was haunted by strange dreams that I couldn't make sense of. They wore me out more than being awake. I was running–being chased by something, or someone, I couldn't see. Then I was pursuing, killing ... Gregory. I woke up scared and breathless. I fell back down, but finally wrestled myself awake around 6 a.m. I quietly got up and went downstairs.

I went into the kitchen and started a pot of coffee. The first light was coming up over the mountains. A thick fog had set over the mountains like a down comforter during the night. As the sun began to rise, the fog slowly receded, as if God himself was pulling the comforter back off the mountains for the morning to begin. I poured a cup of coffee and grabbed the cordless phone and went outside to sit on the deck and watch the sun rise.

"Good morning." I sat down and wrapped a thick blanket around me.

"Good morning to you."

"Did I wake you up?"

"Naw, Brennan woke me up around 6."

"Oh right, you're an hour ahead."

"Yeah. How are you? Why are you up so early?"

"Couldn't sleep."

"Aw Shel, this is getting serious. You must be so exhausted."

"Mmm. Kind of, I wanted to hear your voice. Besides, it's not as fun sleeping with the girls as it is with you."

He laughed. "I'll take that as a compliment."

"I just wanted you to know how much I love you ... I know I never say it. I want to apologize for never being around ... apologize for not being there for you like you are always there for me."

Silence.

"Michael?"

"Apologizing is the sexiest thing ever. I wish I were there," he said in a deep, smoky voice.

"I wish you were here too."

. . .

I took a nap all afternoon. When I woke up and wandered into the kitchen there was a note from Claire.

"I had to take Evelyn to the airport. Evelyn's doctor's office called right after you fell asleep. Her doctor has to go out of town for an emergency and wanted to reschedule her appointment for tomorrow afternoon. Evelyn agreed and wanted to get back to Chicago as soon as possible. Found her a flight out, will be back around 6 p.m.

Vivian left to see Bart before the phone call and doesn't know Evelyn left. She'll be back this evening for dinner. Please tell her and wait for me so we can all have dinner together." -- Claire.

I set the note back on the counter, shrugged and looked for a snack. I grabbed a diet soda and some cheese and crackers and headed over to Mr. Adams' study. I walked down the hall and hesitated for a minute outside his office door. I stood there with a can of soda in one hand and a plate in the other and just stared at the door. I argued with myself on whether or not I should pursue this any further.

Vivian was right ... what was a Jewish girl doing with a stack of Bibles ... in a pastor's office? I've cried enough. I should just go upstairs and watch a movie.

I caved. I went up to Claire's room and looked over her movies. I popped a light comedy in the VCR and sat on the bed.

But as I set my snack down on the night-stand, the presence I had felt before was back. It was gently nudging me, telling me to go downstairs. *Go down to the office.* I tried to ignore the feeling. My soul was burning. I picked out another movie, a fluffy chick flick and nestled down on Claire's bed. I couldn't concentrate on what I was watching. I turned the movie off and flipped through the channels looking for the news. The feeling of something pushing me from the inside out was back, stronger than ever. I knew my mind would not be at rest until I went down there. I flung the covers off, turned off the TV and put the remote control on the night-stand.

I had never really believed in spirits, or ghosts, or whatever ... but something was quickly filling up the house and it was definitely heavier than air. I slowly walked down the stairs. I felt hot. The house was stuffy. I went into my room and changed out of my long-sleeve flannel top and into a white, cotton T-shirt.

I crossed the foyer and went into Mr. Adams' office. The air was still thick, but different. As I turned on the floor lamp behind the desk I felt a faint positive charge. The air was cooler, not stifled. I looked over at the window, assuming it was open. It wasn't. But it had started to rain. I sat in the chair and watched the rain fall.

It started out light, like any other afternoon shower in the mountains that comes and goes pretty much every day during the spring and summer. It starts with light droplets falling through the sun. It feels cool and refreshing. Many people stay outside to enjoy it and see if it passes or gets worse. Clouds thicken and gray mixes in with the turquoise sky as the clouds rolled in over the mountains from the west. But the storm didn't pass. It began to rain harder and harder. The wind picked up. The trees swayed, then rocked, then appeared to be tossed around against their will by the wind.

Thunder rumbled somewhere in the distance, over the mountains. The lighting cracked down out of the sky a minute later. It shone blue and white and quickly started cracking closer and closer. I swiveled around toward the desk. I didn't want to watch the storm any more. The room had grown dark, except for the floor lamp behind the desk that I had turned on. It's little light did not give off much illumination.

I got up and walked over to the bookcases. Claire had, at some point, come in and put the Bibles back on the shelf where they belonged. I looked over the other books. Shelf after shelf of books. Many had "commentary" in the title. I assumed they were commentating on books of the Bible, or maybe the whole Bible, I still wasn't really sure how it worked. I stood there, mesmerized by the colors of the jacket covers and the titles and wondered what all the books were for. I noticed a couple with "Hosea" and "commentary" in the title and pulled them off the shelf.

"J. Hampton Keathley, *Hosea*," I said out loud to myself. "Now that's the name of a scholar. Keathley, it sounds British, but he's probably from New Jersey."

I started flipping through the book and sat back down behind the desk. I lay the book down flat and bent over it, trying to cast the least amount of shadow on the book.

"Hosea was to manifest God's patience and love. Some wonder if Gomer was already a prostitute when they got married or if she became unfaithful later. They think that it presents a moral dilemma.

I have heard the arguments that she became unfaithful after they were married, and they are pretty good too. The phrase 'adulterous wife' is similar to the phrase 'quarrelsome wife.' You don't typically go out and marry a quarrelsome person. You marry someone whom you think is nice and will make you happy and find out later that they aren't so nice.

Hosea's choice of a prostitute was exactly like God's choice of Abraham. Abraham was just another sinner like the rest of the people in the world. He did not deserve to be chosen. But that isn't what the Jews thought. They thought Abraham was special because of his own merit and upright character. God may be using Hosea's marriage to a prostitute to make this point.

The problem was that they were pursuing their own agendas or goals and they changed their concept of God in the process because it was too painful to have the real God around ... "

"No shit," I whispered and collapsed down onto the book.

If it is too painful to have the real God around ... and I can attest to that ... why would I want the real one around? Why would I want to believe in God anyway? I've had enough. I don't want any more gifts or blessings from God. Abraham didn't deserve to be chosen ... I definitely don't deserve to be chosen. Definitely too fucking painful ... what does God want from me anyway? I don't have anything he could possibly want. I'm not like Michael. I'm not like Claire. I moaned. *I'm more like ... like ... Gregory ... I am ... I am ...*

I began to sob.

XX.

My shoulders shook in tempo with the driving rain and I hiccuped on cue with the thunder and lighting. I finally pulled my head up. I stood up and wiped off my face. I started to walk over to the box of Kleenex on the table by the door.

I was looking at the doorway, but it took a minute to realize the doorway was darkened. I tried to gasp, but I hiccuped instead. "Claire? Viv? How long ... "

"Hello Shelby," came the deathly cold reply.

I half-shrieked, half-gasped. I began to shake all over. *How long had Gregory been standing there and how the hell did he get in the house?* He had always had the creepy habit of not making any noise when he walked in a room. It was often impossible to tell how long he'd been standing there watching you.

"How ... " My legs went out on me. I grabbed the desk for support.

"Oh no ... you had your fifteen minutes of fame," he said. He stepped forward through the threshold and into the pale light. I could see him wagging his finger at me. I could see he was dressed in all black, including black leather gloves. In the darkness, backlit by the pathetic light, he looked like a floating head, his body absorbed the darkness around him.

"Now it's my turn. You are going to listen to me for once." He continued toward me. "I have been waiting for this moment for a very, very long time," he said in his usually languid cadence.

I took a step back, hoping the desk would rise up and save me. It didn't.

"You always thought you were better than me ... better than everyone. Know what happens to people who put themselves up on high horses?" he paused. "Do you?" he smacked his palm down on the desk. I sucked in my breath and frantically shook my head no. He took another step forward. I regained my footing and began to walk backward around the desk. I didn't blink. I didn't want to take my eyes off him for one second. "The horse underneath gets sick and tired of her big, fat, dead weight constantly kicking him in the gut and throws her off."

I tried to take another step back and edge around the desk, but I wasn't as far as I thought. I bumped into the desk. My heel caught the foot of the desk and I scraped my foot on the rough under side of the desk. I squeezed my eyes closed to keep from yelping in pain. I lost my balance and fell back and over, torqueing my side and back over the corner of the desk. Gregory seized the moment and rushed toward me. He pushed me the rest of the way to the floor with the full force of both hands. I went flying into the bookshelf behind me.

"You are going to get thrown off," he said again. I looked up to see his face in the half–light. His face was contorted and he was sweating. The light created a long shadow over him. It looked like he had a long, black hood over his head. He had the look of a heroin addict, dangerously close to going too long without a fix.

The sky was black as pitch from the storm and I realized I wasn't sure what time it was exactly, but it shouldn't have been late enough for the sky to be so dark. The rain continued to pound against the picture window. It sounded like a thousand fingertips of rain pressing against the glass, begging to come in, threatening to crash through the glass. The thunder and lighting crept closer to the house.

Lighting hit the mountain. The sky lit up in an electric white–blue flash, searing the earth and pulsing up from the ground back to the sky. It wasn't more than a mile or two up from the house. I started sobbing again, although I wasn't sure which scared me more: the lighting or Gregory.

I pulled myself up against the side of the desk. Gregory reached out and with one bear–like swoop, backhanded me across the face and sent me flying into another bookshelf. I prayed that my stitches hadn't popped open, but realized he had hit the other cheek. Books and knickknacks came crashing down around me. I tasted blood inside my mouth.

"Get up! You come marching into my office ... accusing me and getting my secretary fired. Tony's been arrested and now they're trying to arrest me too. You got the fight you wanted; you'd better not cower in the corner now. Get up!"

He tried to sound commanding, with a booming voice, but he sounded more garbled and like someone was choking him. It still managed to induce fear. He stepped on my feet and jerked me up by my arms. As soon as he let go I fell back down like a rag doll. He went to hit me again, but I ducked. He hit the shelf instead. I heard glass shatter.

"Bitch!" he wailed, fist recoiling.

"Why, dammit? Just tell me why," I asked. I was too scared to cry again.

"Because," he grinned, "because I can. Because I should have long ago when you dumped me ... "

"Gregory!" I cried out, finally coming to my senses, "you got me drunk and then married me and I don't remember any of it!" I started to get up. He put his hands on my shoulders and pushed me down.

"Of course you don't! Why would you want to remember me, right?"

"I ... was ... drunk ... " I said slowly and exaggerated, drawing my hands and arms out. He slapped me again, this time hitting my injured cheek. I shrieked.

He picked me up and tossed me into the other corner as if I were a feather. Books came crashing down on my head again. The corner of one caught my eye and I cried from the sting.

"You ... are ... going ... to ... pay ... " he said, mocking me. He started beating me about the head and shoulders, kicked my legs and tried to kick my gut, but I was curled up in a tight ball and not going anywhere. He picked up a heavy volume and swung it like a baseball bat into my leg. I heard a bone crack. I almost passed out from the pain.

Suddenly, I felt a presence around me, sustaining me. Keeping me conscious and somewhat calm and collected. It was the same presence that had held me close as I cried a few days ago. The room seemed to be getting brighter. The small light now seemed to glow, but the shadow around Gregory seemed to grow and darken. It looked like the black hood around his head was now enveloping his whole body.

Great, I'm hallucinating. I'm going to be knocked unconscious and then he'll really loose it. They'll find my cold, dead body curled up in the corner of Mr. Adams' study. Gregory caught the eye that had been hit with the book with a sharp jab.

I moaned and rolled over. "God have mercy ... have mercy on me," I mumbled.

"What?" he laughed. "Have mercy on you? When have you ever shown mercy to me?" He pulled his arm back to hit me again.

"No, no no! Not you! Adonai, Adonai ... Harachaman, Harachaman ... " *Have mercy, have mercy ...* I strained to say it as loud as I could.

Gregory began to laugh, a sickening, wicked laugh. I looked up, half-expecting to see someone choking him for the sound he was making. But his eyes were flashing and he was almost falling over backward he was laughing so hard.

"What the hell is all that gibberish?"

Then, the presence that had been surrounding me descended. It seeped in through my skin. I felt it cursing through my bloodstream. The pushing I had felt inside exploded out and at the top of my lungs I began to chant, "Hoshaanot ... Hoshaanot ... Hoshaanot ... "*Please save me ... Please save me ... Please save me ...* I began to chant the prayer of Jonah in Hebrew. It welled up inside me and bubbled over. I had no idea what I was saying. Gregory was so shocked he took a step back and stood there in horror. He probably thought I was calling down ancient curses on him. I wish.

Jonah's Prayer

In my trouble I called to the LORD,
And He answered me;
From the belly of Sheol I cried out
And You heard my voice.
You cast me into the depths,
Into the heart of the sea
The floods engulfed me;
All Your breakers and billows
Swept over me.
I thought I was driven away ...
The waters closed in over me,

> *The deep engulfed me.*
> *Weeds twined around my head.*
> *I sank to the base of the mountains;*
> *The bars of the earth closed upon me forever*
> *Yet You brought my life up from the pit ...*
> *I called the LORD to mind;*
> *And my prayer came before You ...*

I chanted, louder and louder, somehow rocking while still curled up, half–buried by books.

"If you are begging God for mercy then I've done what I came to do," Gregory snorted. His eyes burned and his face became ashen again. He shook with rage. He picked up a thick volume and knocked my head into the bookshelf with it. My head hit a picture that sat on the edge of the shelf. I felt the glass shatter against my forehead.

Right before I lost consciousness I heard a loud crack ... a gun-shot, not lighting. *I'm dead*, I thought. I felt my body go limp. My mind drifted off into pitch black.

. . .

I was at the bottom of Lake Michigan. It was so cold. I was stuck there, sunken in the mucky, mired sand and silt at the bottom of the lake. My eyes were open. I could see everything around me, above me. I could see all the way up, through the layers of algae and foamy, green water. The sun reflected high above the surface creating a clear layer at the very top, separating the above from the below. I had no idea how long I'd been there, or how I knew, but I knew exactly where I was.

Suddenly, I realized I wasn't stuck to the bottom anymore. I had started to float up. I was rising up and out of the deep. I floated to just below the surface. All I could see was the dazzling sunlight bouncing off the water's surface. I couldn't see anyone floating above me. No ships passing over, no sailboats, no swimmers.

I heard a faint beeping. Then a faint voice. It was Michael's voice.

"I am so sorry. I am so sorry. I should have been there. This is all my fault. I am so sorry. I should have been there. This is all my fault ... this is all my fault ... this is all my fault."

I struggled to figure out if it was a dream or real. The voice, Michael's voice, just kept saying it over and over. I looked frantically all over, turning over and over again underwater. I was searching but I couldn't see him. I reached out and but couldn't find him. I couldn't feel the air. There was no breeze, no stirring of the air. I was still under water. I tried furiously to shake my body free from the layers resting heavily on me. I couldn't feel my hand ... my left hand. I started thrashing around, trying to break free. I tried to figure out if I was still wearing my wedding ring. I felt a panic coming over me as I thrashed around, trying to see my hand. I couldn't see my left hand.

Break above the waterline ... breathe. I struggled again to rise above the surface of the water. I was so close. Somehow I could tell I was coming up and I wanted to get above water for air. Fresh air.

"Shelby? Shelby ... can you hear me?"

Michael's voice sounded a thousand miles away. I moaned and tried to move around. I started to come to my senses. My mouth was dry. My tongue was swollen and sticking to my teeth and the roof of my mouth. I could still feel the irony taste of blood in my mouth. My eyelids seemed to be pasted shut. I felt like I was thrashing violently, but I slowly realized I was barely moving. My leg was cemented to something. I couldn't move my right arm. I couldn't feel my left hand. I tried to wiggle my fingers and toes.

"Shhh, just lie still baby. Everything is okay. You are okay. Don't move Shelby," Michael said. He was speaking softly into my ear. I could finally feel his warm, sweet breath. It was on my ear. My left ear.

I was confused. Where was I? Was I home? Still at Claire's? My mind waded through the stickiness to remember. The last thing ... what was the last thing I remember?

I jerked. My abdomen sympathetically folded me in half. I gasped for air and finally opened my eyes. A nurse was standing over me, adjusting an I.V. in my right arm. Michael was sitting in a chair, pushed up to the bed. My left hand was firmly in his grip. He was moving my wedding ring back and forth with his thumb. He was so surprised he dropped my hand. I was covered in sweat. My hair was matted down against my head. I could feel gauze and cotton tape on my forehead. My vision was blurred, but I could see a cast on my left leg. There was a wall of electronic gadgets to the right of my bed. I was in a private, very pink, hospital room.

"Hi," he smiled. He looked tired.

"Hi."

"Know where you are?" he asked. I shook my head weakly. He started brushing his fingers over my forehead and cheeks, which suddenly burned. I moaned and tried to pull away. He stopped and put his hand back down over mine. "You're at the medical center in Vail. Grego beat you up pretty bad last night." He kissed my fingers.

Last night? Just last night? It all came flooding back. I tried to sit up, but he and the nurse pushed me back down. Not that they needed to. I could barely move.

"Not yet, Mrs. Maxwell," the nurse said.

"It's Thursday night," Michael said when the nurse had left the room. "Vivian came home last night and heard Greg and you in the study. She crept upstairs and found Claire's gun. She came back down and heard you screaming something in Hebrew. She saw Greg raise his arm up; she saw that he had a gun. She fired and hit him in the leg. He knocked you out, but she tore up his left calf and shattered his tibia. Claire had just pulled up in the driveway. She heard the gunshot and ran in. They called 911. The police brought you and Greg here. This morning the doctors bandaged Greg up well enough to be transported to Denver. He's under 24–hour police protection. He should be well enough to be arraigned in a couple days. The police aren't going to let him leave Colorado for a real long time."

"Viv ... saved ... me," I said weakly.

"Yeah, Viv is a real hero," Michael smiled. "Claire called me about 11 p.m. last night. I was able to get here this morning." He started stroking my hair.

"Water?" I asked.

Michael stood up and poked his head through the door. "Can I get some water for her?" A different nurse came in with a cup of ice chips. Michael fed them to me, one at a time. The melting ice trickled down his fingers and my chin. Neither of us cared. It felt good.

"There's one more thing," he said once the ice was gone. His face brightened and the tiredness seemed to fade away.

I looked at him with wide eyes. "What?" I whispered.

He smiled his Cheshire cat grin and his bangs fell down across his forehead as he leaned in over me. "Well ... " he whispered, "it seems we were better than we thought that afternoon ... after the club ... "

My jaw dropped, what little it could from how sore my face was. "What?"

"Yeah, this morning the doctor came in and said, 'Good news, Mr. Maxwell, it seems the attacker didn't harm your unborn child ... '"

I gasped. "Ch ... ch ... " I was unable to finish the word.

"Yeah ... child." He kissed my nose, then my hand, then my stomach. "January."

"Oh ... my ... I ... "

"Are you okay?" He suddenly looked worried, like I might not think this was so great. I had certainly never mentioned having another child after Brennan.

I looked at him and smiled. I shook my left hand free of his, slowly lifted my arm up and brushed his bangs back off his face. "Couldn't be better."

I tried to scoot over on the bed. He pulled himself up over me and carefully leaned down to kiss me. My lips were dry, my tongue still felt swollen, my face battered and bruised ... and it was the sweetest kiss we'd ever shared. "You are so beautiful. Even when you are six different shades of purple," he laughed and lay down next to me.

"God has shown mercy ... he has given me the gift I have been seeking my whole life ... "

"What's that?" he asked and looked confused. "Another baby?"

"A second chance."

XXI.

After a week I was released from the Vail Medical Center and able to fly home. Michael proved once again to be a wonderful nurse. He never left my side and often in the first weeks I had to plead my case to get up and leave the confines of my bedroom.

Katie agreed to move into the house for the summer to keep me company and watch Brennan since I couldn't maneuver around the four-story townhouse very well with crutches and a cast up to my kneecap.

I was a pretty easy patient. Being pregnant and severely injured took up most of my energy. I slept and read. Katie and Brennan ate their meals up on the balcony with me on bad days. On days I was feeling well, I forced myself to go down to the dining room. But, I spent the summer in between clean, crisp white sheets with my foot and head propped up on mountains of pillows. I was practically folded in half. The blood slowly drained from my head, although it was three months before I didn't have some shade of purple, blue or green rimming my eyes and cheekbones. The cuts on my forehead and cheeks healed and amazingly enough didn't leave ugly scars. Vivian took this as the strongest proof yet that maybe God really was watching out for me. I told her she was crazy, but secretly agreed with her.

After a few weeks of being stuck in bed a bad case of cabin fever set in. It drove me mad to be able to see the bright blue sky and hear birds chirping and children and dogs playing out in the world below. Katie took Brennan to the beach or the park almost every day.

He would run in and tell me about his day, covered grass stains and trailing in sand. I would smile and hug him and then send him away to pout over my invalid state.

I finally became so unbearable that Michael and Brennan transformed two of the lounge chairs on the balcony with layers of soft blankets and pillows so I could hobble out and spend my days outside on the balcony. Michael brought up flowers, cards and gifts from friends. He called all my friends and asked them to send me a copy of their favorite books. I received probably twenty or thirty books and I read them all by Christmas. It was a wonderful diversion.

In August Toby came to Chicago to support me during Gregory's trial. In the two weeks he stayed we forged a new-found friendship. Funny how weak bonds of friendship, based on history and inertia, can grow strong and refined while the world crashes down on you like a flood.

He stayed with me while Michael was in Denver and at the courthouse everyday. I didn't go. I did not want to be anywhere near the courthouse for any of the trial. The doctor happily agreed and wrote a letter saying I was not allowed to fly or travel under any circumstances. The District Attorney had worked it out so I could give a video deposition and not take the witness stand unless absolutely necessary. It wasn't necessary. No defense attorney in their right mind was going to let a battered pregnant lady up on the stand and testify against their client. Normally I would have balked at such and outrage, but I found myself pleasantly content to hide behind my scars and growing belly.

I was able to avoid the Loop and Chicago society for weeks after the trial, happily hermitted away with no reason or excuse to go downtown. I had no energy to be in the public eye or anywhere near Gregory's residue.

Toby helped me down to the living room on the first floor every night after dinner and we stayed up late every night laughing and crying over the same old stories from college days that we had told a thousand times. They were still funny. Somewhere in the midst of the stories and support in the courtroom, my bitterness and resentment for what Toby had done to Vivian and me in college melted away. It had only been fourteen years. I guess it was time to let go.

One night, after the trial was over and I could breath clean, deep breaths again, we were snuggled into the overstuffed couches and sipping coffee. I had all the pillows in the room under my leg. Michael was finally home, and falling asleep against the hard arm of the couch. He finally excused himself. He kissed my forehead, shook Toby's hand and stumbled off to bed.

Toby seized the moment and asked for forgiveness.

"Of course. For what?" I asked, surprised by his sudden request.

"For what I did to you and Viv ... being with both of you, at the same time. I did it on purpose."

"Oh."

"I saw it as a conquest ... the coup of being with two women, two best friends at the same time, without their knowing ... it was a frat thing."

"Huh." I was suddenly unable to form words.

"Still want to dish out that forgiveness so easily?" he asked quietly.

"You were willing to jeopardize our friendship ... your friendship with Vivian and the friendship of Vivian and me ... all for some stupid fraternity thing?" I asked.

He couldn't look at me. His eyes were fixated on his coffee. He clutched the mug with both hands and swirled it around.

"Yeah, I was. But I was also young and stupid and I wish I could take it all back. I would never, have never done it again."

"Toby, look at me." He slowly looked up. I took a deep breath and looked deep into his eyes. "I forgive you," I said emphatically.

"Really?"

"Really." I shifted my weight and motioned for him to come over. He sat down on the coffee table next to me. "I just have one question," I said.

"What's that?"

"If you could go back ... "

"Uh–huh," he said, nodding his head, a smile creeping slowly across his face.

"Which one would you have chosen?"

"I fell in love with you the first time I saw you," he laughed, knowing full well what I was asking him.

"Oh really?" I cocked my head to the side and propped it up with my fist.

"You don't believe me, do you?"

I shook my head.

He took a deep breath and looked directly at me. "You were a freshman. It was a beautiful day, the second or third day of classes and the lake was perfectly calm. You were sitting out on the rocks, remember? The ones down at the lakefront campus? You were hanging out with Vivian, Claire and Evelyn. You were all talking and laughing and I was walking by with some of my buddies."

"Cruisin' for chicks."

"Uh, yeah. You were wearing a pink shirt and white shorts and your hair was down. It wasn't as long then. It was curlier. You pulled it back and I could see your face. Your cheeks were flushed and pink from laughing and your eyes were bluer than the lake. I fell in love right then, right there. I was with your brother. I asked him if he knew who you were. He told me you were his sister and if I touched you he'd kill me."

I laughed at the thought of Toby and my brother Seth, then a senior at Northwestern, hanging back somewhere behind us, talking about us when we were completely unaware. The two of them were the same height and build. The idea of Seth hurting Toby was comical.

"After he graduated I started bumping in to you every chance I could. But Vivian pursued me at a party one night and I was drunk and we hooked up. I didn't know her well enough to know I should have just ended it then. That I ... anyway ... I didn't," he sighed. "Then some of the guys found out and started making some suggestions ... kept pressuring me. It just kind of all snowballed from there."

He shifted his weight again, but kept his gaze steady and locked onto me. "I've spent the week ... I've sat here, watching the news reports of the courtroom drama everyday, watching Gregory and wondering what might have happened if you and I had seriously gone out. If Seth had given me his blessing, or at least not threatened to kill me. Maybe we would have become serious. Maybe you would have fallen in love with me, married me ... or at least not married Gregory."

"Toby, you can't think things like that. I thought like that for awhile after I detangled myself from Greg. It can't do any good to think about what if, it'll only drive you crazy. Life is too short. No one can change the past. Besides, I am happy with my life. I always have been. Things happen. Who's to say it's not the best way? I've come to realize that everything happens for a reason. If Seth hadn't been there that afternoon, if we would have dated, would anything have ended up any differently? Maybe, maybe not. I've spent a long time being angry at God, you know? When I was a kid I hated going to temple. Know why?"

"Boring?"

"No." I smiled. "It drove me crazy to see all those really nice mothers, *sober* mothers. Together families, to hear the rabbi talk about God and how he loves us. The thought of a loving God sticking me in such a crazy family was incomprehensible. It was easier just to believe he didn't exist. But then, things started happening ... I thought I was going to come unglued in every possible way. I told Viv out in Colorado that right or wrong, I couldn't not believe in a God anymore. I couldn't accept the fact that my life was falling apart because of atoms bouncing off each other out there in the universe somewhere. When I was reading Claire's Bible ... I definitely felt a presence in the room. I felt it again when Greg was beating the crap out of me. Something protecting me. When I pray now, I feel God is listening, that he hears me. Call me crazy, I know, but I can't explain it. It's the same feeling. I feel like Amelia's death was a wake-up call–a vision of my future if I didn't change my path. I know it in my core. Greg wasn't the only one sending me a message. I realized that if there wasn't some reason for me to still be alive, there is absolutely nothing that would have keep Greg from killing me."

"I don't think you're crazy. I know exactly how you feel." He looked over his shoulder and quickly kissed me on the cheek. "I hope Mike doesn't kill me for that."

"For what?" I smiled. I swatted at him playfully, "Toby, you are my friend. We've been through a lot together. Michael is not the kind of guy who would tell me who my friends are or who not to hang out with, even if it is someone he knows I was in love with once upon a time. He knows he has my whole heart now. That's all that matters."

"Yeah. That's all that matters."

"I'm sorry honey. It never would have worked out, you know. I never would have stayed with you if you hadn't broken up with me. You are not exactly a patient person. Hell, it's taken Michael eight years of saintly patience and understanding ... C'mon," I said, holding my arms out for him to pull me off the couch. "grab my crutches, I need some sleep."

"Michael won't mind you sleeping with me?" His eyes twinkled.

I slapped his arm. "You can find the guest room yourself."

. . .

The memories of that horrible night in Damascus and the weeks that followed didn't fade easily. Slowly, my wounds healed. My broken leg healed and the cuts and bruises faded away. It was seven or eight months before I slept a whole night without crying or having nightmares that left me exhausted and soaked in sweat.

By December I felt strong enough to go out and about. My first taste of freedom came on a cloudy, dreary Tuesday. Evelyn and I went to Marshall Field's for a day of Christmas and maternity shopping. We had a wonderful time. I was quite the sight, eight months pregnant and using a cane. We had several good laughs at my feeble attempts to hobble around and the looks I got from other shoppers trying not to stare. I finally gave up and we collapsed at our favorite corner table in the Walnut Room for a late lunch. It was right next to the windows, although our magnificent view of South State Street was considerably reduced. The sky was still a blanket of thick, pearl–gray clouds and it was beginning to snow softly.

"Wait, wait," Evelyn giggled, "we need to keep our bags separate or we'll take the wrong stuff home!"

"How many bags do you have, girl?"

"Um, let me see ... " she looked down and rifled through the bags. "Four."

"Then these are mine."

I swung three bags over my lap and set them down on the other side of the table. I propped up my foot on a spare chair. We enjoyed the quiet, richly paneled room, empty of all but a few patrons and wait staff in crisply starched gray and white uniforms. Evelyn and I sat and gazed up at the Christmas decorations, magically transported back to those days of being little girls in Chicago at Christmas. Every girl lucky enough to grow up in Chicago loves coming down to the Loop, the peanut and chestnut vendors in their antique red and gold carts, the ice rink and especially the windows at Marshall Fields and the Walnut Room.

Evelyn's mother took us every year to the matinee performance of *The Nutcracker*. We would put on new dresses, white tights, patent leather shoes and velvet coats with fur trim, our hair curled and put up in bows. My mother was never fond of children or large gatherings, so she would dress my brother and me up and send us off with the Cohens. After the show we would skip and leap all the way to Marshall Field's, gaze up at the large picture windows, each year decorated with different animated characters depicting a Christmas fairy tale featuring Uncle Mistletoe. Once frost–bite had begun to set into our little toes, we would head up to the Walnut Room. Every Christmas it was transformed into a winter fantasy world with a Christmas tree rising up in the middle of the room, brushing the vaulted ceiling above.

I came back from memory lane to notice a waiter glaring at me. I pointed at the cane leaning up against the wall and rubbed my protruding belly. He softened and came over to the table.

"Can I get you anything, ma'am?" he asked politely, with a soft Mexican accent.

"I don't suppose you could find me a pillow for my foot? I'm recovering from a broken leg."

"I'll see what I can do."

"I love this place," I smiled.

"Give the lady what she wants!" Evelyn said.

"God bless Marshall Field."

Another waiter came up to us with glasses of water and menus. We perused the menus and finally decided on salads and ice tea.

"So, how are you doing, anyway? No one's seen much of you. The rumors are flying."

"I bet. Blame Michael. He won't let me out of his sight. Today is my first day out without him."

"I've heard it all, everything from you're really dead, but no one will admit it, to Michael left you in Colorado."

"Nice."

A woman, who was sharply dressed in a maroon suit and matching pumps, her hair pulled back severely into a bun, came swiftly up to the table carrying two pillows.

"Hello, Mrs. Maxwell. Mrs. Auer. How are you?"

"Fine. How are you Mrs. Lillton?" Evelyn and I responded.

Mrs. Lillton was one of the event coordinators at Marshall Field's and had helped us through many parties. The waiter had pointed us out to her and she scuttled off to housewares to find pillows. She brought two and said she could bring more, if needed. I thanked her and accepted the pillows.

"Do you want to hear something funny?" I asked, after Mrs. Lillton had scampered off to assist someone else.

"Always."

"It's more strange, really."

"What is it?" she asked, sipping her ice tea and cutting her salad into tiny bites.

"I spent all summer and fall cooped up in the house, right?"

"Mmmhmm," she murmured while chewing.

"And in August I had that chat with Toby, I told you about that, right?"

"Of course."

"Well ... since then, I've, I don't know ... not felt as scattered, as crazy. Watching Mrs. Lillton scamper around everywhere made me think of it. I feel like I used to be like that, running four different directions all the time and never getting anywhere. Now I feel this crazy sense of calm. It's weird."

"If it's too unsettling for you, I'd be happy to trade."

I smiled at her. "I think it'll be okay. I just need to get used to it."

"So, what changed?"

"Near–death experience?" I shrugged.

"Possibly," she said dryly.

"No, I'm serious. I don't know what. All I know is I've been stuck in my room and reading all these books my friends have sent over, looking at all the flowers, wandering around my house. I've even read through the entire Torah, I'm so bored."

"Well then, that's it."

"What's it?" I said, exasperated at Evelyn's eternal zen–like state.

"Silly, you really don't see it?"

I shrugged again and stuffed an obscene amount of food into my mouth.

"You almost died. You had a religious experience that touched you deeply. You are now able to take the time to appreciate you family, friends, intellect, home, etc.–all that you have–you're able to put it into context and appreciate life. You've figured out how to travel through life lightly, with open hands ... just like Feldstein said."

I sat there a moment, chewing my food and thinking about what she said. *She was right. Damn it, Evelyn was always right.*

"You're right. You're absolutely right," I said, astonished and half-laughing.

"Absolutely fabulous, you mean."

"Right. Absolutely fabulous."

. . .

Michael had never really liked living in the city. He enjoyed the short commute and the park across the street filled with pigeons, dogs and old men playing chess. It helped him feel like he was in a small town, but he complained every summer about not having a yard of his own to take care of–a lawn to mow, projects to work on on the weekends. Man stuff. He had loved hardware stores as a child and building things with his hands. He built shelves and cabinets for our townhouse, but there was only so much he could do around the place before it started looking like a guilded lily. I was partial to my home. It had been my grandmother's home and the place I loved as a child, my refuge.

However, that Christmas, my mother decided she had had enough the city, of charity balls and cocktail parties. She was going to live in Lake Geneva year round. My father decided he was not going to live in Lake Geneva at all. They didn't divorce, as was normal in their strange, vaudevillian world. They lived two hours apart, never saw each other again, and yet, remained married.

My father moved into the townhouse and we moved out of the city. As Lake Shore Drive winds up and out of the city, curling around Lake Michigan, it turns into the quiet, leafy Sheridan Road, which carves a quiet path through the heart of some of the oldest ring of suburbs.

We fell into a comfortable suburban existence among the perfectly spaced brick homes with manicured lawns, large oaks and red maples, kids on bikes and joggers down by the lake. Our backyard, hedged in on both sides by fifty-foot evergreens and cedars, goes down to a little strip of lakefront. Now, I watch the sun rise each morning over the pale green water from my kitchen. During the three months of the year it is nice enough to be outside, I take my coffee out to the deck, prop my feet up and imagine the Rocky Mountains rising up behind Lake Michigan.

On the last day of January our daughter, Hope, was born. She was bright pink with a tuft of black hair and a nose so tiny, we were afraid she wouldn't be able to breathe. She was perfect. She looked up at Michael, all of two hours old, smiled and reached out her tiny hand and put it on his cheek. He was gone. He never left her out of his sight and she never let him forget who ruled the palace.

I was exhausted for weeks, my body still healing from the previous spring. After two months I felt well enough to bring Hope down to the office so everyone could see her. Everyone swarmed around the baby. I left her in the good care of the assistant editor and wandered into Pete's office.

"Hey."

"Hey," he said, looking up from his desk.

"I know you're not a big baby person ... "

"Right, sorry. I'll come out and see him, I bet he's cute."

"Yeah, she's gorgeous."

"Sorry."

"Don't worry about it. With any luck, in about eighteen years she'll be hanging around and jumping on your last nerve."

"Shelby," he smiled, "if I'm still here in another eighteen years, it'll only be because I've died and no one noticed."

"Pete," I took a deep breath.

"What? You quittin' again?" he asked and accidentally flung his pen over his shoulder.

"Yeah," I whispered. "For real."

"Right." He was only half paying attention, searching the floor for his pen.

"I'm serious. I can't do this anymore." I picked up his pen, which had rolled under his desk, and set it on a stack of papers.

"You'll be back."

"If it makes it easier for you."

"Seriously, Shelby, you can't give this up! It's in your blood. I saw it the day you walked through my door, without knocking I might add ... I saw it in your eyes. You've always been hungrier, wanted it more than the others."

"I'm sorry. I don't any more. I want to write my book, hopefully with out further incidence, and maybe write some more books. I don't know what I want. All I know is I have two children, I don't know them at all ... I can't make the same mistakes I made the first time around. Maybe I'll come back. I don't know."

"Okay, okay," he got up and hugged me. "Just don't steal anything on your way out."

"Okay," I smiled.

"And you'd better not forget to mention me in your Pulizer acceptance speech."

"I won't. I promise."

I went back out and said good-bye to everyone. J.P. gave me a big hug and told me to take care of myself. I started to cry.

I told Michael that evening that I had quit my job. He almost passed out.

"What?" he tried not to yell and wake up the kids.

"Really."

"Why?"

"Because it's not there anymore. I've lost the drive to go out there every day."

"Well, if this is what you want," he said.

"It is."

"Well then, okay, you know I support you no matter what." He wrapped his big arms around me and we sank down in to the couch. A snug and content tangle of arms and fingers, legs, ankles and feet.

. . .

Brennan spent a year watching me like a hawk. Every day he'd ask me if I was going to leave that day, go on a trip. I just smiled, kissed his forehead and said "no."

I had the greatest time of my life learning all about him. His favorite book, song, teacher, subject, birthday cake flavor, what Michael does after a trip to the dentist, everything. I was constantly amazed at how much Brennan and I were alike. It broke my heart to think I had never known any of those things before.

For every good day I had staying at home it seemed one bad day balanced it out. I quickly realized why it was easier to run to work each morning, to leave child and husband behind for the glamour of lights and the electric charge of a highly anticipated news conference. It was simply easier to run away and be alone than to ask forgiveness of those you love day after day. The feelings of incompetence and wanting to bolt bubbled up again. I was frustrated and confused. Wasn't all supposed to be joy and peace and smooth sailing once you decided to change your life around? Where was the reward for my diligence, my sincerity?

The reward was the tiny fingers of a baby girl, curling around mine and holding it snug against her bottle while she drank in absolute peace and safety. It was in the smile of a son who ran through the house each afternoon until he found me and then threw his arms around me and hugged me for an eternity.

I've never had an alderman or federal employee run up and hug me after a story I wrote. I was no longer propelled. I was sustained. I survived the adventure. I found truth. I found justice. I came home.

XXII.

The year after Hope was born Abigail arrived. Now, instead of overnight news from a dozen sources and drinking my third cup of coffee at my desk by eight a.m., I start each morning with a prayer for sanity and one cup of coffee in my kitchen as the sun rises. I look in the mirror and see that my skin is filled with wrinkles and scars forged through walking through violence and finding grace waiting for me on the other side. I can now see me as Michael sees me, as Brennan sees me. And I love how I look.

Sealed up within my healed bones and skin is a forgiveness I could never deserve or repay. Forgiveness is the most powerful thing I have ever experienced. Georgie was right. The thing ... the thing I couldn't put my finger on *was* grace ... *is* grace. The tears finally washed me clean. The blood I could not wash off because it was not there is no longer clinging to my skin.

I spent thirty years ignoring God but he chose me anyway. I don't know why. I often wonder if it's all a dream, or a scam or one huge mix up. Some days I still feel more like Jacob the scheister than David the king. More face down in the pavement than floating along with cherubs on heavenly clouds. "Holy hell," I think, "It is a mysterious thing indeed."

. . .

"Yeah ... so there are four shows I am going on ... one Sunday morning and all three morning shows on Monday," I said to Viv.

I was trying, only somewhat successfully to pack my suitcase and balance the phone on my shoulder.

I no longer needed to go out into the world and seek its stories. I now had enough material for a hundred stories. I wrote the book that I had been working on when sent to Syria in the first place, a book on the connection between Chicago and Israel. The second was an account of the murder of Meelie and the trial that put Tony and Gregory away. I didn't think anyone would want to read it. It has been selling surprisingly well. I start a book tour in two days. I turn 40 in two months.

"But I have to get back," I continued, "because the kids have just started school and sports and I can't leave Michael alone with all three children. Abbey and Hope have dance classes and Brennan has football and I can't wait till that boy can drive!"

"I don't know how you do it. How old is Abbey now? Her birthday is next week, right?"

"Five ... and it was last week. Aunt Viv owes her a birthday present."

"Yeah, yeah. I'm on it. So you're coming in Saturday and leaving Tuesday?"

"Right. Brennan has his first high school football game ever that Thursday. Rosh Hashanah service then, Friday night. I fly in Saturday afternoon and fly out Tuesday afternoon. We could get together Saturday afternoon or Tuesday morning. Sunday I'm hanging out with Toby and Monday I think I have a book signing thing in the afternoon."

"Hmm, lemme see here ... I made plans last week to be out of town that weekend. One last trip to the Vineyard for the summer. Couldn't you have worked your book tour out so we would both be in New York at the same time?"

"Sorry. I guess I could have held out till October, but I think my publisher would have gone completely bald from the stress. Besides, I'll be back in November."

"How about Tuesday, then? You can come up and see my swanky new office and we can have breakfast. I can take you to the airport after that."

"You sure? You won't have important work to do?"

"Ah, what's the fun of being a big executive if I can't dump work on my assistants?" she laughs.

"I'm glad I'm not your assistant."

"Okay, so Tuesday ... that's what? The eleventh?"

"Uh-huh. Are you writing me into your day planner?"

"Palm pilot."

"Great."

"Hey ... I'm 40. My brain is rapidly turning into applesauce. Two more months and you'll see. You'll wake up on your 40th birthday and Bam! Applesauce."

"Thanks for the warning."

"Good to be prepared babe."

"Right."

"See you in two weeks."

"See you in two weeks. Bye."

"Bye."

. . .

Michael and the Skirts had convinced me to sit down and write. I ended up with two books. The first was pretty much finished, just much delayed. The second was therapy and I was convinced no one was going to want to read it. Vivian sent a copy to a publisher friend in New York. My publisher is insisting on an extensive book tour around the country. "People love this stuff," he keeps saying. I convinced him to let me do it in small chunks, around my children's schedules. This means two trips to New York. One in September and one in November.

I guess most people would be happy to have found truth and reached revelation by the time they are 30. It seems so young. It's still seems young. Ten years later and am I any smarter? Or just older? You put off wisdom, telling yourself you still have most of your life left to live a better life. It just doesn't always work out that way. Sometimes, all God asks is that you find the truth.

. . .

Brennan and his freshman football team won their first game against Evanston on Thursday afternoon. I cheered, louder and more exuberantly than I have ever cheered for anything. Who knew I had it in me to be a sports parent? I was, however, still violently opposed to being an active member of the parents' boosters club. Some snobberies die hard.

It appears all the hurt from his selfless sacrificial love of his first six years had melted away. He forgave me as he always had. He relished my newfound homebodiness more than the girls will ever be able to. Twice I overheard him telling the girls stories of when he was little and I was not around as much. Once, when Hope was six months old I heard her crying and I was on the phone. When I got off she had stopped crying. I went up to her room and Brennan was feeding her a bottle through the slats in her crib. He was nine. The second time he was rocking Abbey to sleep, last year, right before her fourth birthday. I ran and got my camera and took a picture.

The freshman team won their first game of the season and their fledgling egos could not have been bigger as the final buzzer rang. We celebrated with pizza and cokes.

. . .

"Are you sure you want to do this?" Michael asked me.

"Yes. I never did. I feel like I need to do this," I answered.

I looked over at him as we sat in the car, parked in front of Lake Michigan. The kids sat in the back holding three lily plants. The September sky was clear and blue, not a cloud for miles. A soft breeze rustled the trees and swirled down through the open sunroof.

"Okay, let's do it!" He smiled and squeezed my hand.

"Thanks for indulging me," I squeezed his hand back.

"No problem ... as always," he smiled and leaned over and kissed me. The kids started screaming and so we kissed some more.

We finally climbed down out of my new Urban Assault Vehicle ... I mean SUV ... and headed down to the waterfront. I carried our yearly loaves of bread, part of the Rosh Hashanah ceremony. The kids carried the lilies.

The Tash leik is a ceremony where Jews take a loaf of bread, as a symbol of our sins for the past year and cast it into the sea ... or lake or river or any handy body of water. It symbolizes God taking away our sins, drawing them out of us and making them disappear into the endless sea. It is done each year on the morning of Rosh Hashanah, before Yom Kippur, which is the Day of Atonement. It is easier in the modern world to use bread than goat sacrifices.

We took off our shoes and lined them up on the beach. Michael helped Abbey and then held her hand to keep her from diving in the water herself. I handed out the loaves to Michael and the children. Keeping a sense of humor, and perspective, even where sin is involved, Hope was given a large Kaiser roll, Abbey a dinner roll, Brennan a baguette and Michael and I had full-sized loaves.

Michael pulled out his Bible and read.

"Who is a God like You, Forgiving iniquity and remitting transgression; who has not maintained His wrath forever against the remnant of His own people, because He loves graciousness! He will take us back in love; He will cover up our iniquities, You will hurl all our sins into the depths of the sea. You will keep faith with Jacob, loyalty to Abraham, as you promised on oath to our fathers in days gone by."

"Amen," we responded.

We hurled our sins into the sea together. One fluid, collective motion.

I took the Bible from Michael and flipped over to Hosea. Michael and the kids plucked lily flowers from the plants and passed them around. I took one and tucked it in my fingers, underneath the Bible.

"Hosea 6, verses 13. 'Come, let us return to the LORD. He has torn us to pieces but he will heal us; he has injured us but he will bind up our wounds. After two days he will revive us; on the third day he will restore us, that we may live in his presence. Let us acknowledge the LORD; let us press on to acknowledge him. As surely as the sun rises, he will appear."

I paused and looked up. The morning sun was sparkling on the water. A rainbow of pink, orange, yellow, blue and green. Its brilliance blinded me and made me catch my breath. I looked back down and flipped out a piece of paper I had stuck in the Bible.

"But about the resurrection of the dead–have you not read what God said to you, 'I *am* the God of Abraham, the God of Isaac, and the God of Jacob?' He is not the God of the dead but of the living. I tell you the truth, you will weep and mourn while the world rejoices. You will grieve, but your grief will turn to joy. I will see you again and you will rejoice, and no one will take away your joy."

"Amen."

We all looked at each other and then shielded our eyes and gazed out over the water.

"Any time you're ready," Michael whispered.

I took a deep breath, set the Bible down in the sand. "Bye, Meelie. I love you."

I tossed the lily into the water and watched the little ripples of water lap it out away from the shore. The rest of my family whispered their own good-byes and tossed their lilies in the lake.

I smiled through the tears as I watched the water lap away the flower. I had said good-bye to Amelia, but also to my past, to the fidgety, angry person I had been for so long. It felt good to let go. I felt it slip between my fingers like silk as the flower fell to the water.

Abbey looked up at me, unsure what to do. She and Hope had never met their cousin. She reached up and took my finger in her soft, little hand and patted my wrist with the other.

"It's okay Mamma, it's okay."

I started crying. Michael wrapped me up in his strong arms and helped me back to the car. Michael passed out apple slices and honey in the car as we drove up to the Rosh Hashanah service. We had moved from our congregation downtown to a much smaller congregation up in the suburbs a few years ago. It was informal and many members of the congregation shared the various leadership roles during the service. It was cozy and intimate and felt like we were worshipping with family, in a home. The children actually enjoyed going and seeing friends each Friday night.

It was still warm. As we entered the building the warm air lingered on our skin as we sat in the air conditioning. We sat down again on the plastic folding chairs, dressed in polo shirts and jeans. Brennan sporting ragged sneakers, the girls in sweet pink sundresses. Michael and Brennan wore matching white satin yarmulkes,

Brennan's hanging on by pure determination to his peach fuzz of a head. The football team gets shorn each August for the season.

As the service for Rosh Hashanah, the Jewish New Year, rolled on I found myself tearing up. Maybe it was the book and going on tour to promote it, maybe it was something else, but the poignancy of the words and hymns and the service as a whole hit me. My heart trembled. They were tears of joy, of thanksgiving, of relief. Amelia and I had been sisters in our lust for life, our unquenchable thirst for the next thrill. I now knew why I was so exhausted at the hotel in Damascus. I hadn't been living life; I'd been chasing it. Chasing all over the globe in hopes that just once I would find what I needed to quench my thirst for life. I still couldn't explain the change, I can't tell anyone what that something is that I was chasing so hard or why I don't need to chase it anymore. All I know is I am full.

The race was over. I felt an assurance, as I looked ahead to Yom Kippur that I had not just been forgiven for this past year, but all the years past and all the years ahead. I was forgiven.

XXIII. ───────────────

On Saturday, everyone piled in the car and we headed to the airport. Brennan hugged me at the gate, still sweaty and covered in dirt and grass from a pick-up soccer game with friends that morning. I smiled and wore the dirt smudges as a badge of honor.

The day I left for Vail eight years earlier, and him asking to come with flashed before my eyes as we hugged.

"Want to come with?" I asked.

He looked at me like I was speaking in tongues. "What? I have school on Monday. And practice." I just smiled and kissed his forehead. Michael and I looked at each other and he remembered that day at the airport.

"That's right ... he's got to keep his old man on the straight and narrow," Michael said. "Besides, he has no luggage and has to go to school." Michael patted Brennan on his back.

"You both are too weird," Brennan said and rolled his eyes.

I hugged the girls good-bye. They were both still dressed in their little green and blue New Trier cheerleader outfits. Abbey insisted on wearing hers everywhere since we found it. I can't wait for her to grow out of the wearing strange costumes and combinations phase and start dressing normally. I was assured by her kindergarten teacher that a few weeks of school usually cures it.

"I love you. I love you all. I'll see you in a couple days. Be good."

"I love you," Michael said. He wrapped his arms around me. I buried my head in his chest and breathed in.

"I love you too," I whispered. I kissed him good-bye, the kids all groaned and I boarded the plane.

. . .

I woke up early Sunday morning. I lay in bed for awhile, half-asleep, half-awake. I thought about calling home, but Chicago was an hour behind and it would be too early. I finally rolled out of the bed and opened the curtains in my hotel room.

From my vantage-point on the top floor, with a window facing west of the Waldorf-Astoria, it was a sunny, crystal clear morning. The Manhattan skyline sparkled in the still-bright sunlight of early fall. I took a quick shower and threw on a pair of jeans, a black sweater and boots. I grabbed my black leather jacket, room key and purse and walked out of my room and down out of the hotel. I walked out onto the sidewalk and tucked my key and wallet into the inner pocket of my jacket and put my sunglasses on. Rays of sunlight bounced off the gleaming glass and steel of Midtown.

The air was perfect. Crisp and fresh. The summer haze and smog had started to roll out to sea. I caught a cab and headed over to Rockefeller Center. The Sunday morning TV circuit was not my favorite, and I was delighted that so far only one had called for an interview.

After the taping, I headed due west, scooting across the southern border of Central Park. It was Sunday morning and the tourists were still asleep. I relished the quiet, one-mile walk over to Toby's apartment building on the southwestern edge of the park. I was in an amazingly good mood, my heart felt light and I hummed a tune as I strolled through the park. The trees were still green. The grass was worn from a summer full of dogs and children and weekend football and soccer games. There was a cool breeze and a gaggle of pigeons, who, in true New Yorker style, glared at me and refused to move when I started to walk through. I laughed, but thought twice about walking through a flock of ornery birds and circled wide around them.

I knocked on Toby's door two minutes before noon. I had twisted his arm to get him to have brunch with me. I hadn't seen him in a year and wanted to talk to him. I had called him up to let him know I'd be in town, but I had a strange, deep feeling that I needed to see Toby while I was in New York. He said I was being stupid, but I insisted. He finally bent and agreed to give up his cherished Sunday morning. A confirmed bachelor, he had finally tied the knot two years ago and now considered his Sundays more sacred than ever. I suggested a noon brunch and told him I'd pay.

"You're early ... dammit, you are always early. That is so annoying," he said while still opening the door. He didn't need to wait and see if it was me, no one else would ever dare to knock on his door on a Sunday.

"Wonderful to see you too, sunshine," I smiled at Toby and gave him a peck on the cheek.

"You look fabulous," he said quickly bouncing back.

"Thanks. I'm also starving. You ready?"

"Yup."

"Where's Jenna? Is she coming?"

"Nope. You lucky thing, you. She's in LA on business. Left yesterday. She won't be back till next week."

"Oh, that's too bad. I was looking forward to seeing her," I said.

He shrugged. "Eh, what'da'ya gonna do?"

"Brilliant," I laughed. "Hey, I've been craving waffles for some odd reason. Wanna go up to that Belgian waffle café place on Madison?"

"Sure." He started to step through the doorway and I looked down.

"Wanna put on some shoes there, Lee Roy?"

He looked down and then looked back up and smiled. "Huh. Probably would be a good idea."

"Right."

I followed him into his apartment and waited for ten minutes while Toby rummaged through his apartment for two matching shoes.

"So, do you always forget to put on your shoes when the wife's away?" I teased.

"I'm ignoring you," he called out from his bedroom. "Hey! Is it cold outside?"

"Uh, a little ... kind of ... "

"Okay!" he called again. He came bouncing out of the room, this time fully, and more appropriately dressed. I tried not to make any comments about his rumpled khakis and wrinkled white shirt. He put on a blue and cream plaid shirt, but left it completely unbuttoned. He grabbed his leather jacket and keys. "Okay! Let's go."

"You're going to get your New Yorker card taken away by the fashion police," I said as we stepped out of the building and I put my sunglasses on.

"What do you mean?" he asked, looking down as his ensemble.

I just laughed and started walking up the street.

"Cab?" he half-asked, half-whined.

"Cab?" I turned and answered incredulously. "It's a gorgeous day. The restaurant is just on the other side of the park." I laughed and flailed my arms out in front of me. He groaned and pretended to stumble and fall. I ignored him and kept walking. He finally trotted up beside me and we walked together through the park up to the northeast corner.

"So ... " I finally said after we'd been walking for about five minutes in silence. "Have you read the book?"

He looked over at me. "I'm sorry Shelby, I just can't. I was there, remember?"

"I remember," I nodded and looked at the ground in front of me. "I do appreciate you letting me write it and talk about you ... us, everything we went through."

"You didn't need my permission."

"Yeah, I did. You didn't have to say yes, but you did. I really appreciate that. You let me write about everything. You honored Meelie's memory. You are a good friend," I said quietly, looking down.

He put his arm around my shoulders. "I didn't do anything, Shel. You are the one who honored Meelie's memory and has been the good friend. You and Viv. I probably would have wasted away to a dirty, shriveled ... I don't know what. You saved me from becoming one of those mental cases who never showers or shaves or leaves their homes ... talks to himself and eats garbage ... " he trailed off.

"Don't forget, 'collects newspapers and aluminum cans and piles them up to the ceiling in his apartment so when he dies no one can find him,'" I smiled.

He looked over and smiled. "Yeah."

"You know, it's okay if you don't read the book. It's okay if you never read the book. As long as you are happy now, and moving forward ... that's all that matters."

"I am."

"Good," I said. "I'm so happy for you and Jenna. I like her."

"I like her too."

He dropped his arm down and we walked side-by-side through Central Park in silence the rest of the way, basking in the warmth of the sunshine.

· · ·

"So Jenna wants to have a baby."

I spat the coffee I was sipping back into the cup. "What?"

"Yeah, can you believe it? Me? A father?" he choked on the words. "Shelby, really ... I'm forty-one years old! I don't even like children. And I've been blessed to live in a place where lots of people I know don't like children! I'm not even considered a monster ... if you don't count my mother."

I laughed at him. "Toby, has Jenna said, 'Toby, I want to have a baby.' Hmmm? Those exact words?"

"Yes."

"Dang."

"Exactly!" he threw up his arms in exasperation.

"Well, what did you tell her?"

"I told her I'd think about it," he mumbled sheepishly.

"Are you? Seriously?"

"I don't know. I'm too old to have a baby! Not to mention Jenna travels to the West Coast about once a month. Not that I mind ... it's like marriage therapy, only she gets paid for it."

I snorted and rolled my eyes and wondered how Jenna managed to live with him, even with the traveling. "You know, you guys could adopt an older child."

"Huh."

"Obviously, you hadn't thought of that already," I said. I waved my fork around in the air and then took a large bite of waffle and strawberries.

"I'll think about it. I got married, didn't I? I think that's enough. I don't think I'm getting the credit due for actually getting married."

"Right."

"Hey, I didn't have the greatest track record going there."

"I know."

"I mean, really, one could say it all began with you ... that it's your fault I was so messed up," he said defensively, sitting up straight in his chair.

"One could say that," I said and threw him a dirty look over my coffee cup. "Or one could be a grown-up and admit that shit happens and it wasn't anyone's fault."

"Sorry Shel."

"So'right."

"Still, it sucked. I lost you to my stupidity and your brother's threats because I wouldn't stand up for myself ... but then he died and it became really hard to argue with him. Then Gregory ... then Michael ... then I lost Amelia ... " Toby had stopped using her nickname shortly after her death and rarely uttered her name at all. Jenna had first heard about Meelie from Vivian.

"But now everything is great. You have a beautiful wife who loves you ... Lord only knows why ... "

"Hey!"

"Sorry," I laughed. "No regrets, remember?"

"No regrets."

"As sketchy as things got at times, think how screwed up they could have been if we'd been able to choose how our lives would turn out ... clearly we weren't doing so hot there for awhile."

"Yeah, you're right."

"As always."

"As always," he smiled. He put his hand up and I smacked it. He pulled my fingers through his and gripped my hand tightly. "You are one of my best friends. You know that right?"

I smiled and nodded.

XXIV.

"Oh ... my ... "

"Impressive, isn't it?" Vivian smiles smugly.

"Dang, girl. Impressive doesn't even begin to describe it. You can see everything up here. The windows are so narrow ... it's kind of like a fun house mirror," I say, peering directly down 90 floors, my forehead presses against the window in Vivian's office.

"Yeah, supposedly the guy who built the towers was afraid of heights or something ... can you imagine?" she laughs. "So he made sure all the windows were no more than shoulder width apart, so you would never feel like you were falling out."

"Makes sense." I pull my head back up and turn back around to face Vivian. She is standing behind a large mahogany desk. The furniture is a dark brownish-red leather. On the walls are photos of Colorado and Chicago. "Well, Madam Vice President. I am so proud of you! This is great! I hope you will finally start enjoying life again now that you received this promotion."

"Yeah, well, that's kind of why I went out to the Vineyard this past weekend."

"Good for you. Go with anyone in particular?"

She starts picking up papers on her desk and making a pile. She picks up a paper clip and starts unfolding it. "Maybe."

"Maybe?" I raise my eyebrows and smile.

"Max Carpenter."

"Senator Carpenter's son?" I shriek.

"Shhh!" she flaps her hands at me. "Yeah. He works over at Merrill Lynch. We've been seeing each other for a few months now. But he's moving down to

Washington to take a job with the Senate Finance Committee. He asked me to go to the Vineyard with him one last time. He wants me to move down there with him ... "

"He what?"

She nods.

"Did he propose?"

"Not really."

"Are you going?"

"I don't know. I'm not sure," she smiles.

"You're not sure ... " I say slowly, "but you're smiling. You're seriously thinking about this!"

"Yeah. I guess I am. He left yesterday. I told him I'd go down for Columbus Day weekend and let him know then."

"That sounds reasonable."

"I guess. So, you ready to go down for breakfast?" she asks, ready to change the subject.

"Sure." I look around the room and find my purse on the floor next to the couch. Vivian's phone rings. She looks down at the caller ID and frowns. "Hang on, I have to take this."

"Okay."

She picks up the phone and starts talking. I reach in my bag and pull my own phone out. I walk over to the far corner of her office in front of another window and punch in the number for Michael's office.

"Hey babe."

"Hi! Where are you?" Michael asks.

"Vivian's new office. Very impressive."

"Really? Wow. What's it like."

"Very Wall Street. It's on the 90th floor. I think I see Philly from up here."

"Cool."

"Yeah, she had to take a call, but we're going to go to breakfast here in a minute and then she'll take me out to LaGuardia. What are you up to?"

"I just got in. I have some paperwork this morning. A lunch meeting with Rich and then I'll pick up Brennan and Hope from school, Abbey's going to be at a friend's house. We'll all be at O'Hare to pick you up around four."

"Marvelous."

"I do have to go to a meeting tonight though ... I can't get out of it. Some of the Aldermen are pretty pissed off at Rich right now. He wants me there just in case it gets ugly."

"What? City Council get ugly? Mad at Richie Daley? Unheard of," I say dryly.

"I know, I know ... hard to believe," he says sarcastically. "What's the weather like? Is it nice?"

"Beautiful. Clear blue sky ... not a cloud to be seen. Perfect temperature. You couldn't order up a better day in New York."

"Mmmm. Same here."

"See, we're not so far apart," I say dreamily.

"Not so far apart," he replies.

I straighten up and notice a plane. I look over at Vivian. She is sitting at her desk, madly scribbling away notes and saying "yes sir" every minute or so.

"Hey Michael, you won't believe this ... it looks like a plane flying right toward me. I didn't know planes flew directly over Manhattan. It looks like it's going to fly right over ... that is so cool. It must be an optical illusion, right?" I say in disbelief. I strain my brain to remember any other time I'd seen a jet fly so close to the Trade Towers.

"Really? I've seen planes from the Hancock before, but none that were close enough to look like they were flying directly overhead. You know, ones flying over the lake from the east heading out to O'Hare."

"Yeah ... " I trail off. Something in the way he says it makes my blood run cold.

"Shel?"

"Uh–huh ... uh, Michael ... it really looks like the plane is flying right at me. That's not right ... is it?"

"I don't know. I've never been in the World Trade Center."

"Hey Viv!" I yell. She looks up and throws me a dirty look. She holds up one finger and then looks down again. "Uh Viv, you might want to get over here and see this. It looks like ... "

"Hey Shel ... gimme a minute, okay? I need to get this down before we leave."

"Don't worry about it Shel, you're probably right. It's probably just an optical illusion," he says reassuringly.

I scream and drop the phone.

Don't you go walk in the rain without me
Don't you go walk alone
Keep your eyes steady on my face
I will settle down the angry place
Ain't no calm in the storm but me
Only I am peace ... only I am peace.

Don't you go down to the desert without me
Don't you go down alone
I will follow you across the sand
Carry you water in my sun–burnt hands
Ain't no water in the desert but me
I am the well and the spring ...
I am the well and the spring.

If you get lost in the darkness darlin'
If you can't see the light
I will be everywhere you are
Rising you like a morning star
Ain't no light in the dark but one
I am the moon and the sun ... I am the moon and sun.

Author's Notes

I need to thank several people, without whom, this book would never have been written. First, to whoever dropped their roll of film outside the Marriott Wardman Park Hotel in Washington, D.C. I am forever grateful. Unlike Shelby, I did not pick the roll of film up and so I have no idea what was really on it. I assume it was tourist pictures of the pandas at the National Zoo, and not grizzly murder photos to bring down two minor mobsters.

To Bill Judd, my author's advocate at Author House. Bill is hands down, the greatest advocate and cheerleader a writer could ever have. Thank you, thank you, thank you, thank you! With out his support and encouragement this book would never have been published!

To Matt and Kari MacKellar, for their support when the idea for this book was in its' infancy. They read the first 30 pages and enthusiastically encouraged me to keep writing. I probably would have abandoned the idea if it were not for their support. They were a continual sounding board and editorial advisors throughout this process. Kari also helped me with the cover art and author's photo.

To my former roommate Dan Mack, who let me use his computer to write the first draft in the summer of 2002.

To my other friends who edited drafts of the manuscript: Karen Lentz, Jim Byrne and Lisa Tedder, a.k.a. Georgie Armstrong, for being the coolest person I know. I love to "sit at her feet and listen to her stories." She is one of the best friends I have. I asked if I could use her songs and her likeness as part of the story, she laughed and said I didn't need to ask permission. "Just do it!" she exclaimed. I will not even try to take credit for the beautiful lyrics to her songs I have put in the book. "Isaac," "God Does Not Remember," which she did actually write for someone, and the poem at the end, "Deep," a song she sings a capella. My only regret is that readers will not be able to hear her sweet "bluesy-bluegrassy-rock-Melissa Ethridge" voice while reading her words.

To Kimmie Pasquesi, who let me use her last name for Vivian. Kimmie and I grew up figure skating together and had lost touch when I started writing this book, I based Vivian on Kimmie and four years later I ended up back in Chicago and coaching at my old home rink ... with Kimmie P. Thanks babe, you're the best!

The story is a modern retelling of the story of Hosea and Gomer from the Torah, but from Gomer's (Shelby's) point of view, which is not given in the Scriptures. I have loved Hosea's story since introduced to it by my roommate my freshman year of college, Amy Ferguson. Amy was in a class with Dr. Rosalie DeRossett. Two years later I had the privilege of taking two classes with Dr. DeRossett. Her words and teaching came back to me while writing this book, guiding me as I wrote. She was even gracious enough to edit the manuscript. I could never have written this story with out her.

The story of Hosea and Gomer is an analogy of God's love of Israel and her future as a nation. For several reasons I thought it was important to show that Shelby was successful in her restoration as a child of God. Shelby relished her success at redeeming her marriage over any other success she had in her life. She learned the lesson I am still learning every day: life is an adventure and it takes you places you'd rather not go. But in the end, you have to live with no regrets.

The ending may upset some, but it is not my intention to try to profit from the horrible events of Sept. 11. I was in Washington, D.C. that day, I knew people at the World Trade Center, Pentagon, White House and Capitol that day. The images are burned into my mind forever. As I read all the obituaries in the NY *Times* in the months afterward, I kept thinking about all the people ... their lives and what they were really like. They were my age, Gen Xers. Our tiny generation became that much smaller in the span of a few hours. It was crushing. We then went on to survive anthrax and snipers. It was a rough year. This book is dedicated to everyone in New York City and Washington, D.C. who survived. I hope it honors all their stories.

I knew that Shelby had to die at the end of the book. I think it's important to show that sometimes things like that happen to people and we never get an answer to "why." I think that was one of the important lessons of 9/11.

The "tiny Dryer Bible College" is Moody Bible Institute, where I went to college. "Dryer" is to honor Miss Emma Dryer. She left her teaching post at Illinois State University to come to Chicago and help Mr. Moody start his school. She taught English. The Communications Dept. gives out awards each spring for student work, they are called The Emma Awards. I received one, for photography.

Dr. Michael Rydelnik teaches Jewish Studies at MBI. Even though my grade did not reflect it, I probably learned more in his class than any other class I had. I had Dr. Rydelnik read the manuscript for "Jewish correctness and consistency." I also want to thank my other Old Testament profs for everything they taught me: Dr. John Walton and Dr. Paul Benware. You made learning fun. Thanks.

Michael, however, is not named after Michael Rydelnik. I wanted to juxtapose Michael and Gregory ... good versus evil with Shelby in the middle. Gregory isn't necessarily pure evil ... he's named after a pope on purpose. He's the embodiment of what can happen to people when they get a distorted view of their own power and importance and put themselves above everyone else. Michael is named after the archangel ... God's messenger to humans.

One more nod to Moody ... J.P. Wilson, the darkroom tech, is a real person. J.P., or P.J., or Rufus, (depending on how late at night it was) was the Photography Editor of the school newspaper my sophomore year when I was Sports Editor. Everyone loved J.P. Wherever he is, I hope he is still taking pictures, and singing as he works.

A good chunk of what Rabbi Feldstein and some of what Georgie Armstrong tells Shelby is gleaned from Dr. M. Craig Barnes. He was another big influence on the theme of this book. He was my pastor at National Presbyterian Church in Washington, D.C. for five years. Dr. Barnes preached about grace every Sunday. The things Feldstein and Georgie say are a compilation, a generalization of countless sermons, and Dr. Barnes' book *When God Interrupts: Finding New Life Through Unwanted Change*, IVP 1996. Dr. Barnes' sermons can be found in print and on tape at the NPC Web site: **http://www. natpresch.org**.

I found Dr. J. Hampton Keathley, IV, Th.M., and his commentary *Hosea* on the Internet while doing research for the book. I really liked what he had to say about Hosea and Gomer. It fit in perfectly with what Michael Rydelnik taught me in class and what Dr. Barnes preached on every Sunday. I researched several commentaries on the Internet and went through my old college textbooks while writing this book, but decided Keathley's comments best fit the story line and what Shelby needed to hear. His commentary can be found at: **http://www.bible.org/page.asp?page_id=967**. Dr. Keathley is a 1995 graduate of Dallas Theological Seminary.

The International Bible Society Web site was a wonderful resource in the writing of the story. It has Bible passages in pretty much any translation (and language) and one can flip back and forth between translations. The quotes from the King James Version and New American Standard Version in the book were taken from the editions found on the Web site. The passages were edited down to fit the story, but the exact wording was not changed. The complete passages of Hosea that were edited down and used in the book, along with the entire books of Hosea, Job and Jonah, or any other Bible passage can be found at: **http://www.gospelcom.net/ibs**.

The opening passage from "The Torah," Hosea 2; the passage Michael reads at the end, on the beach, Micah 7:18–20; and the first half of Shelby's reading on the beach, Hosea 6:1–3 are taken from the Tanakh. The Tanakh is an acronym for the three sections of the Torah, or Jewish Bible: Torah, Nevi'im and Kethuvim. To make life interesting, Christians refer to it as the Old Testament, put the books in a different order and base translation on the Greek, or Septuagint, ancient text instead of the Masoretic, or Hebrew, text. I used both Christian and Hebrew texts while researching and writing this book. The version I used in the writing of this story is *Tanakh: A New Translation of THE HOLY SCRIPTURES According to the Traditional Hebrew Text*, the Jewish Publication Society, 1985.

Three passages are from the New International Version, Student Bible, (Zondervan 1986): Jonah 2, Job13:26–27; 15–16 and the second half of Shelby's reading at the beach, which is Matthew 22:31–32 and John 16: 20, 22b.

Grace & Peace ... wherever you are on the journey.

Carrie Ann Alford

- an excerpt from the upcoming novel -

Conquering Washington
Carrie Ann Alford

"I am embarked on a wide ocean, boundless in its prospect and from whence, perhaps, no safe harbor is to be found."
~ George Washington, June 1775

I. Boundless In Prospect

The sky seemed to be slipping away behind her as they drove toward the airport. She was sure she was being hurled toward the place where the sky ends. Her courage was melting away as quickly as her father was driving. The blood rushed to her cheeks. She felt seasick. She pressed the edge of the window button down. The warm air rushed in over her face and ruffled her auburn curls, slapping them against her forehead, eyes. She breathed in deeply and tried to relax.

"Hey, kiddo," her father said. He patted her knee and smiled. "Excited?"

"Uh, sure," she said absent-mindedly.

She was too busy multi-tasking to be excited. Don't freak out, ignore mother chattering away in the back seat, Mother's yippee dog chirping along, block out brother and sister arguing, keep breakfast down, don't scream to turn the car around. They wouldn't do it anyway. She knew it was irrational, but couldn't help feeling this was the last beautiful spring day she would ever see. The last time she would ever be in Texas. The last time she would be young and carefree. She wanted to soak it all up. Remember every scent on the air, every leaf, flower and cloud. She memorized every building they passed and the way the Jeep vibrated as it hummed along the road. What if it all disappeared? What if she never made it home again? What would she do without the big Fourth of July bash? Was she coming home for Thanksgiving? Christmas?

She'd been so confident for the past year. What happened? There was no guy begging her to stay. No real job offers. She hadn't applied anywhere to tempt her to stay. Maybe she should have made plans to stay here. It was safe, predictable, familiar — she knew the rules. Everyone knew her here. She pictured the state house and governor's mansion. All the cocktail receptions with the worst small talk. All the balls and parties with the best music and guys. She was only 22, and yet had already accomplished so much. Why did she want to trade Austin for Washington? Who was crazy enough to jump to the bottom of one ladder before getting all the way to the top of the first?

"Quinn! You're not listening!" Her mother gave a disapproving look, that Quinn couldn't see from the front seat, but knew was there.

"What?"

"We're almost to the airport, dear. What airline are you on?"

"American."

"American, Bruce. That's terminal 2. Slow down, you're going to miss it."

"Thank you for that brilliant back seat driving, Lill."

"I am just trying to be helpful."

"Thank you, hon."

"Not a problem."

Quinn rolled her eyes. On second thought, maybe Washington, D.C. wasn't far enough away after all.

. . .

"Can you fit this over on that side?"

"Um, yeah, I think so."

Corrie caught the pillow her father lobbed over the car with both hands and jammed it into the last corner of space in her maroon '84 Cutlass.

"Okay, that has to be it. There is no more room," she said, slamming the car door shut.

They all stood around the car and looked at it, waiting for the doors to burst open and the contents to spill out like a tidal wave. Boxes, plastic containers, dress bags, pillows, a stereo, a 13-inch television, food, blankets and CDs were piled up to the roof of the car.

"Ah, to be young and move to a new city with all your worldly possessions in only your car," her father exclaimed. "Drive safe, peanut."

"Dad," Corrie sighed.

"Sorry. Princeton-graduated peanut."

Corrie rolled her eyes. She was anxious to get on the road. To go to a new place. But, part of her wanted to set a match to her car and all her worldly possessions and go back home with her parents. To be the big fish in a little pond. She could work for the government back in Boise. Or the Sierra Club, or Greenpeace or any one of the thousand anti-something groups out west. If Princeton had taught her anything, it was that there were thousands upon thousands of people who were more driven, more intelligent and more cutthroat than her. And most of them were headed to Washington as well.

She slid into the driver's seat, said a quick prayer for survival and drove off.

. . .

"Here." Quinn's dad handed her a cup of coffee and a Wall Street Journal and sat down next to her. "Have they started boarding yet?"

"Naw, should be soon though."

"You're going to do great."

"Thanks."

"I mean it. Washington is a magical place. Blinding. Full of energy and people from all over the world. Brilliant people who want to make the world a better place…"

"Daddy, you always said you hated D.C."

"I do. But you're going to love it. It's your kind of city. Austin is too small for you. Too Republican."

They shared a laugh.

"The promised land," Quinn said.

"The promised land. Just do me a favor while you're out there making the world safe for the little guy."

"Sure, what?"

"Call your mother once a week, go to a museum once a month, find non-politicos to be friends with, find a good Presbyterian church and never forget where you came from."

"Sure, no problem," she smiled.

"It's harder than it sounds."

"Come on, Honeygirl, they're boarding your flight!" Lillian Archer said. Quinn's mother was standing over her with her arms open wide. She was swinging Quinn's brand new Yves Saint Laurent carry-on bag in one hand and her matching handbag in the other.

Quinn tried hard not to roll her eyes. She hadn't wanted those stupid bags. Her mother had insisted.

"Are you excited? Isn't this great? What an adventure you're about to begin!" Her mother hugged her with false enthusiasm. Quinn could see the tears bubbling up from all the way under her mother's pink twin set. She was worried the same cruel world that had once crushed her and her husband was about to do a repeat performance on her youngest daughter. "I am so excited for you. Part of me wishes I could go with you."

Quinn tried not to show panic at the thought of her mother coming with, but smiled broadly and said, "yeah, me too. It's going to be great. Bye Mother."

"Now, John Henry going to meet you at the gate, right?"

"Yes mother, he's meeting me at the gate. I'll call when I get there."

"Lillian, lay off. She's 22. She's moving to another city not Mars. She's a big girl. I hardly think something's going to happen to her on a non-stop flight."

"You never know," she shot back defensively. "She was only five when we left D.C. She doesn't remember anything."

Quinn laughed to diffuse the tension. She quickly hugged her family good-bye. She looked back as she handed her boarding pass to the airline employee. Her mother was waving and tearing up. Her brother and sister were smiling. Her little brother, Ryan was leaving in a month for college, and big sister Cricket was getting the hell out of Texas herself for grad school at Notre Dame. Her father put his arm around her mother, smiled and gave a little half-wave half-salute. He was just hoping none of his children would be moving back in.

. . .

The breeze off the bay gently rustled her hair against her neck. The sun was a smoldering blaze of orange and red behind the bridge. She breathed in deeply, wanting to remember every second. She had a wave of nostalgia come over her and she vacillated on her decision to move. His arms were wrapped tightly around her waist and he was softly kissing her neck.

"Quincy?"

"Yes?"

He turned her around, but still held her close. He looked deeply into her eyes and smiled. He kissed her and hugged her.

"Don't go," he whispered.

"I have to go," she whispered back. Her face turned from soft and romantic to puzzled and fear with those two words. She had convinced herself this wouldn't happen. He wouldn't do this to her. Not on her last night.

"I can't live without you." He would. "We could be so happy here," he continued, ignoring her face and body language. He was positively gushing. "I'm getting a raise. I want us to look for a place here in town, near a park. We could raise beautiful children and be happy."

She took a deep breath and closed her eyes. Happy. His definition of happy. It was always his definitions, his plans over hers. He never listened. She'd finally found the courage…and now this. Sigh. She was crushed. He had promised weeks ago to let her go. Not to make a fuss about her new job and to trust that it would all work out. There was nothing for her here anymore. If he thought their relationship was the real thing, he'd find a way to follow her to Washington. This was her opportunity of a lifetime. To be twenty-five and offered a job at one of the best universities in the country, surely he understood that. He was all opportunities and life plans.

"Aaron, we agreed." She tried to keep her voice even and not get emotional. She hated emotional girls who always cried to get what they wanted. "This is a great opportunity for me. I love you, but if I don't go out there, I'll always regret it. We have our whole lives ahead of us. You don't want to live with someone who ends up bitter and living in the past, do you?" It was more of a plea than a question.

He pulled back and looked at her. His face hardened. He dropped his hands and backed away. She could see tears welling up and him fighting them back.

"I've changed my mind."

"You changed your mind?"

He quickly changed his tactic. He dropped to one knee and scooped up her hands.

"Miss Quincy Anne Lane, I love you more than anything in this world and I want you to be my wife. I can't live without you. Please say you'll marry me." She gasped. "Please..." he whined softly.

"Aaron, you can't ask me to marry you just to keep me here! What kind of marriage is that?" she screamed.

She didn't care who heard. She was furious. Struggling to get her hands free, she realized she how loud she had screamed. Deep breath. Calm down. She put her hands up to her face and tried not to cry.

"Of all the stupid, manipulative things to do to someone you say you love!" She surprised both of them with how strong her words were. She felt a surge of power rush up and down her spine as she stood her ground. Maybe this new job and move was giving her even more than she'd thought.

"Hey! I'm serious," he said. He jumped up to his feet and tried to pull her close.

"Don't! Don't touch me," she said. She backed away and started crying. "Don't come near me again. Ever. Again. I can't believe you. You were supposed to support me in this! You were going to be there for me. I am going to take this job. I am going to move. If you can't handle that, then I don't want you around. You were supposed to find a way to come out to me, not the other way around. A promotion? Did you weasel that out of your boss so you'd have an excuse to stay? I can't do this...it's, it's hard enough without people trying to hold me back. My mother, my father, my sisters, everyone! You were the one person....How could you do this to me?"

She couldn't believe this was happening. She was trembling. Tonight was supposed to be romantic dinner, a walk, one last night together before her flight for Washington in the morning. Now she was reduced to rage and runny mascara. Romance and the Bay Bridge had dissolved into a crying, arguing mess.

. . .

On the plane. In the air. Finally. One small step for girl from Texas, one giant leap in the right direction. Hope to God. I am going to hurt that cranky near-blond, frosted-within-an-inch-of-her-life flight attendant, Quinn thought and sipped her diet Coke.

A black leather journal was lying untouched on the tray. She was determined to record every second of her adventures in Washington. There was only one problem—she didn't have any yet. The journal was new, a graduation gift from one of the many great–aunts who hardly saw her, but still sent gifts. "To Quinn, a new slate for a new adventure" was scrawled in a smushed and creaky script on the inside cover. She was pretty sure it was from the one who had financed most of her father's congressional campaigns.

Her mind was a million miles away from the journal and Congress. She was thinking about College Station. She stared out the window at the bright blue sky and endless sea of foamy white clouds. Scenes of all her friends at her going away party the other night at the Dixie Chicken, floated across the clouds. They had tried to make it a surprise. Never tell a secret about a party to drunken frat boys. They were lousy at hiding things and she'd found out a week ahead of time.

"Attention everyone! Attention! I would like to make a toast!"

Dirk Clayton, her fellow intern, clinked a glass with his knife and waited for everyone to quiet down. They had been close friends, and she was touched he'd put this together. They had interned together twice and in some ways, he probably knew more about her than her real brother. He was standing on a chair. He was a head and shoulder above everyone else anyway and absolutely towered over the crowd now. His white button down shirt was still tucked into his neatly creased pants, but he'd lost the navy tie and even unbuttoned the top button. This was a major statement for the self-proclaimed future Governor of Texas. His hair was neat and closely cropped. Quinn looked at him and wondered what would be the final straw to make him finally let loose and not worry about perceptions. She wanted to be there when he cracked. She also wondered how someone who worked twenty-hours a days had time to get a tan. If he ever becomes governor, it's going to be a scandal-licious administration, she thought.

"To Quinn Archer, Wunderkind, Superstaffer, Golden Girl...off to Conquer Congressman Hill's office, Capitol Hill...Washington. The world. God help us all."

Everyone laughed and said, "God help us all! To Quinn!"

Quinn laughed. She'd already had several drinks and was well beyond the point of caring that Dirk was mocking her for the last time. He grabbed her hand and pulled her up on the chair. They balanced there for a minute, cheek to cheek. Everyone howled.

Quinn blushed. Dirk clinked her beer bottle, gave her a peck on the cheek and jumped down.

"Speech! Speech!" he yelled, smiling broadly up at her.

Quinn feigned shyness for a minute and then quieted everyone down.

"Thank you to Dave for that lovely toast. Who are you again?" Everyone laughed and several guys smacked Dirk on the back. "No seriously, I'll miss Dirk. And the J-Squad. Jenna, Joe and Jeff and everyone else I worked with in Senator Stafford's office. I can't say I'm going to miss sorting mail, making copies, coffee or answering phones...oh wait, that's what I'll be doing in my new job, too," she laughed and smacked her forehead with the palm of her hand. "I'd just like to thank y'all for coming tonight and being my friends and supporting me..."

"Bullshit, we just want you out of the way so we look better, you overachiever!" Jeff said.

"Okay, okay. You're right...I am the best. I hope the Texas state house doesn't fall apart while I'm gone. I'll have my cell phone. No seriously, I just want to say that, well, I'll miss knowing what the hell I'm doing and you'd all better come and visit..."

"Excuse me, how much longer?" Quinn handed her cup and empty pretzel package to the flight attendant as she walked by.

"About forty-five minutes."

"Thank you."

Quinn pushed her seat back a little and flipped open her journal. "I can at least write about the trip so far," she said to herself. She started writing about her new job.

"June 22, 1995.

My job will be great. 22 years–old and working in the U.S. House of Representatives for Congressman Hill. A Member from North Texas, on several committees I'm interested in and, seemed real nice when I met him. Who wouldn't be excited? Who wouldn't want to work there? Okay, probably lots of people. Pull it together-you're going to do great. They're going to love you. Yes! I'm giving myself a written pep talk? Maybe I shouldn't journal after all. I need to relax. My mind is wandering to John Henry. I shouldn't get my hopes up. Top of his class, 6-feet and 3-inches of gorgeous dark and handsome. Deep brown eyes and long black lashes. Looks equally good in tailored black Washingtonian suits as blue jeans, cowboy boots and white T-shirt. Wondering if dreamy JH will fall madly in love with me. Mmmmm. We could be such a gorgeous power couple. New Jack & Jackie, the Texas version...I will be professional Hill staffer, exuding confidence and class, matching suits, pearls, hair always in place and lipstick shimmering (matched perfectly to nails and suits–of course). Rushing between important meetings and hearings will call JH in middle of crazy day and say "Hi! How's your day going? Strategy Dinner? Oh... what? What's that? Romantic dinner? Even better." I am being stupid.

I need to focus on my career. I am not silly girl who gets married right out of school and subjugates herself to her husband and his career goals. Will work hard. Will make best coffee ever. Take best notes, write best letters. I will treat constituents like royalty. I will definitely be youngest chief–of–staff since Dick Cheney. But must also remain humble and willing to climb ladder out of mailroom basement. Cannot get too cocky or ahead of myself. No one likes conceited brown–noser. Must find balance.

John Henry, fellow Aggie, God was my father happy when he met JH last fall during election. Only two years older, but has already worked in the State House and now at DNC Headquarters for a year. I hope our paths cross often...its nice to have at least one acquaintance in town. Not to mention him setting me up with a friend of his who needed a roommate. I'm so fine.

. . .

"This cannot be right!" Corrie screamed.

Her five-hour drive from Princeton, New Jersey to Falls Church, Virginia was now entering its seventh hour. She was beginning to hate this town and hadn't done anything but drive around it. She had pictured herself driving down through the rolling hills of Maryland, into the heart of the District. Driving past marbled federal buildings and shiny law offices. She would pass the Capitol building and the Washington Monument and Jefferson Memorial, sail over Memorial Bridge and past Arlington Cemetery. Swing around the Iwo Jima memorial and through downtown Arlington to Falls Church. It seemed so easy. She had carefully mapped out the route, not the quickest or best, but most dramatic. She wanted to feel like she was arriving. Her cousin had told her how to do it, given landmarks, explained the Beltway. She had the directions written down to the last turn, with landmarks on every last corner to guide her way. How is it possible for the Capital of the free world to have the worst marked roads?

She saw an exit and, while she was pretty sure this was not Virginia or anywhere near where she wanted to be, she pulled off and into the shopping center parking lot at the corner. She yanked out her map, but it was completely uncooperative and she had nowhere to extend it out, since the passenger seat was full of stuff. She smacked the middle fold to try and get it flat, but all that did was create a large rip down the center of the map and honk her horn loudly. She started to cry, for probably the third time in her life.

Don't be ridiculous, she scolded herself. No need to cry. I am perfectly capable of figuring out where I am and reading a ripped up map. She looked around, trying to remember what exit she had just used. Useless. Completely useless. She folded up the map the best she could, wiped the tears from her eyes and took a deep breath. She got out of the car and started walking toward the Home Depot.

"Someone in there better know how to get me to Falls Church," she muttered.

The college-age clerk in the store was not much help. He apparently never went beyond the store.

"Is there anyone else I could ask?" she asked as politely as she could. Her voice was squeaky, her Idaho twang creeping up. She was ashamed that she could still feel the tears on her cheeks. She never cried.

"Anyone else?" he asked, genuinely confused.

"Yes." Deep breath. "Someone else in the store who might know how to get me to Virginia. A manager perhaps?" She asked through clenched teeth. She tried to remain calm, but realized she was overemphasizing words and sounding sarcastic.

"Ooo, we sell maps!" he exclaimed.

She rolled her eyes and took another deep breath. "Lovely. I have a map. What I need is a person." She waved the poorly-folded map in front of his face.

"Okay, dude. Calm down. My manager is over in plumbing. I'll go find him."

He wandered off to find a manager. She bet herself twenty bucks he would never come back. Ten minutes later a large man with hairy arms and a bald head came over.

"You the lost girl?" he asked. Before she could answer he grabbed the map and laid it out on the Customer Service Desk.

"Hello there. Name's Bob. Oh yeah, you're on the other side of the Beltway hon." he said in a thick Baltimore accent.

"Fabulous. How did I do that?" she said more to herself.

"Oh, well you see here…" he answered her, pointing at the map. "When you came down from Jersey here into Maryland, you took the wrong half of the split. Easy to do, hon, both sides go to Virginia, it being a large circle and all."

"Virginia is a large circle?" she asked stupidly. As soon as she said it, she regretted it. Of course Virginia isn't a circle! She wanted to yell at him for continually calling her "hon" but didn't want to offend him and have him not help her.

"No, no, hon. The Beltway. Not really a circle though, not a perfect circle. It meanders here and there, but it does go 'round. Not real well marked on the Virginny side, easy to miss the exit."

She sighed. She didn't really want a geometry lesson on the Capital Beltway from a home-improvement store manager. She was over two hours late at this point. Her cousin was probably wondering why she couldn't follow simple driving directions and her triumphal entry into D.C. was ruined.

"So, what's the best way to get to Falls Church?" she asked, hoping to get him back on track.

"Hmmm. That is a tricky one. A sticky wicket as the Brits would say."

The Brits? Sticky wicket? Have I driven into Alice in Wonderland? She took a deep breath to avoid screaming at a fairly nice man in the middle of a Home Depot.

"So, probably at this point in the day, you're still okay to stay on the Beltway. Getting to be rush hour though…"

"It's 2:30 in the afternoon!"

"Yup. Starts pretty early around here. Did you know that in…'52 I believe it was, hmmm, anyway, President Eisenhower, I think it was Ike, could've been Kennedy in '62…anywho, one of our presidents took the Russian Prime Minister Khrushchev up in a heli'copter to show him rush hour on the Beltway. Very impressive back then. Big deal I guess to show the Russians how many cars we had in Washington. Only gotten worse since."

"That's nice," Corrie said dryly. "So the exit I need would be?"

"Oh right. Sorry about that. Get off on a bit of a tangent every once and awhile. Former history teacher, you know. This is my fun retirement job."

She smiled politely at him and raised an eyebrow. He made some noises to give the impression of thinking hard while he studied the map.

. . .

"This is the final call for flight 1577 to Memphis, connecting on to Washington-Dulles, all passengers should be on board. Thank you."

"Quincy, honey…"

Quincy had been staring so hard she had to blink a few times before seeing her mother. Her mother was sitting next to her, stroking her blond curls and massaging her shoulder. "Hon, he's not coming and you're going to miss your flight. This job is too big of an opportunity."

"Yes," she whispered hoarsely. She swallowed hard. "I know. I need to go. Bye Mom…Dad."

They hugged her and tried not to look too sad.

"I know I wasn't that supportive, before. But now I see that you need to leave. You need to get out there on your own and away from all distractions. You are going to be great. You're students'll love you."

"Thanks, Mom." Quincy stood up and felt a little dizzy, but righted herself quickly.

"You go knock 'em dead girl. You show those East Coast know-it-alls how it's done." Her dad slugged her on the arm and smiled broadly.

"Thanks, Dad," she said. She managed a smile and quickly hugged them and grabbed her bag. She tried not to be annoyed that her sisters hadn't bothered to show up. She had three, and two of them lived in the area. One of them could've bothered to come and say a collective good-bye.

They waved her onto the plane and she sighed, both of sadness and relief. It wasn't the day she'd been hoping for, but maybe it was better to have a complete break, if not a clean one. It would make moving 3,000 miles away easier in the long run. If nothing else, she'd have lots of saltwater to wash away the memory of Aaron Burkie. She'd meet other guys in Washington. Now, she would not feel ashamed if she was attracted to them. She would not feel guilty for accepting offers for coffee or dinner. And hell, she figured, the best part was not getting stuck with a ridiculous name like Burkie for life. It always reminded her of burpy or some other junior high word.

She straightened up, thrust her shoulders back and pushed a curl behind her ear. You my friend, are going to be fine, she told herself. It will all be fine. She took her last breath of West Coast air and boarded the plane.

. . .

Quinn pressed her head against the cool Plexiglas window. She was straining her eyes to see every detail as the City of Washington came into view below her. Her parents had had such a horrible final campaign that they never wanted to return or even talk about it, when her dad left for the last time. Her mother was right. She hadn't seen D.C. except in photos and on television since she was five years old. It was depressingly average. Suburbs with cookie-cutter homes and requisite malls, roads and highways, it could be the suburbs of Austin.

The plane took a sharp turn and started its decent and Washington finally came into view. She caught her breath as the Capitol, White House and monuments came into view. The full force of the picture below her hit her like a club. This was it. She was here. This would be her new home. The plane swooped down and appeared to be headed straight for the Potomac River. She jerked her head up, but no one else seemed to be alarmed. The flight attendants were calmly buckling themselves into their seats for landing. She tried not to panic. Looking down, she could see the airport off to the right and what appeared to be a pencil-thin strip of concrete. The plane landed gently and a chorus of seatbelts unclicking rang out. Quinn didn't move. She was staring at the Capitol Building and thinking of everything it held inside. She was going to work there. Starting Monday. She tried not to cry. It was the most beautiful thing she'd ever seen.

. . .

Printed in the United States
94199LV00004B/1-18/A